A Mother's Mistake
by
K.T. Marshall

This is a work of fiction. Names, characters, organisations, places, events, and incidents are either products of the author's imagination or are used fictitiously. Any resemblance to actual persons, living or dead, or actual events is purely coincidental.

PROLOGUE

All I wanted was my mum. The room was pitch dark with not even the tiniest bit of light coming from anywhere, and it was creeping me out because it looked the same whether my eyes were open or closed. That was why I couldn't tell what was in the room beside me. Well apart from the bucket that is, the smell of my sick was a constant reminder.

The cold from the stone floor made its way through the shabby blanket that I had wrapped around me. A piece of cardboard or something like that would have made it a little more bearable but I didn't dare to move from that spot. It made me think about homeless people sitting on cardboard boxes. I finally understood why they do that. I kept thinking how those people were better off than me; although they'd probably say, 'at least you've got a roof over your head.'

Maybe it was because I was so ill; my brain was pounding like a giant pulse and I was weak from spewing up so many times, but I'm certain I kept drifting in and out of consciousness. I spent quite a while arguing with a homeless person inside my head, and soon realised that I was definitely worse off. At least you can hide on the streets… and I had yet to do the toilet in the bucket.

Was this where I was going to die, or was he coming back for me? I had no idea. There was no chance of my mum ever finding me. If anyone saw what that man had done to me, they would have phoned the police or followed us. They would have saved me already, I knew that much.

I was going to pay for my stupid mistake. We learned about Stranger Danger in nursery, and after what happened to that other boy, I should have known better. I watched the news, I knew about serial killers and paedos. There was nothing else I could do, except pray – for the first time in my life – because I didn't want that to be my fate.

1
CAROLINE FRANK

22tnd March 2018

A week had dragged by since that moment I switched on the TV to break the unbearable silence, which had become all too familiar in recent months. The Scottish accent of a female news presenter filtered around the room:

Exactly one year on from the day that teenager Jase Frank's skeletal remains were discovered in a field in Blackbridge, a second teenager has been reported missing.

Fifteen year old Evan Shelby was last seen during his lunch break from Blackbridge High School in Fife at around 1.15pm this afternoon, near the wooded area next to the High Gate underpass. Evan was last seen walking towards the break in the hedge here, often used as a short cut to the school. He hasn't been seen since.

The police have said that Evan may have come into contact with someone and possibly entered a vehicle. Police are appealing for witnesses who were in the area at or around this time. Evan was wearing his school uniform: black trousers, a black Super-Dry jacket, white shirt and blue and white Nike trainers.

With my hands masking my mouth, I sat down on the arm of the sofa. All I heard from then on was my own voice inside my head pleading, *please no, please God not again,* while the images flashed up on the screen of the blond boy and a similar jacket and trainers to the ones he had been wearing.

All I wanted was to get through that day as strong as I possibly could. It had been six weeks since my last flashback but there it was again, the feeling of being stuck in a simulator with no escape, watching the sickening images of the day that my son's bare bones were found in that field.

Despite having never met this boy, Evan Shelby, or his parents, from the minute I first heard it on the news, I felt involved. Enough so that my mundane life immediately went on hold. I called in sick to the charity where I'd been volunteering and avoided calls from my best friend - probably my only friend, in fact - Tony. Instead, I sat at home following every inch of the investigation and cursing Police Scotland for once again being out of their depth.

The vehicle believed to be involved in Evan's disappearance was found burned out ten miles away, a stolen Citroen Picasso. The owner was cleared of any involvement and so far, there were no CCTV or dash-cam sightings of the car. It was mentioned that a second or possibly third vehicle could have been involved.

With my Jase's killer locked up, they were confident that there wasn't a serial killer on the loose. The most popular theory to date was that it was some kind of copycat kidnap. Not exactly the sort of thing Evan's parents needed to hear.

They had been on the news, the Shelbys. Rebecca, a petite little woman with blonde hair and her husband Ray, well-built and dark. As soon as I saw her sitting there in front of the microphones and cameras, I felt the terror in her as if it was radiating from the TV, that exact same feeling I had when I sat in front of the nation and pleaded for someone to give me my boy back.

In that moment I knew I had to speak to her, which was the very reason I decided to go to the underpass where he went missing.

I sat in my car, watching the gap in the trees for over half an hour. I knew she would be there, or at least I suspected it. I was drawn to the exact spot where Jase went missing. I kept returning in the hope that there would be something I had missed, something that would lead me to him. I suppose you might call it a mother's instinct because I was right, her white 4x4 was sitting next to where I was parked.

Offering my support felt like the right thing to do, but as I sat there waiting, my head started telling me otherwise. I found my phone and dialled Emma – Detective Sergeant Emma Harper, that is – who was my liaison officer when Jase went missing and was now Rebecca's. I still had her on speed dial but it went straight to the answering machine.

I was indecisive whether I should leave a message or not, but before I could make my mind up, I heard the beep.

'Hi Emma, it's Caroline Frank. I'm just hoping that you could pass on a message for me.' I sighed because I had no idea what the message was. There's nothing worse than an answering machine putting you on the spot. 'I want Rebecca to know that I'm here to offer support if she needs it. If she needs someone to talk to … or someone to listen. I just want to help, Emma. Thanks, please call me back.'

The remaining walls of snow from the 'Beast from the East' still lined the paths despite the rising temperatures. I focused on them, wondering how long it would take them to thaw, when a small figure appeared between a gap in the trees.

It was her. Rebecca.

My mind started racing, I didn't know whether to wait on Emma speaking to her first or whether to face her there and then. Although I'd had many a conversation with her in my head, suddenly I had no idea what I would say: 'Hi Rebecca, I'm Caroline.' Then what? As she headed in my direction she continued to stare at the ground in front of her. I could have easily jumped in the car and driven off but

5

instead, I took a couple of steps forward, praying that the right words would come naturally. It must have been enough to catch her attention because she stopped and stared at me. I felt so stupid, even more so when she spun around on her heel and began running towards the play park.

Why on earth did I think she would want to speak to me?

I shouldn't have been surprised and couldn't really blame her. People were talking, saying that history was repeating itself and that her boy's bones would soon be discovered somewhere nearby. Just like Jase's had been. It wasn't fair on her and it wasn't fair on me. I saw how people had been looking at me, like I was some kind of symbol of what was to come. Like a bad omen.

Rejection had become a part of life for me. It was as if people were thinking: *It's a shame what happened to you, to Jase, but we can't be bothered with it anymore, we have moved on.* I had unreturned phone calls, invitations being 'lost in the post', or 'oh sorry, I couldn't find your number'. Not that I've ever really had friends – except for Tony – it was more acquaintances that had appeared during that darkest period of my life; I suppose that says it all. Regardless, I became nothing more than an awkward intrusion on so many perfect little lives. But, I have to say, this was the first time someone had looked straight at me and ran away.

It's strange because if I didn't know who she was, at that moment and from that distance, Rebecca Shelby could have been mistaken for a child, swinging back and forth without a care in the world. She could be no more than 5ft tall, her blonde hair tied tight in a ponytail. But everyone around here knew who she was, so there was no mistaking, that sitting there, on a swing, was a grown woman trying to escape her own mind.

Despite the fact she clearly wanted me to leave her, I still had this urge to go over to her, hold her tight and say, 'It's ok. Everything will be ok.' But, that would be a lie, wouldn't it, a false hope, because, if I'm being honest, I didn't believe that any more than anyone else around here. I prayed to God, for her sake it was true. I know it must sound awful but for a moment, I thought about how she might end up being the only person that could possibly understand how it felt to be me. When people told me they knew what I was going through, they didn't. They couldn't even begin to imagine. I wished they could.

I got in the car and before I drove off, I glanced back and noticed the swing coming to a halt as an elderly woman wearing a purple coat approached her. I could tell by her stoop and the reluctance in her arm as it reached for Rebecca's shoulder, that she was a stranger. Rebecca accepted a tissue, wiped her eyes and nodded. The lady took her hand, cupping it between her own and said something comforting. Or something intended to be comforting. People don't know what to say at times like these, and often get it wrong. I remember one woman who approached me in the street and said, 'Oh honey, I hope your son's not been taken by one of those paedophiles.'

I slapped her. It came as a natural reaction. I soon realised that some people don't think before opening their mouths and some, simply, are as thick as shit.

I thought of Tony as I stopped the car around the nearest corner. I needed to speak to someone and I knew I couldn't avoid him forever. After dialling his number, it rang a couple times before he answered.

'Hey you, what's up?' The familiarity, and confidence in his voice, soothed me instantly.

'I've done something stupid,' I said.

'What have you done?' I could sense the panic in his response.

'Oh no, nothing like that.' I reassured him, realising he thought I was suicidal again. 'I went to see Rebecca Shelby.'

'For goodness sake, Caroline I thought you had–'

'Sorry. No, I'm fine, I made you a promise, remember?'

'Why haven't you been answering my calls?' he asked.

'I just needed to be alone.'

'Well as long as you're ok. You should have phoned me before now.' He sighed. 'Right, tell me what happened with Rebecca Shelby.'

'She took one look at me and ran away.'

'Did she? Oh Caroline, don't take it personally, I'd imagine she's pretty messed up at the minute. Where are you now?'

'Victoria Park.'

'When do you get off work?' he asked.

'Em, that's me finished now.' A complete lie after realising he assumed I went to meet Rebecca through my work for the charity.

'Right, go home, give me an hour and I'll come over.'

'It's ok, you don't have to do that,' I replied.

'Caroline, I haven't even spoken to you since this Shelby boy went missing. I need to make sure you're ok.'

'Alright, if you insist. I'll see you then.'

It was Tony's idea for me to volunteer at the Missing People Charity. It was supposed to be my chance to turn a negative into a positive, to use my experience to help others. The idea of it made sense but the reality was very different. Focusing on other people's troubles was also meant to take my mind off my own but again, let's just say it didn't really work out that way.

2
CAROLINE FRANK

As I pulled up in the driveway, I took a minute to savour the house, our family house. 17 Hartley Drive. A Victorian, ivy covered haven on the waterfront of Blackbridge. The house I would soon have to sell. The thought of another family living there, unsettled me. I imagined them filling the rooms with their things; making a layer of memories over ours.

I have a lot of regrets, but moving to Fife isn't one of them. It has little picturesque villages, full of character around the coastline. Elie for example, it's not even thirty minutes away but Jase would say, 'Mum, it's like being on holiday,' and he was right. It has endless sea, sandy beaches, boats, water sports, and a pretty little lighthouse.

Unfortunately, there is a side to Fife that you don't get to read about on tourist information sites. It mainly comes down to drugs and lack of education. Ironic really, given that I gave up my education and married a drug dealer.

Blackbridge falls somewhere in between. It's neither rough, nor (in my opinion) picturesque; although an aerial view would probably look like an exotic garden labyrinth. Everyone has conifers. I have no idea why. It's as if one of the garden centres were giving them away at some point in the seventies or eighties. They're good for privacy. But on the other hand, when someone breaks into you shed or steals your child nobody sees a thing. It is therefore, a criminal's paradise.

I knew it was for the best – selling up. It was never really a happy house. There were more bad memories than good, but all the good were of Jase. His first steps were in that lounge. As for his dad, Ronnie, he committed suicide a year before Jase went missing. I was sorry that Jase lost his dad but not for my loss, I refused to play the grieving widow. Truth is, if I had been on that cliff beside him, there's a good chance he wouldn't have had to jump.

***

After a quick tidy for Tony coming, I heard the front door opening as I slipped into my comfy joggers. 'I'll be down in a minute,' I shouted.

I heard the kettle boiling and the clinking of cups as I paused in the doorway of the kitchen, where the smell of Emporio Armani lingered.

'Come here.' Tony summoned me with his forefinger.

Walking over, I knew what was coming. The way he held me caused all the tension in me to release, feeling like I would slither to the floor if he let me go.

'How you really doing?' he asked.

'Not too bad, I suppose. I'm kind of gutted that she didn't want to speak to me. I was sure I was doing the right thing. You're always telling me to follow my instincts but I obviously misread them.'

After a second or two he said, 'Maybe it's not your instincts you're following.'

'What do you mean?'

He placed his hands on my shoulders, held me at arm's length and said, 'Maybe there's some other reason.'

I couldn't quite make out if he was making a statement, asking a question or receiving some kind of message from the spirit world. This was something I was quite used to from Tony. He often came out with something random and in his eyes, philosophical, but to me sounded more like a riddle. 'Oh Tony, what's that meant to mean?'

'Never mind.' He turned away to pick up the cups.

I shook my head, and led the way to the sofa.

'Tell me how you've really been feeling,' he said.

'I'm not sure about all this that's going on with Evan.' I sounded like I knew the boy personally.

'Brings it all back, doesn't it?'

'It all seems so similar. It said in the paper it might be some kind of copycat thing, obviously because... *he's* still locked up.' I couldn't even bear to say his name out loud. The sound of it alone, those three syllables, ran through me like a shiver. *Patt-er-son.*

'Could be.'

'I know you haven't been keen to use your gifts, you know, since we found Jase, but,' I had to ask, 'would you consider helping Rebecca find him if she asked you to?'

We both focused our eyes on the muted TV above the fireplace, both looking through it. I wondered what he was seeing. The image that jumped into my mind was Jase's skull. Tony's hand brushing away the mud from the smooth rounded top. The acid having burned away his skin and hair. Both of us throwing up.

'I'm not sure I could go through it all again, to be honest,' Tony said eventually. 'D.I Watson might be gone, but the police is still riddled with narrow-minded homophobes.'

'What about Evan, do you think he's dead?' I asked.

'Not yet.'

'Oh my God, Tony. You think he's alive? Why haven't you said anything?'

'Because, it's not my place.'

'Are you kidding, you should be out there now.' I jumped off the sofa as if ready to lead an army to find Evan Shelby.

'Leave it, Caroline,' he said.

'How can I leave it? You've just told me he's alive.'

'I might be wrong.'

'You're never wrong Tony, please.'

'I'm pretty sure that if Rebecca Shelby came to me personally and asked for my help, I'd be unable to say no. Unless that happens, there's no way I'm getting involved.'

The doorbell rang and I could have screamed with frustration. I wasn't expecting anyone.

'Back in a minute,' I said. As I reached the door, I could tell through the mottled glass that it was Emma. It had been a while but her silhouette remained the same with her unmistakable mass of shoulder-length brown curls or frizz depending on the day she'd had.

'Hi Caroline, is it ok to come in?' she asked.

I held the door open as an invite. As we entered the lounge, Tony had his jacket on ready to leave. I wanted to beg him to stay. I couldn't bear for the conversation to be left hanging like that.

'Hi Tony, long time no see, I hope you're not leaving on my account.' Emma smiled.

'Oh no, Emma, sorry I was ready to leave anyway, I need to be somewhere.' He looked at me. 'I'll catch you later. I just wanted to make sure you were ok.'

'Could you not stay a bit longer?' I asked.

'Sorry, I really need to go.'

'OK. Well, thanks, for coming.' I tried to mask my disappointment.

Emma sat down as Tony let himself out. 'I've just seen Rebecca Shelby,' she announced.

'Listen, Emma, I'm sorry,' I interrupted. 'I know I shouldn't have gone, it wasn't fair on her, or you.'

'No, Caroline, you shouldn't have. Why did you go there today? I'm pretty certain it wasn't through the Missing People because Rebecca has made it pretty clear that she doesn't want any support from them at the moment.'

'I don't know, I just want to help, I suppose.' Sipping the cold tea from the bottom of my cup I sensed her sigh was one of pity.

'I know this must be hard for you, Caroline, and I think I can understand where you're coming from but Rebecca is pretty upset after seeing you today. She thought you had been stalking her until I assured her that wouldn't have been the case. How did you know she would be there? Or didn't you?'

'Oh God, she thinks I'm a stalker?' I was close to tears through embarrassment and guilt. 'I just had a feeling she'd be there. I didn't mean to scare her.'

'I know that wouldn't have been your intention, but I think it was a shock for her to see you there.'

'I know what she's going through, Emma, I know it too well and I thought I could help, that's all,' I pleaded.

'Listen, if I'm being honest I think it could do her good talking to someone but she's a very private person and she's obviously not ready yet. I've been through the Missing People Charity leaflets with her and explained the kinds of support available but she's dead against the idea. I know you weren't on duty today but I don't think that'll make a difference. I'll have a word with her and apologise on your behalf but unfortunately I'm going to have to ask you to stay away.'

'I will, but tell her I quit the charity this morning in case that's what's putting her off,' I said.

'Did you? I heard you were getting on fine there.' Again I sensed pity and I'm not sure if I also sensed disbelief. Although, that could've been paranoia after having just lied to a detective.

'It's not for me, Emma,' I said convincingly, because that was the truth.

'Well, I'm really sorry to hear that. I'm sure you were a credit to them.' She stood up, scooping up her keys and handbag from the sofa. 'I better get going. Now you take care of yourself. You've got my number. Ok?'

'Ok.' I nodded as she turned to walk away. 'Tony thinks Evan's alive.' I blurted out. She looked back at me without a hint of surprise or emotion; the look that they must get some kind of training for.

'I need to go, Caroline. I advise that you don't get Tony involved.' Still not giving anything away. The familiar feeling of wanting to shake her returned. To tell her to cut the professional crap and say what she was really thinking. She paused before closing the front door. 'If Tony does get involved, I want to be the first to know about it.'

Emma can be very professional but a lot of the time her moral judgements and personal opinion come out on top. I think that's why we got on well. I couldn't help but wonder if she hoped that Tony would get involved in the search for Evan.

D.I. Max Watson (Emma's partner at the time) put Tony through hell after we found Jase's body in that field. In his eyes, he had to be guilty - psychics were conmen and there could be no other possible explanation. Emma, on the other hand, asked Tony for a private reading. Her dad who had been high up in the police force had recently passed away.

She had obviously been warned, though. I could imagine her boss now, *under no circumstances, should Tony*

Delimonte be allowed near this case. To say they were embarrassed when Tony found my Jase's body, would be an understatement.

There was no doubt in my mind that it was the treatment Tony received from D.I. Watson that was preventing him from trying to find Evan.

I made myself a coffee, turned the sound up on the TV and waited for the one o'clock news. The events of the morning ran over in my mind: Rebecca running from me, *her crazy stalker.* I had blown it. I wondered if Emma would tell her about Tony thinking Evan was alive and how she would feel about it. I thought about what I was going to say to Paula, my manager, now that I had no choice but to quit. Most of all, I tried to come up with a way to convince Tony that it would be different this time.

3
REBECCA SHELBY

22ⁿᵈ March 2018

In the afternoon after Caroline Frank had turned up unexpectedly, I returned to High Gate woods knowing it would my last visit. Despite it being nothing more than a gravel path tunnelled by trees, leading to the underpass, it was Evan's last known location. His trail didn't cease there but without knowing the direction in which he was taken, I was unable to knowingly get closer to him.

I kept returning, although nothing ever changed, except the weather and the litter; the snow was gradually thawing and the burst crisp packet that lay on the path that morning was now trapped in the nettles on the opposite side of the path, the crisps being gratefully received by some bird or other, I presumed.

As I turned to look at the gap in the hedge, I could see Evan there, sauntering down the banking with his friends; laughing, flicking the blond hair from his face; his red rucksack bouncing on his back with his earphones swinging like a pendulum across his chest.

That would have been him every other day, but not that day. He wasn't with his friends, he was alone, hurrying to catch up. As I stood there for the last time I was still certain there had to have been someone else there, a man, who had stopped him. I imagined a knife, a blade, thick and ridged. Clear as day I could see the man threatening and then overpowering Evan when he tried to run away. They would have then walked towards the underpass as the monster gripped my baby's arm.

My fingernails pierced the skin on my inner arm as I thought of him being driven away to somewhere secluded: alone, petrified, pleading for me to find him.

I felt his fear and pain. I felt it as skin gathered under my nails, the warmth of blood trickling down to my wrist. Sitting on the largest rock adjacent to the large oak tree, I took in a deep breath as the pain dulled to a throb.

They say it's a mother's instinct to protect her child. But what happens when that instinct is powerless? Out of reach? Well I'll tell you what happens, you feel useless; you question every little decision you have made, until you realise that you are to blame; that you are responsible for not protecting your child. That you should not have forced your child to go to a school he didn't want to go to, or given him medication and sent him to school with a cold; you should have sent him back to bed and taken the day off work to look after him. If I had at least given him a packed lunch, he wouldn't have had to walk through those bloody woods to buy lunch from that chip shop up on the estate.

I hated the place for hosting the encounter and I sat there trying to convince myself there was no need for me to be there. What made things worse, was that for the last couple of days people had been walking past as if I were some form of entertainment. They didn't have dogs like the ones I had come to recognise, who would give a respectful nod or smile. Instead, they either stared or smirked, laughing at me behind my back, no doubt. Caroline Frank's little visit that morning was the final straw.

Here we go again, I thought, as something red caught my eye towards the underpass. This time it wasn't a stranger, it was Ray. There was no smile, so I knew there was no news. I looked slightly in the opposite direction, wishing he would take the hint and leave.

'Why don't you come home? You must be freezing,' he said on approach.

'I'm fine.'

'Emma's been trying to get you on your mobile.' He reached for my hand. 'You're bleeding.'

'It's nothing.' I pulled it away.

'Let me see.'

'It's nothing, leave it. I was just running my fingers through the gravel, that's all.' It was the first thing I could think of.

'Then why are they not dirty?' He took a deep breath as he ran his fingers through his hair. 'You need to see someone about this, Becky. Please.'

'Go away, Ray.'

After staring at me for a while, he did. Ray and I never knew what to say to each other now, so most of the time we said nothing. It was like we were both living inside our own heads, minds racing in different directions, while trying to reach the same finishing line. We were definitely not racing side by side, that's for sure.

As he walked off, I stared at the tree. Above the knot of the police tape, was one of the missing posters - a photo taken six months before, on Evan's birthday. That smile; minutes before the picture was taken, I caught him taking a mouthful of Ray's beer, casual and swift, like Oliver Twist, like he had done it a million times before.

'Hey, I saw that,' I'd said. The innocence in his expression told me it wasn't a common occurrence, that he was just as surprised as I was.

'Don't tell Dad,' he said.

I told Ray, of course, and we both laughed. I took a photo of Evan holding the beer; silly really. I wanted the beer cut out for the poster, though. I could hear the judgements and accusations that would be made otherwise. People can be cruel.

That same morning, we gave him an iPhone for his birthday. We had always promised he would get his own phone when he was old enough instead of being embarrassed about using our hand-me-downs. Our regret was instant; he barely took his eyes from it all day.

'You're so rude,' Ray teased.

'I'm not being rude, nearly three hundred people have wished me a happy birthday, it would be rude not to say thanks,' was his reply. I remember thinking; I don't even know three hundred people. The stories you hear about kids getting groomed these days, dirty old perverts pretending to be young boys and girls, it's sickening.

'Don't worry,' Ray had said, 'I'm keeping an eye on him.'

I don't have a clue about all that Facebook stuff, but Ray does. He said he would be able to tell if there was anything untoward going on. I believed and trusted him.

The police were monitoring Evan's Facebook page and 'doing their best' but if I'm being honest, I got the impression that D.I. McCabe was a bit of asshole. When I first reported Evan missing, he hit us with one of his memorised statistics, 'You know, Mrs Shelby, 91% of missing persons cases are closed within forty- eight hours, try not to worry. Can you think of any reason why Evan might have run away? Troubles at home, or school?'

As much as I kept hoping we were wrong about somebody taking him and that he had run away, I could have smashed the nearby vase of flowers, over McCabe's head, right there, splattering blood all over my sofa and that little note book of his. Evan was just a number to him, another statistic. As I pondered over that ghastly image, I

20

noticed the screen on my phone light up. D.S. Harper calling.

'Hello,' I answered.

'Hi Rebecca, it's Emma. Where are you?'

'What is it? Do you have any news?'

'Sorry, I just wanted to let you know that I spoke to Caroline Frank. She's really sorry and didn't mean to scare you this morning. She thought that she could maybe help because she knows what you're going through, that's all. She's harmless, Rebecca, so I don't want you worrying about it.'

'I'm not worried,' I replied. 'I regret running away from her like that, if I'm being honest. I don't know what came over me. I should have just told her I didn't want to speak to her.'

'I don't think it would do you any harm, you know - to speak to her, I mean. She quit her position at the Missing People Charity. I know that was putting you off too, wasn't it? Anyway, maybe you should have a think about it.'

'I will,' I replied.

'OK. Will you be heading home soon?' she asked. 'D.I. McCabe is planning to head over soon. I won't see you again until the morning.'

'I won't be long,' I told her before hanging up.

Taking one last scan of the area and a final glimpse at Evan's photo, I climbed the banking and made my way to the car park. I recalled crossing that same playing field in the morning to find Caroline Frank standing a few feet away from my Jeep. I recognised her immediately, with her tiny frame and hunched shoulders making her look like she was trying to curl inwards, and her red hair; not natural but bright red from a bottle.

It had to be the overwhelming feeling of not being able to escape the situation that made me run, I have no other explanation. I must have looked like a mad woman.

I saw myself through Caroline Frank's eyes, running until I reached the swings. As my hands had gripped the cold iron rings, I felt a comfort, like a child again, like nothing could hurt me. I started to swing gently, then built up speed and closed my eyes. I remember being tempted to jump so that the pain of landing would take it all away, for a few minutes at least. I didn't know what I wanted. When I opened them, she was still standing there, watching me. *Leave me alone,* I wanted to scream, but I didn't, because deep down, I knew she wasn't there to hurt me.

As much as I was weary of Caroline Frank I did pity her. She had experienced my worst nightmare, similar to the one I was living through, but not the same. I knew what people were thinking but I refused to believe it. Evan was alive, I was sure of it.

Now, sitting behind the wheel overlooking the field from the opposite direction, I imagined what I must have looked like and what she must have been thinking. I considered the fact that she deserved an apology, if nothing else. As I reached into my pocket for my phone, the raw scratches rubbing against the sleeve of my coat made me flinch; I cursed myself for being so irresponsible. In a text message to Emma, I wrote: *Can I have Caroline Frank's telephone number please?* My finger hovered over 'send' reluctantly for a minute or two before I went ahead.

4
REBECCA

Emma had told me over the phone that D.I. McCabe was coming over but when I closed the front door behind me, I heard another voice I didn't recognise coming from the living room.

'Here she is now,' I heard Ray telling them.

As I entered the room, a man with speckled grey hair and a green woollen sweatshirt over his shirt and tie, stood up to greet me. A little less formal than McCabe, who once again was in one of his perfectly tailored suits.

'Rebecca, this is Andrew Landon, one of our computer forensic analysists,' McCabe introduced. 'I've brought him along with me to discuss what was found on Evan's laptop.'

'What have you found?' I asked a little confused. I sat down without removing my coat.

'Mrs Shelby, I've just been explaining to your husband that in October last year, a software known as Tor was downloaded onto Evan's laptop. Do you know what Tor is, Mrs Shelby?' the man asked.

'No,' I replied, feeling stupid that he was going to have to spell everything out to me while Ray sat there possibly knowing more about computers than he did.

'Tor is an anonymity network that can be used to protect a user's privacy. It makes it difficult, or impossible when used correctly, to trace a person's I.P address and monitor their online activity,' he said.

'Isn't that a good thing?' I asked.

'Not if you're using it to access the dark web to buy guns, drugs, hit-men, prostitutes or anything else that's illegal,' Ray answered.

'So what exactly are you suggesting? Evan's not a criminal,' I told them.

'I've already told them that,' Ray agreed.

'No, we're not suggesting that he is a criminal and the good news is that he has had Java script running quite a lot, which allows us to see most of what he's been up to. We are concerned though that he might have gotten himself involved unintentionally in something that could have put him at risk,' he informed us.

'Like what?' I asked.

'We don't know, Rebecca, that's what we're hoping to find out,' McCabe replied.

'This is ridiculous,' Ray accused. 'I've told you everything I can about Evan's interest in computers, he's smart and curious, he's definitely smart enough not to get himself involved in anything dangerous.'

'I agree that's he's smart and I hope you're right Mr Shelby, I must admit that I was impressed at the level of knowledge he reads about, some of this stuff I didn't learn until I was at University,' Andrew said.

'We built our first computer together when he was ten and he's been hooked ever since. He's even taught me a thing or two,' Ray told him and I couldn't help feeling irritated by his bragging.

'Yeah and if you find out he is involved in something dangerous, are you going to be proud of yourself then for teaching him all this shit,' I said before I stood up and had to leave the room.

I was no good in there anyway, computers are Ray's thing not mine. He would fill me in, if anything crucial came to light; not that I expected it from the way they were talking. I know the basics and how to use the software and programs for my accountancy work but beyond that, I'm lost. The reality of there being a whole different dark, sordid world out there is scary enough without having to listen to the details. Ray was right about one thing, Evan was too smart to get mixed up in anything like that.

The sound of their continued conversation faded as I closed the bathroom door and removed my coat, slowly peeling away the lining from the dried blood on my arm. Three raw claw marks etched on my forearm left me feeling ashamed. I had never dreamed of self-harming before and I always presumed it was a conscious decision. Maybe it is, I can't be sure, but this was the second time in three days that I had used my nails in this way and both times I felt no control over it.

The first time was when Ray told me he thought that Evan was dead and the overwhelming anger and fear that I felt in that moment displayed itself it the form of gouges in my thigh. I was wearing short pyjamas at the time, with my bare legs curled up beside me on the chair. When Ray saw the blood, the colour drained from him in horror.

After cleaning my fresh wound of dried blood and fluff, I reached inside the medicine cabinet for the nail scissors. I trimmed each nail as far to the quick as I possibly could, leaving them stubby and useless – a pathetic attempt at trying to regain some sort of control.

5
REBECCA

23rd March 2018

The following morning, the house was quiet. The distant clanging of ladders from outside, and the low grumble of Ray snoring coming through the roof were the only sounds. It was 8am and I should have been shouting up the stairs, reminding Evan that he needed to get up in time to have breakfast. The lack of routine and uncertainty that had replaced our settled, everyday life was torturous.

The sound of a van pulling up outside set the next door neighbour's dog off. I peered out the crack in the curtains expecting it to be reporters but it wasn't, it was a parcel delivery van. Emma pulled up beside it and took the small box from the woman driver after asking to see her I.D badge. I wasn't expecting anything but soon remembered Ray mentioning that he had ordered a new tablet to keep him going until our laptops were returned. She let herself in.

'Morning,' she said softly holding up the box. 'Parcel for Ray.'

'It's a tablet,' I told her.

She placed it on the coffee table along with the daily newspapers. 'Do you want another coffee?' she asked, holding out her hand for my empty mug.

'Please,' I replied. I listened as I heard her laying her bag and keys on the kitchen table.

As far as family liaison officers go, I presumed she was good at her job. In any other circumstance, I'm sure I would have struggled with the inconvenience of having an outsider in my house day in, day out. But she made it bearable. Emma had a way of knowing what to say, when to say it, and when to back off. She tried to prepare us for the worst but I was having none of it. I gave her the benefit of the doubt because I knew she was just doing her job. Ray however, had no excuse. If he wanted to give up hope, well that was up to him. If he wanted to believe that Evan was dead, then God help him when Evan did come home to find out that his own Dad gave up on him, was all I kept thinking.

As I heard movement from above, the creaking of that one annoying floorboard, I reached for one of the newspapers so that I didn't have to look at him when he came down. The headline read: *The Blackbridge Curse* and I immediately felt the urge to bin it. So I did.

It wasn't new, this curse of Blackbridge nonsense. It was insulting. Some idiot came up with the idea which gave everyone an excuse for all the bad things that happens around here. Nobody is to blame or God forbid, take responsibility for anything, everything is a consequence of that bloody curse. It was probably crazy Mrs Sheldon. Apparently, she had been down in the caves doing all her vigilante witchcraft and walking about the streets burning white sage. Apparently she grows her own and occasionally gathers all of her nutty friends to carry out the ritual every time something bad happens.

Of course, it was nothing to do with all Blackbridge's precious trees and hedges. I've always been convinced that if they were all cut down and the town was opened up, there would be nothing to hide behind. It would either deter criminals or at least allow the possibility of them getting caught.

Tony Delimonte was another example of all the weird and wonderful things that went on in this town; the psychic

27

who found Jase Frank's remains. Caroline was with him at the time and I couldn't even begin to imagine how she must have felt. Seriously, you couldn't write this stuff.

Like everyone else, we were quick to judge. Ray and I didn't believe in that kind of thing so when it turned out that he was innocent, my brain struggled to work out the odds of that actually happening. Apparently, people were hounding him for readings afterwards that could have made him a fortune but he refused. Rumour has it that he had some kind of breakdown.

'Here's a coffee for you Ray,' I heard Emma say as he reached the bottom of the stairs. 'And there's a parcel on the table for you.'

Still in his pyjamas, Ray lifted the parcel and a newspaper and sat on the sofa at the back of the lounge. Emma also took a newspaper and sat on the chair next to the fireplace.

'A few more possible sightings are being followed up this morning,' Emma informed us, but we both knew she was only telling us because she had nothing more substantial to report.

After our appeal was broadcast on the previous Sunday, hundreds of possible sightings were reported from all over Britain. Nothing came of them. As much as they told us that publicity has its rewards, I couldn't help wondering if it was all just a set-up to see how we would react; so they could get the body language experts on the case.

I hated every minute of it: the reporters, photographers, everyone standing around, staring meticulously waiting on a sign that we might be hiding something. Even though you've nothing to hide, you're aware of this and become anxious and the more natural you try to be, the more you realise how unnatural you feel. Ray appeared to take it in his stride, 'too emotionless' according to a local that was interviewed.

They surely knew by then that we had nothing to hide, but it didn't stop them digging. *So, I see you had post natal depression Rebecca, how do you think that affected your relationship with Evan?* Seriously, what the hell did that have to do with anything? They didn't seem to take into account that Evan was a happy, clever boy and surely that had been our influence, our parenting.

I tried not to take my grievances out on Emma, I knew it wasn't her fault. D.I.McCabe and his team did appear to be working hard, I was just sick and tired of them getting nowhere.

'So what was this Max Watson like then?' Ray asked Emma.

'What does it say?' she asked as she got up and walked over to him. 'Can I see it?'

Ray handed over the paper and Emma returned to her seat. We both watched her as she read it.

'Max is an exceptionally good detective,' she said when she was finished. 'But he made a mistake leading the Jase Frank case.'

'He was only thinking what everyone else was thinking. Why did he resign though?' Ray asked.

'His pride maybe? Max never makes mistakes,' she replied.

'Do you still see him?' he asked.

'He's a good friend,' she replied.

'Well I'm still not convinced he got it wrong. That Tony Delimonte, I mean, come on? You don't honestly believe his psychic powers led him to that exact spot do you?'

'My beliefs are irrelevant and private, Ray,' she said, putting an end to the conversation.

Ray took the last mouthful of his coffee and took his new tablet through to the kitchen where I knew he'd sit for an hour or so playing about with it. It drove me insane. Emma had previously brought him a laptop that he could use for a couple of days and he thought it was perfectly acceptable to sit down all day fiddling about with it.

He said he *was* doing something and that wasn't his fault that I'm 'as thick as shit' about computers, Mr I.T. Specialist himself. I'm an accountant, I know what I need to for my job but I've just no interest in the rest, especially social media. Why anyone would want their secrets and life in pictures all over the internet is beyond me. Yes, I'm sure there is a lot to learn on the internet but I knew that Google didn't know where Evan was.

'Did you phone Caroline?' Emma asked.

'Not yet. I'm still not sure if I want to,' I replied.

'Did you speak to Ray about it? Maybe you could speak to her together.'

'No, he won't be interested.' I knew he wasn't going to be happy when he found out I had her number. His reaction was the main reason I was putting it off. There was no doubt in my mind (or anyone else's that I know of) that Caroline didn't have anything to do with her son's murder, but I remember Ray making that accusation. I had no intention of telling him.

'Do you want me to have a word with him?' she asked.

'No, I'd rather you didn't mention it. I'll tell him later. I'm away to have a shower.' I got up from the sofa.

At the top of the stair, Evan's bedroom door was ajar. Every time that I looked in, I expected to see him either sitting at his laptop or playing his X-box. The room was tidy but I wished it wasn't. The night before he went missing, I was tired and hormonal and felt like I was running the house and family single handed. I threatened him with changing the Wi-Fi password if he didn't get his bedroom tidied. To him, this meant an end to his world. It took him the best part of two hours. 'Happy Now?' he said, rather pleased with himself. And I was happy. To me, it was a big thing. It was nice to be reminded that his carpet was indeed blue and not a mirage of colourful football strips, video game cases and dirty dishes.

His effort was ravaged when the CID came in. They left one hell of a mess. You would think it was a drugs raid. So it wasn't even Evan's effort in front of me, it was mine. What I would have done to see his dirty clothes scattered on the floor, or the Pot Noodle tub, with the fork he had just eaten from. I promised to God, that when he came home, I would never complain about these things again.

I picked up his pillow and inhaled a combination of Lynx Africa and sweat. I was glad I didn't get around to washing his bedding that day as planned. When I say sweat, I don't mean stale. Not like an adults, but that sweet odour he'd had since he was little. It took me back to a time when I'd complain that I couldn't take my eye off him for a second or he would have been up to something.

All of a sudden, he's grown and I didn't have a choice but to take my eye off him, and this is what happened. I considered that a law should be brought out to ensure all children are supervised at all times until they are sixteen, for their own safety and the peace of mind of parents. I know how outrageous and unrealistic that sounds but this is what our world is coming to. I spent another few minutes in his room before heading to the bathroom.

Having spent the last couple of days spraying my hair with dry shampoo and having a wash at the sink, I decided to take a shower. I had had no motivation to make any kind of effort lately but if there was a chance I was going to be meeting Caroline Frank to apologise I didn't want to turn up with greasy hair and add to the embarrassment I already felt at running away from her.

Around 9.30am I decided that I was going to phone Caroline Frank and get it over with. After a flood of anxiety at the thought of actually meeting her in person, alone, I decided an apology over the phone would suffice. Emma had left and the sound of the bath running, told me that Ray was shaving and wouldn't be out for another twenty minutes or so. I took a deep breath and pressed dial.

It rang and rang. *She's in bed,* I thought but as I was getting ready to hang up. I heard her voice.

'Hello.'

'Hello, Caroline?'

'Yes.'

'It's Rebecca Shelby. Sorry for phoning so early, did I wake you?'

'No, no, it's ok I was up,' she said but I knew from her slightly gruff and confused tone that she was still in bed. 'I'm glad you called.'

'I wondered if you would like to meet somewhere?' Thrown back to my original plan out of nowhere, I shocked myself. It had to have been the anxiety, I have no other explanation.

'Yes, of course, just let me know where and when,' she said before coughing to clear her throat.

I was silent. What the hell was I doing? I felt too committed not to answer.

'What about that little cafe down by the Miners cottages... about one o'clock?'

'Today?' she asked.

'Yes, but it's ok if you're not free, I know it's short notice.' My fingers were crossed. Was I going to get out of it?

'No, no, I'm free. Yes that'll be fine,' she said.

'Ok, see you then.'

'Ok,' she replied. 'Bye.'

'Bye.'

It's not a big deal, I told myself. A quick apology, one coffee, no big deal.

It was around that time of the morning that I would usually head down to High Gate woods, but as I had made the decision not to return, I was lost for what I could do instead, I had to keep myself busy.

Ray was still in the bathroom, so I went back downstairs to make another coffee and have a proper read of the papers.

The local newspaper with the spread about the Blackbridge curse had been removed from the bin and placed back on the coffee table, so I binned it again. It would have been Ray no doubt. The paper I picked up was the one with article that Ray and Emma had been reading- *'No Connection'- Says Detective.*

The article was about former Detective Inspector Max Watson, who had resigned and was now working as a Private Investigator in Edinburgh. It didn't say anything that we didn't already know. It did mention quite a bit about Tony Delimonte though and it made we wonder about what kind of relationship he and Caroline had. Were they friends? Were they lovers? The whole thing was a bit weird but I guessed there was a chance I would probably find out soon enough.

Instead of keeping myself busy like I should have done, I spent the rest of the morning staring out the window trying to psych myself up to meet a woman that I couldn't quite

33

make my mind up about – was it the unknown that I was afraid of, or her?

6
REBECCA

The newly painted green and white sign informed me that Jeanie was now the new owner of the cafe. It's changed hands so often you'd think someone would learn that it's not worth the bother. Below the sign was Caroline's unmissable red hair. She was sitting on one of the cold metal bistro chairs smoking a cigarette. She recognised me immediately and smiled as I climbed out of the jeep. I attempted to smile back but it wasn't genuine, neither was hers. It was more like the kind of smile that people exchange at funerals, a polite smile, not a happy one.

'Hi, Rebecca, it's nice to meet you,' she said awkwardly.

'It's nice to meet you too,' I replied.

The little bell above the door rang as she held the door open for me. The smell of coffee and fresh baking appeared wasted as there was only one other customer; an old man eating a butter scone, wiping the crumbs from his newspaper. He didn't look up. The girl at the counter, too young to be Jeanie, I imagined, was engrossed in her phone. She finally looked up and put it to the side as Caroline approached her.

'Two coffees, please.' She turned to seek my approval and I gave a nod.

'I'll bring them over,' said the girl.

Caroline led the way to the table furthest from the window. 'I can see now why you chose here,' she said.

'Every time I've passed it's looked quiet,' I told her. 'I'm sick of the press, to be honest. I'm surprised they haven't followed me.' I gave a nervous smile.

'They should all be shot, if you ask me,' she replied with contempt in her face, and it made me think of a rumour that circled about her a couple of years ago; that she had killed her husband for the insurance money. I quickly shook the thought from my head. I could only imagine what was said when her son went missing after that - I'm sure Ray wasn't the only one. It made me wonder what gossip was going around about me – what assumptions were people making?

'I'm sorry about yesterday. I'm not really feeling like myself at the moment,' I said just to get it off my chest.

'Don't apologise. I'm sorry for turning up out of the blue like that. I honestly don't know what I was thinking. The last thing I wanted to do was frighten you.'

'It's ok,' I replied. I realised straight away that this first impression I was getting of her was completely different to the image I had created in my head. She didn't look threatening or like a junkie, she looked like a woman who lacked confidence. With her being a drug dealer's wife, I half expected her to be twitchy and have rotten teeth. On the contrary, her teeth weren't bad regardless of being a smoker and she was surprisingly amiable. The bold and brashness of her hair certainly didn't match her personality.

'Rebecca, I hope you don't mind me saying, but the reason I wanted to speak to you was to let you know that I'm here if you ever need to speak to someone that understands what you're going through. Or if there's anything I could do, please-' She stopped as the girl put down the coffees.

'Thanks,' we said, perfectly synchronised.

'Like I said, if there's anything I can do, please let me know,' she continued.

'Thanks, but I really don't know what else there is to do,' I replied.

I didn't want to cry, not now. I took a couple of deep steady breaths in an attempt to pull myself together but saying those words aloud, for some reason, triggered tears that welled up in the corner of my eyes. It was true and it was killing me. *Stay at home* they said. But how could I? Evan wasn't at home. I had knocked on doors, I had searched gardens. I even searched someone's house. The police were apparently doing all they could but it wasn't enough.

'Just don't give up, that's all you can do,' she said and pulled her chair close enough so that she could put her arms around me. She was a complete stranger and despite how uncomfortable I felt, I didn't resist her. At that moment I wanted her to tell me that everything would be ok, that it wouldn't be long now, but she didn't. Instead, she cried with me.

I remember when Jase Frank first went missing and how I tried to play it down to Evan. I told him that the boy was probably staying at a friend's house and had forgotten to tell his mum. I then gave him a lecture about the importance of him making sure that Ray or I knew exactly where he was at all times. As the searches got underway and it was all over the newspapers and news channels, I went out of my way to hide them from him so he wouldn't be scared. I thought I was doing the right thing. 'You can't wrap him up in cotton-wool all his life,' Ray kept saying.

When Jase's remains were found all those months later, I couldn't play it down. I left it to Ray to explain. I think I was partly trying to protect myself from the truth. Caroline didn't have the option of pretending it wasn't happening though, did she? The realisation of what she had actually been through, hit me. We can read things in the newspaper or watch them on TV, and it's sad, but there's a distance there. I could appreciate how she felt when Jase went missing, but to think about what she had gone through since, I couldn't; and I didn't want to.

From the corner of my tear-filled eyes, I could see the young girl running to the door, fumbling with her keys. Caroline released me. I turned around as she locked it and drew the yellow chequered curtains. 'If you go out the back door, the alley leads to Main Street,' she informed us.

Caroline took my hand. 'Come on.'

Before I knew it, we were running like we were being chased. I had no idea if we were or not. As we reached Main Street we slowed down and stopped next to the library. I bent over with my hands on my knees trying to catch a breath.

'Sorry,' she said, 'a couple of photographers were at the window. I thought you could do without it. So did the girl obviously.'

I didn't have the breath to answer but they were right. They were running out of things to report, so I'm sure they would have had a field day with this. I was already embarrassed at letting her hold me the way she did.

'We can go to mine for a coffee if you fancy it? I'm just down by the waterfront,' she suggested.

'Ok,' I managed. I'm not sure why I agreed but reminded myself to keep my guard up.

The path she led me was a succession of left turns, braes and steps. I was grateful that the only people we saw were too engrossed in their own business, to pay us any attention.

'You're looking for him aren't you?' she said, noticing that I was scanning every area that we passed.

'I can't help it.'

'Of course you can't, it's only natural,' she said.

We continued to walk at a fast pace, a bit too quick for any kind of meaningful conversation.

'How do you get on with Emma?' she asked.

'She's been really good with us.'

'What about her partner? What's he called?'

'D.I. McCabe. He's ok, I suppose.' I shrugged.

'Really? That's all you need,' she said as if reading my mind, or more likely my face. 'D.I. Watson used to be Emma's partner. He was nice enough to begin with but as soon as we found Jase, he wasn't long in showing us his true colours. Luckily, he resigned. McCabe has to be an improvement, surely.'

'What do you mean, his true colours?' I asked.

'He couldn't accept that Tony's psychic. He tried to have him charged with murdering Jase, even though there was absolutely no evidence. And when they caught the guy that did do it, he didn't even apologise, he just resigned.'

'That's terrible,' I replied. I didn't know what else to say. When Jase's body was found, Ray and I said the same thing. Afraid of offending her, I left it at that.

'Do they have any new leads?' she asked. 'Other than what's already been reported.'

'No, they keep saying they are following up every lead, but they're clearly not getting anywhere. There have been hundreds of phone calls about possible sightings of Evan from all over Britain and abroad, but they've all been false alarms. A few things came up from the door to door statements about a man acting suspiciously, but again it came to nothing. They're still checking CCTV footage and running car number plates, but have had no luck there either.'

'It was the same with my Jase. It was like they were out of their depth.'

'Well, I couldn't disagree with that,' I replied.

We didn't say another word until we reached her house. 'That's us here,' she said and I didn't let on that I already knew where she lived. Everyone in Blackbridge knew where she lived. Just like they all knew where I lived now too.

7
REBECCA

The house was a lot bigger than I had imagined. I'd driven past it many times, but from the road, the view is obscured by the conifers. From the outside it looked a bit run down. The house was overgrown with ivy and weeds, but the inside was immaculate.

'Your house is lovely,' I said as she led me through to the lounge. Unlike our house, there was no clutter, everything had its place. The neutral colours against the dark wood finishing gave it a grand feeling. I must admit, I was surprised. Caroline looked strangely out of place in it.

When she headed through to the kitchen to make us a coffee, I glanced around the room. There were neatly placed photos all around the units and walls. They were all of Jase at different stages of his childhood, up to the point where it had suddenly been cut short. There wasn't a single one of her husband, which struck me as being a little odd. On the unit below the large mirror to my right sat one of Caroline with short brown bobbed hair, holding Jase when he was a baby. A man's arm was wrapped around her but the rest of him had deliberately been cut out.

'Looks like me, doesn't he?' she said as she placed the two mugs on the side table.

'Your double,' I replied. 'I don't know how you do it, Caroline.'

She sat on the soft leather armchair beside the one I was sitting on and brought her feet up by her side. 'Do what? Get out of bed? Leave the house? Not commit suicide?'

'Sorry, I didn't mean that, I just meant... cope in general,' I replied, taken aback by her abruptness.

41

'Sorry, I know you didn't mean anything by it. But the truth is; it took me a while to get out of bed, a lot longer to leave the house and I did try to commit suicide. I failed obviously and now I'm trying to make a go of living. I'll never get over losing Jase but I'm hoping that one day I'll be able to accept it enough to feel that my life is worth something without him. Most people have other children, a husband, or family to live for. At the moment, all I have is Tony. I wouldn't be here today if it wasn't for him.'

'Have you had any counselling?' I asked.

'If you could call it that. I spoke to one woman with some crazy ideas and she put me off seeing anyone else. That's when I decided I'd prefer to work through my feelings in my own time and on my own terms,' she said.

She waved her arms towards a pile of books in the alcove next to her: *Cognitive Behavioural Therapy*, *Stages of Grief*, *The Psychology of Happiness* and a few others. They were all academic books, which made me wonder if she really understood them. I pitied her even more.

'Sometimes self-help can be more beneficial,' I said, forcing something positive.

'I studied Psychology at University which helps a little,' she said and I was stunned and a little confused by this revelation. She went to university? I heard the famous quote in my mother's voice; *Don't judge a book by its cover, Rebecca,* and it just goes to show that you really shouldn't.

'You have a degree in Psychology?' I asked.

'No, I left after my second year, that's when I met Ronnie, the man I married,' she replied. 'Big mistake.'

I gave a consoling smile because I wasn't sure how to respond, but now it made sense. She obviously had the chance to make something of herself but then chose to give it up for him- the infamous Ronnie Frank. Not that I had heard of him before he died but according to the papers he quite notorious.

'I take it you had a tough marriage then?' I responded.

'You could say that.' She gave a half smile.

'I'm sorry to hear that. Was he violent?' I asked before being concerned that I shouldn't have; worried, that she was about to tell me to mind my own bloody business. But she didn't.

'He was violent towards me but never Jase. He hid that side of him well. I'm pretty certain Jase had no idea what his Dad was capable of,' she replied with ease.

'Were you still together when he...' I didn't know how to word it.

'Killed himself? Yes. I had planned to leave him many times but was always too scared.'

Again I thought of the rumour that went around about her killing him for the insurance money. But then I looked at her and couldn't imagine someone so small and frail being able to push a big man like Ronnie Frank off a cliff. Either way I had no sympathy for him.

'How's your husband doing?' she asked, bringing me back to reality.

I let out a sigh. 'I don't know. He's not saying much.' I appreciated her openness about her family but I wasn't ready to do the same.

'Men tend to bottle things up more than us, don't they?

'Yeah, Ray does anyway,' I said.

'And what about you?' she asked.

'I'm terrified that if they don't find him soon it'll be too late.'

'Do you think someone has him?' she asked sounding reluctant.

'I don't know. I don't know what to think. I'm sure he's still alive though, he has to be.' A lump formed in my throat as the tears returned.

'I'm sure he is,' she said. 'You need to stay positive.'

'That's what my mum keeps saying, but she's about the only one,' I told her. 'How long did you manage to stay positive for?' I regretted the question instantly. It was insensitive. 'I'm sorry, ignore me.'

'Four months, then I hit the bottle,' she replied calmly. 'By then I felt it, I just knew. So, if you believe and feel that he's still alive then that's a good thing.'

'Do you think so?'

'I honestly do,' she replied. There was hope in her face that made me think that she believed it too. She believed that Evan was still alive. And coming from someone that I'd probably expect otherwise, I was sort of grateful.

'Can I use your toilet?' I asked.

'Sure. You'll need to use the upstairs one, the downstairs one doesn't flush. Turn left then it'll be on your right hand side.'

'Thanks, I'll just be a minute.'

As I reached the top of the stairs, I turned left. I recognised the bathroom instantly because I could see the black and white checked floor tiles. Crossing the hallway I noticed that the door to my left was slightly ajar. Being nosey is not in my nature but as I walked past I knew straight away that it had been Jase's bedroom. It looked untouched. The walls and bedding were blue and school books still lay on the pine unit.

As soon as I sat on the toilet, I put my head in my hands and sobbed. The sobs came uncontrollably as I imagined Evan never coming home to his bedroom, his bed never to be slept in again.

Five or ten minutes must have passed when I realised that Caroline would be wondering what I was doing, why I was taking so long. I pulled myself together as best as I could, checking my face in the mirror and headed back down to the lounge.

Caroline's mobile started to ring as I entered the room. Reaching into her pocket, she pulled out the phone and looked to see who it was. 'Tony,' she said as she rejected the call. 'I'll phone him back later. Are you ok?'

'I'm fine,' I assured her as I sat back down. 'How did you meet Tony?'

'Fate, I guess. Jason had been missing for six months. I went off the rails and spent most nights in the Lister. Tony was sitting at the bar one night and we got talking. He was reluctant to tell me what he did for a living. You could imagine why he doesn't go about shouting about it. When he told me he was a psychic, I'm sure I asked him if Jase was dead. He wouldn't tell me. When he was leaving, I followed him outside and in my drunken state, begged him to tell me. Things just went from there.'

'I wasn't sure how much was true about what happened,' I said. 'You know what the papers are like. Maybe it's just ignorance but I've never believed in that sort of thing.'

'Neither did I, to be honest, I do now though.'

'How does it work, does he hear voices or use a crystal ball or something?' I asked in all seriousness but she found it amusing for some reason. I could feel myself beginning to relax a little.

'No, I don't think it works like that, I can't explain it. You would have to ask him.'

That was never going to be an option so I found this a strange thing for her to say. 'Has he said anything?'

'Well... no, not really,' she said unconvincingly.

45

'He has hasn't he? What did he say?' I asked, uncertain that I really wanted an answer.

'He said that Evan's alive.'

For a split second, I could imagine Ray's reaction to this. He would have exploded. I didn't know how to react. Should I be glad? Should I be angry?

'I want to know what else he has to say,' I told her.

'I'm sure he'd be fine with that. Do you want me to ask him if he'll see you?'

I told her I did despite the fact that I really didn't want to meet him, I just wanted to know what this so-called psychic had to say for himself.

8
CAROLINE

24th March 2018

My phone was flashing 'Tony calling...' Without lifting my head, I reached over, pressed answer and held it to my ear.

'Caroline?'

'What?' My annoyance escaped involuntarily.

'I take it you're still in bed?'

     'Yes, what time is it?'

'Nine-thirty. Well if you're still in bed you won't know that you're on the front page of the paper looking cosy with Rebecca Shelby.' I let out a sigh of further annoyance and kicked the covers off. 'Oh, and the best bit is the headline: *Is Psychic Tony looking for Evan?* What the hell, Caroline?' I sat up. Now I was awake.

'What? Wait a minute. Maybe if you hadn't been ignoring my calls yesterday you would know that I met her. Yes, she asked me about you but the press couldn't have known. It's paper talk, that's all. What was I meant to do? Not meet her so that they couldn't jump to bloody conclusions.'

'I'm not saying you shouldn't have spoken to her but there's a ton of reporters outside my flat and now I don't want to go home.'

'Where are you?' I peeled back the curtain an inch, I saw cameras and microphones poking out under a canopy of umbrellas. 'Yeah they're here too. It's hardly my fault though.'

'I'm at the shop. They caught me off guard on the way out. All I wanted was some milk and a bloody newspaper.'

'Well if you're not even home, then I'm sure they'll be gone by the time you get back,' I suggested.

'I hope you're right. I'll call you back in a bit.' He hung up without a goodbye.

In my attempt to remain unseen by the reporters outside my gate, I avoided the front of the house. The curtains were all drawn so the only chance of them seeing me was through the glass in the front door. Edging my way down the last few steps on my bottom, swinging my head around limbo style, I crawled to the kitchen. I needed my coffee and cigarette.

With my coffee and phone in hand I made my way back up the stairs. I never smoked in the house, always outside the back door but it wouldn't have been the first time that reporters had entered my property and casually made themselves at home in my back garden.

I closed the bathroom door behind me, opened the window a couple of inches and switched on the hot water in the hope the steam would diffuse the smoke out quicker. I lit up and inhaled. I inhaled until it filled my lungs; held it for a second before releasing it slowly and blissfully. Each draw after that was filled with disgust as I watched the cloud of nicotine clinging to my voile curtains.

After spraying the bathroom with half a can of air freshener, I decided to read the article that Tony was talking about - *Is Psychic Tony Looking for Evan?*

Not only was there a photo of me and Rebecca, but one of Tony too, taken outside the police station last year – he looked rough and exhausted. The photo of me and Rebecca had been taken through the café window and zoomed in, showing the details of my face. Rebecca's head rested on my shoulder as my arms wrapped around her. The look of anguish and surprise made it possible for me to tell the second it had been taken. It was when the young girl made her first leap towards the door.

The article itself was complete nonsense- it made out that Rebecca had organised the whole thing in the hope that Tony would help her find Evan. I imagined Rebecca reading it and never wanting to speak to me again. I had no doubt Emma would have seen it, advising her on what to do and what not to do.

As I stepped into the shower a few minutes later my thoughts were still on Rebecca. The truth is - after she left my house the previous day, I hadn't stopped thinking about her. I kept hoping that Tony had been right about Evan. It was disturbing to think though, that if he was alive, where was he? What had he gone through? What was he going through? I had no idea what happened leading up to Jase's murder but the thoughts of what could have happened still haunted me. Rebecca came across like she was holding it together but only barely so.

While rinsing the soapy lather off my skin, a thud on the bathroom door made me jolt. There was someone in my house. My doors were definitely locked- they always are. I instinctively scanned the steam-filled bathroom for a method of defence. A candle in a jar? I reached out for a towel and the candle.

'Caroline, it's me.'

'For Christ's sake, Tony,' I yelled back.

9
CAROLINE

I quickly dried myself, threw on a robe and headed down the stairs. He was already sitting at the kitchen table hugging his coffee, his wet hair clamped to his forehead. 'Do you not wash your face in the shower?' he asked. I used my fingers to wipe away mascara streaks that I could only imagine were smeared the length of my face.

'Yes but I don't normally get disturbed in the shower like that,' I replied. 'How did you get here? How did you get in?'

'Well, the journos didn't leave. They probably guessed I wasn't going far when they saw I had my slippers on.' He held a leg out from under the table to display a brown suede moccasin. 'And I got in with your back door key that you didn't put much thought into hiding. Why do you even hide a key?'

'I forgot it was there. Please don't ever do that again!' I demanded.

'Sorry. I promise I won't.' He smiled slightly and it was enough to calm me down.

'How are you?' I sat down facing him.

'Well, I shouldn't be surprised. I saw this coming you know? I knew I'd be dragged into it somehow.'

'You don't have to get involved. If you steer clear then they're not going to have much to say, are they?' I said this with instant regret, knowing that the reason I was desperate to see him was to convince him to meet Rebecca, to get right in there and find her boy.

'I suppose,' He shrugged.

'I have to be honest with you though, Rebecca does want to speak to you.'

I didn't say any more. I watched his reaction. He stared into his coffee and I had no idea what he was thinking. He closed his eyes and the silence dragged out for at least a few minutes.

'I don't want this media attention,' he said finally. 'I hate it. I hate them. I don't want to get involved Caroline, not with all the press hounding me like that.'

'So is it just the press that's stopping you?' I asked, trying my hardest to sound sympathetic instead of hopeful.

'Oh, I don't know.'

Again, I left it there. I didn't want to pressure him and jeopardise that little bit of hope he was giving me. Some people are easy to manipulate, and I'll admit that if I feel it's for a good cause, friend or no friend, I will pull that card.

'Let's change the subject,' I suggested and he smiled in agreement.

'What're your plans for today?' he asked.

'I've nothing planned, what about you?'

'It looks like I'll be here for a while so maybe we should make a start packing up those boxes,' he suggested.

'Oh, I don't know,' I said.

'You can't put it off forever if you want make a fresh start somewhere else.'

'I know. I'm just dreading it that's all.' But he already knew that because I had been putting it off for weeks now.

When is the right time to box up your child's room? Pack it all away, knowing they are never coming back: a month, a year, two years, ten years, never? I knew he'd never walk through that door again, I had accepted that. I dusted and vacuumed his room regularly, leaving everything in its place. Clearing it away meant removing the only comfort I had left.

'You know you don't have to get rid of anything, right? All Jase's stuff will be safe and protected inside the boxes until you get to your new little house, wherever that may be. You'll still have your memories with you too.' He placed a hand on my shoulder.

'You're right, I know. I need to get out of here I really do. I'll do it soon, I promise,' I replied. 'You can help me have a clear out if you want? Get a load of stuff ready to go to the dump. I reckon I'll need about fifty runs,' I exaggerated.

'It's ok, your secret's safe with me.' He winked, referring to my overflowing, junk-ridden cupboards. 'I'll grab some boxes, I'm sure the charity shop will welcome some of your crap.'

Tony didn't know about my money troubles, only that I wanted out of Blackbridge. When Ronnie committed suicide, his life insurance didn't pay out. The house was paid for but it was the rest, the bills and the upkeep that I couldn't afford. I thought about going back to my psychology degree; pick up where I left off all those years ago, before I fell in love. It was hardly an instant solution to my problems though. Not that I could possibly be that Caroline again anyway. That was twenty years ago. I had come a long way from being twenty-two and carefree. I was confident and happy back then. I could see myself, how I looked, how I held myself but it was like watching a stranger.

I followed him to the cupboard under the stairs where we had stored the boxes. 'We may as well start in here,' he said.

'Whatever.' I was already regretting the task that lay ahead of us. Years' worth of junk had accumulated and a sense of anticipation washed over me at the thought of possible reminders of Ronnie and memories of my Jase that I might soon be faced with. I let Tony take the lead.

'So what's she like then?' he asked while trying to find the end of the duct tape.

'Who? Rebecca?'

'Yes, what was she like?'

'She was nice. She wanted me to meet her at that Jeanie's Café so I did. It was quiet and after we got talking she got really upset. She's really struggling, Tony, it was so horrible to see, and when I put my arms around her to comfort her that's when those bastards must have taken that photo. The wee girl behind the counter locked us in when she saw them and we ran out the back way. Then, she came here for a coffee. I just wish there was something I could do.'

'I take it Emma and her cronies aren't getting anywhere?'

'Nope, same old shit,' I replied as he handed me a holdall full of other empty holdalls. Tossing it to the side, I quickly returned my gaze to the back of his head waiting on further comment. Instead he began making a pile next to him with paint pots and tools. 'I said I would give her a call after I spoke to you. Do you just want me to say that you don't want to get involved after the way you were treated the last time? Or, what do you want me to say?'

He sighed and I knew he was feeling guilty for not wanting to help. How could he not? Knowing me better than anyone, he probably knew that that was my intention.

'It's not that I don't want to help. I just can't. I don't want my name all over the papers - slagging me off and making up shit for the sake of entertainment. They don't care whose lives they ruin, do they?'

'I know Tony, but you have to look at the bigger picture. What if you find him…alive? Isn't that more important? I'm not saying his life is more important than yours obviously, but he's just a boy. Could you honestly live with yourself knowing there was something you could have done? I know I couldn't,' I said. I realised how that sounded and didn't want him feeling any worse than he already did but it was true. I often wondered how different things could have been if I met Tony sooner. Maybe he would have found Jase alive. Rebecca deserved that chance. 'I'm sure we could arrange it so that the press wouldn't know. She hates them as much as we do.'

'You're not going to give up, are you?'

'I can't. I'm sorry, not when it's this important to me,' I replied.

'OK, I'll speak to her. But on the condition that nobody else knows about it.' He let out another sigh as I grabbed him around the shoulders. 'I mean it. If word gets out, I'm done.'

'Thank you, you're doing the right thing,' I assured him.

10
REBECCA

24th March 2018

Ray had gone out and I had no doubt he'd be searching over the same places again; the places that had already been covered, but I understood because I did it too. No matter how futile it was, at least you felt like you were doing something.

I had been staring at Caroline's name on my phone for over half an hour. Underneath her name was the green phone symbol that read 'call' and a yellow speech bubble for 'message,' My finger hovered between the two and I tried to convince myself, that the reason she hadn't called was because she hadn't spoken to Tony yet.

Psychics or mediums, or whatever else they call themselves, were not something I had ever believed in; it was all a bit far-fetched. It's not that I don't believe in the after-life, because I do. I just couldn't believe that someone that's very much alive can have a conversation with somebody that's dead and buried. I just thought that if it was possible, then surely there would be a psychic working for every criminal investigation team in the world. Surely, there would be nobody missing or getting away with murder.

There's that other stuff too. People say it's 'spooky' when you're thinking about someone and they call you, or something happens in your day and you think *wait a minute, I had a dream about that last night.* It has to be coincidence, surely? I couldn't say I had given it much thought, but what I did want to know, was what made Tony

Delimonte think that Evan was alive. What explanation could he possibly have for having this prediction or whatever it was? Any normal person wouldn't toy with people's emotions like that.

Emma didn't say much about Tony when I asked her about him that morning. Only that, 'He found Jase after everyone else had failed.' I already knew this but hearing her admitting failure and his triumph gave me the impression that there was admiration there. I had a feeling she was trying to sway me in his direction, like she did with Caroline. There had been no warning against him. Only, that she 'has to advise me not to get him involved.' Not that she did, just that she *had* to.

The mention of Max Watson however, provoked more of a reaction. As soon as I mentioned the word *nasty*, she jumped to his defence. 'Max is a good man. He made a mistake,' she said. 'Tony is not the reason he left. There's a lot of money to be made working as a private detective if you are as good as Max.'

'So why didn't he find Jase if he's that good?' I asked.

'I'll tell you it wasn't for lack of trying, I'll tell you that much. Patterson was calculating, he knew exactly what he was doing. He was very clever in covering up his tracks,' she replied. I was beginning to see a glimpse of the real Emma. Her professionalism was wavering and she knew it. Needless to say, she had somewhere else to be after that, leaving me worried that history was repeating and that this was the very reason they were getting nowhere with the investigation.

I jumped when my phone finally vibrated and the screen changed to *Caroline calling...*

'Hello,' I answered.

'Hello Rebecca, it's Caroline.'

'Did you speak to Tony?' I asked immediately.

'Yes, he's just left. Did you see the article in the Mail?'

'Yes. I take it you've seen it too?'

'I read it online. It's a disgrace,' she said. 'They'll write anything to sell a story. Tony was a bit upset about it.'

'I could imagine,' I said although I didn't really care what he thought. I was upset about it. Ray was more than upset, he was furious. Luckily, Emma was there to de-escalate the situation – she told him that it was her idea and that she thought he knew about my rendezvous with Caroline. She turned to me and I simply apologised and said I hadn't gotten round to mentioning it – as if it was no big deal. He gave up and stormed out.

'Tony said he's happy to see you but wants to avoid the press. Do you think that would be possible?'

Initially I thought there wasn't a hope in hell, but then I recalled the night that I had switched all the lights off early and the reporters all left because there was nothing left to see.

'Yes, later on in the evening shouldn't be a problem,' I said, knowing I'd have to worry about getting round Ray later. Meeting Caroline was one thing but if he knew I was away to speak to Tony, I'm certain he would somehow put a stop to it.

'We were thinking the same thing. Tony suggested going to his mum's house. It's not far from here.'

'If you text me the time and address, I'll be there.'

'Perfect, see you tonight,' she replied before ending the call.

Not having Ray on side meant that I had to speak to my mum, I needed someone to confide in.

'Hi, Mum, it's me,' I said when she answered.

'Hi, honey, has something happened? I was getting worried. I just said to Harry that I was going to give you a call.'

'Harry? So he is aware that his nephew is missing then?' I hadn't even received as much as a text from him and it hadn't gone unnoticed.

'Of course he does, he just doesn't know how to deal with it, that's all. Please don't be like that, sweetheart.'

'Do you know what? I don't even care. I've got more to worry about than Harry.'

'Yes, you do. So, has anything changed?' she asked again.

'No, nothing. I was waiting on a phone call from Caroline Frank, Jase's mum?'

'Oh right, why was that?' she asked.

'Well, I met her yesterday.'

'Really? How is she?' she asked with genuine concern. My mum would mother everyone, given half the chance.

'She's doing ok, better than I would if I was her,' I said.

'We're all stronger than we think, honey.'

'I'm going to meet that Tony guy, you know, the psychic?'

There was a pause. 'I thought you didn't believe in stuff like that?' she said eventually.

'I don't, but he said to Caroline that Evan is alive, and I know that he is mum. It was a bit of a shock to hear that somebody actually agrees with me. I really just want to go and see what he has to say for himself.'

'How does Ray feel about it?' she asked.

'He doesn't know. I think he'd freak out.'

'Oh Rebecca, you shouldn't be keeping things from him,' she said.

'I know. But you agree that I should go?'

'Definitely.'

'Ok, thanks. Well, I'm going with Caroline to meet him tonight. I'll probably be home late, but I'll phone you first thing in the morning.'

11
REBECCA

I dimmed the lights early that night as planned. From the upstairs window I waited to see the last reporter leave.

9pm, 42 Rowan Court. Could you please bring something of Evan's? The text read an hour after I had spoken to her. It was going to be a three mile cycle, according to Google Maps.

Ray looked at me in what I could only describe as either disbelief or disgust when he saw me with my Lycra on. 'I need to get out of the house,' is all I said. He wasn't stupid but surprisingly, he let me go without an argument. The one we had that morning about the article must have exhausted him.

Ray always said that I shouldn't trust people so easily, and that just because I didn't see the bad in people, it doesn't mean it wasn't there. I always retaliated by telling him he watched too much TV; he said I didn't watch enough. I wasn't naive, I knew what went on in the world, more so now than ever, but I've always preferred to look for the good in people. It has to be better than living in Ray's world, where everyone had an ulterior motive and nobody should be trusted. Giving people a chance was what I would normally do. But one thing was for sure, I'd never suffered fools gladly.

In Rowan Court, number 42 was the last bungalow on the right. It looked tiny from the front, displaying an oversized front window with its door to the left. As I pushed my bike into the driveway, I noticed the side of the house was over twice as long. I passed two little windows and a larger one before reaching the side door. Through the few inches where the blind didn't quite reach the ledge, I could tell it was the kitchen. While resting my bike against the end wall, I saw the red of Caroline's hair approaching through the glass pane. Scanning the street, she ushered me in. I was welcomed with an unassertive smile and hug. 'Glad you could make it,' she said. 'Come through.'

We walked in a U shape past a dining room, two bedrooms and another door that must have been the bathroom. The living room was on the left. The smell of patchouli grew stronger as we entered, reminding me of my grandmother. Tony stood up and reached out his hand for me to shake. I had seen photographs of him in the paper, so he appeared familiar. He was taller than I had imagined, at least 6ft. His hair was darker too, more rust than strawberry blonde, but it could have been the lighting, or lack of it. There was a little oriental table lamp in the corner giving out nothing more than a glow. The rest of the room was flickering with tea-lights on every shelf and surface; a bit too clichéd, I thought. I took a seat next to Caroline on the sofa; Tony sat facing us at the other side of the coffee table. There was no sign of his mum.

'Sorry about this.' He used his head and eyes to suggest he meant the room. 'My mum's idea, she tries her best to help out and I don't have the heart to tell her that this isn't how I work.'

'That's ok, I quite like it,' I said, because I sort of did after hearing that it wasn't his idea.

'Would you like a drink? Tea, coffee, something stronger?' he asked.

'Coffee, please, I'm driving.' I gave a slight wave of my helmet before laying it on the floor.

'Coffee, it is.' He smiled before heading to the kitchen.

61

'Are you ok?' Caroline asked.

'I suppose,' I replied, grateful at least that I wasn't alone.

'Tony's lovely,' she assured me. 'He's no different to you and me.' I knew what she meant by this, but still found it a strange thing to say. He claimed to speak to dead people for goodness sake.

'I know,' I found myself saying.

'Tony didn't ask you to bring something belonging to Evan but I thought I would mention it. I know it can sometimes help.'

'It's ok I did wonder about that, I brought a ring,' I told her, showing her the ring attached to the chain around my neck. I had no idea what to bring. It was a choice out of the ring and the baby blanket I found that he used to carry around by the label. I figured the ring would be easier to carry.

'That's nice,' she said.

When Tony returned I decided not to beat around the bush. 'Sorry Tony, I don't know anything about this kind of stuff. Could you explain it to me?'

'Of course, I'll try to explain it as best I can,' he replied, then paused. 'I'll try putting it like this; if you ask someone to find something out, like...who was the prime minister in 1933, for example, they'll maybe try to find the answer by looking on the internet. Someone else who doesn't have a computer might go to the library. Someone else might ask a friend who would know the answer. My point is, everyone gets their information in a different way. It's the same for psychics. Some psychics see things, others hear things or feel things but all could end up with the same information. I personally see some things but get most of my information through hearing, I'm clairaudient. A medium means that I get my information from the spirit world.'

'So people that have passed, you mean?'

'Yes. Do you believe in the spirit world?' he asked me.

'I'm not sure,' I replied. 'So you hear voices?'

'Kind of. I don't hear other people's voices as such. It's more like I hear my own voice in my head but the information is coming from the spirit world.'

'Ok.' I hesitated as I wondered how the hell he would know the difference between his own thoughts and information from the spirit world. I decided not to ask. 'So what makes you think Evan is alive?'

'Ever since Evan went missing, some people have just assumed that it's my job to find him. I don't believe it is. I wouldn't dream about getting involved in something important like this without being asked to. It wouldn't be fair. If I'm being honest, curiosity got the better of me, so I asked if he was alive and was informed that he was. I don't know anything else and won't try to find out unless you want me to.'

'I do,' I replied. Despite being unconvinced by his spiel, I couldn't take the chance that this man was not deluded. 'What do I need to do?'

'You don't need to do anything-'

'Rebecca has a ring belonging to Evan,' Caroline interrupted.

'Do you?'

'Yes,' I said as I removed the chain from my neck.

'Can you leave it with me?'

'I'd rather not. Why can't you do it now?'

'Sorry, I presumed you would need to get home,' Tony replied.

'No, I don't have much to go home to,' I heard myself saying.

'Of course, I'm sorry,' he said out of sympathy.

'What about your husband?' Caroline asked.

'He won't mind,' I said. I could have kicked myself. I have never been one for discussing our marriage with anyone but I'm sure I had just made my feelings towards Ray perfectly clear.

'Well I'll be happy to do it now while you're here if that's what you want?'

'Sorry to put you on the spot like this but I can't leave with nothing or without trying at least.'

'That's ok, I'll be back in a minute,' he said.

Caroline and I didn't speak a word while he was away. I don't know about her but I was worried about what he might say, or what I might say. I was sure I'd have a smart answer for everything that came out his mouth. I would be giving nothing away, that was for sure.

'Just try to relax, taking deep breaths will help,' he advised as he sat back in his chair comfortably, holding the ring on the end of his thumb. 'Please bear with me as I prepare.' He closed his eyes. It makes me think of Whoopi Goldberg in *Ghost*, luckily without the theatricals. I took Caroline's lead and closed my eyes too.

'Your father has passed, Rebecca?' He opened his eyes and looked at me for confirmation. 'David, Davie?'

'Yes, David,' I replied.

'This was his ring, his wedding ring. He gave it to Evan when he knew he didn't have long left to live. Is this correct?'

'Yes.'

'Your brother was annoyed because he believed it should have been given to him. Your Dad says he made the right decision.'

'Yes,' I said again before realising that he wasn't asking me, he was telling me. It's true. Harry made a few hints that

64

it should've been given to him. I did agree but it was Dad's decision not ours.

'He wants you to know he's still proud of you. He is saying you're his little mathematician, his little Carol Vorderman. You were worried he would be disappointed when you didn't take that job in London but he wasn't, he was proud that you put your family before your career. He wishes he had done the same.'

My chest was tightening, how could he have known this? I imagined my Dad standing next to Tony, smiling that incredible smile as he was telling me that he was proud.

'Evan isn't hurt; he's just a bit scared and wanting to come home.'

'Oh God. Stop. Stop. I can't take this.' I couldn't breathe. I felt Caroline's arms around me. She was telling me it was ok, that I didn't have to hear anymore. I felt sick. I didn't want to believe him but how could he have known this stuff? It was all too personal.

'Can I have a drink of water?' I asked before Caroline ran to get it.

'I'll be ok, please carry on,' I said.

'Are you sure?' Tony asked with concern.

'Yes.'

'Evan has been moving around a lot. Could you give me more please?' He was saying it like he was having a conversation on the telephone; like he was on the phone to my Dad. 'Ok, thank you and god bless,' he finished. 'Rebecca your Dad is away for now but you've not to worry, he is always here and loves you very much.'

In that moment I wanted to scream for him to come back, to tell me where to find Evan. I was desperate. Instead, I took a long drink of the cold water that Caroline had just handed to me.

'Some kind of ruin,' Tony announced.' 'Your Dad showed me a ruin.'

Maybe I was in shock or having some kind of panic attack, but I just stared. Caroline and Tony were moving around. I know they were talking but I wasn't listening to what was being said. I could see a ruin too, what was left of an old house maybe. Why was I not getting up? Why was I not doing something?

'Rebecca. Rebecca, are you ok?' I snapped out of it as Caroline's voice began to register.

'Yes, yes, I'm fine,' I said.

'Do you want a lift home?' she asked.

'No, I'll be fine. I just need fresh air.'

'Listen, first thing in the morning we will go out and have a look, there's not much we can do in the dark. Go home and get some rest. We'll do some research on ruins in the area, won't we, Tony?' she said.

'Of course,' he answered. 'Caroline's right, you need to rest.'

'Ok,' I said, picking up my helmet. I made my way back through the house the way I came in. I think they were both behind me, but I'm not sure. Confused and drained I wondered what the hell had just happened.

12
REBECCA

I must have been on autopilot because I have no recollection of my journey home. It wasn't until my hand was on the handle of the back door that I remembered Ray had no idea where I'd been. I had that feeling you get when you're a teenager trying to sober up and act normal when you get home to your parents.

He was sitting in his usual position, in front of his laptop at the kitchen table. 'Where the hell have you been?' he asked.

'What's it to you?' I retorted, realising that I did in fact sound like a teenager.

'What's it to me? You're my wife, our son is missing and despite how you feel about me, I have a right to know that my wife is safe.'

'Well, now you know I'm fine.' I snapped, although I did feel an instant guilt.

'I was about to phone the police, who the hell do you know that lives in Rowan Court?'

'Why are you asking that?'

'Because I know that's where you've been,' he answered.

'Wait a minute, did you follow me?'

'No I didn't follow you.'

'So how the hell do you know where I've been?'

'Phone tracker,' he revealed, turning the laptop to face me. 'I thought I better check it before I phoned them.' He stood up using his legs to throw the chair back. It rolled back and stopped with a crash against the fridge.

'Why didn't you just phone me, instead of checking up on me like that?' Our voices were gradually rising with each retaliation.

'Because I knew you wouldn't answer. You still haven't answered my question. Who lives in Rowan Court?' he demanded.

'Tony Delimonte's mum!' I screamed at him before leaving the room.

'How could you be so stupid?' He followed me.

'I had to see him, Ray. I don't see you coming up with any other ideas. Nobody's doing anything and if you must know he told me Evan is alive, and I believe him.'

'So what, you believe in psychics now?' he yelled.

'Go away Ray!' I screamed as I shut the bathroom door and locked it behind me.

Clutching my dad's ring, I slid down the back of the door until I reached the cold tiles. All the things that Tony said were true. He couldn't have been told, or guessed - the odds were too great. I struggled with the idea that my Dad was proud though. I should have taken that job in London, demanded that we relocate. It was bad enough that I decided to stay so that Evan's education wouldn't be disrupted, but I also thought he would be safer here.

Maybe there was a logical explanation that my mind wasn't open to, but no matter how hard I tried to work it out, it didn't matter. I believed him - my Dad was there tonight.

'Oh, Dad, please help us bring him home,' I whispered.

13
CAROLINE

'Was it a castle? What did it look like?' I asked Tony as he tapped away on the glowing screen in front of him.

'No it wasn't a castle. It was more like an old farm cottage.'

'That's what I have in mind but all that is coming up here is castles in Scotland,' I told him.

'No it definitely wasn't a castle.'

I typed *old farm ruins Scotland* into Google on my phone. 'Right, there's photography and derelict property for sale. Maybe you should look through the photographs and I'll look at estate agents?' I suggested, hoping that he would recognise one of them from the image he saw earlier.

'Ok, that sounds like a plan, but could we go to your house to do it? Mum's probably lying awake. She won't settle until the house is locked up.'

'I think that's a good idea.' I thought of the comfort of my own home; skinny jeans off, bra off, pyjamas on, glass of wine. Tony gathered his things as I began the never ending task of blowing the tea-lights out, while checking the ceiling for a smoke detector that was guaranteed to go off if there was one.

'I'll get you in the car,' he said, 'I'll grab some things to stay over. There's not much point in me driving home to come back in the morning.'

'Ok,' I replied. He had stayed over a few times to save him the drive home to his flat in Perth, so it didn't come as a surprise. He practically lived with me for a while after I attempted suicide. It was a comfort knowing there was someone sleeping in the next room, or downstairs on the couch depending on where he chose.

Sitting in the car as he gathered his things, the digital clock on the dashboard read 23.45. Although it was freezing, I decided against turning the engine on, afraid that the hole in my exhaust would irritate or wake the neighbours. I rubbed my hands together instead and blew on them with my vaporising breath.

My attention was drawn to the passenger mirror. A dark shadow blocked the reflection of the street light for a split second. Whatever it had been, was close to the car. I'm jumpy, I told myself. Being around spirits makes me like this; that feeling you get after watching a horror movie. But I wasn't being paranoid. A man in dark clothing passed the passenger window. Tony was now locking the door unaware of this strange man but instantly I knew what was coming, the broadening of his shoulders, his clenched fist.

The next thing I knew, Tony's head smashed off the wall and I was now protecting my own head in horror, like I used to do. I closed my eyes: one, two, three, four, five, six, seven. There was no excuse, I was a coward. As I opened my eyes to peer through the gap in my forearms, I saw Tony sitting against the door with his knees pulled up to his chest. There was blood on his face and hands and the man was gone.

'I'm sorry,' I cried as I knelt beside him. 'I'm so sorry.'

'I'm ok,' he told me, but he was trembling and upset so I knew this wasn't true.

'I need to look at you in the light, give me the key.'

'No, I don't want Mum to see me like this. Let's just go.'

I had an old towel on the back seat so gave it to him for his nose. 'Pinch the soft part of your nose and tip your head slightly forward,' I instructed as I started the engine and pulled out of the driveway. 'We need to phone the police. I'll take you to accident and emergency.'

'No, let's go to yours. It's nothing.'

'You better get it checked out. That gash is pretty deep.' I glanced in his direction. Even in the dark, I could tell that all the blood was seeping out one open wound in the middle of his temple.

'I'm sure you can fix it up,' he said.

'Tony, we need to phone the police,' I repeated.

'I don't want the police involved.'

'Why not? Somebody has just attacked you. Did you see his face?'

'No, but from what he just said, I could guess that it's Rebecca's husband.'

'Oh shit.' Somehow, I knew she hadn't told her husband. I think it was the way she dismissed him like there was no love lost there. So I wasn't too surprised, a thug, like my Ronnie. I wondered if she'd ever been on the receiving end of his vile fists. If she had bruises on her skull or her back or cigarette burns on her stomach. 'He should be locked up,' I said.

'I don't think that would help Rebecca, do you?'

I shook my head, anger rising inside me. 'I wouldn't be so sure,' I wanted to say, but I knew Tony would disagree. He'd say that he's just an angry man, who wants his son back. There could have been truth in that, but it was still no excuse for going around assaulting people. 'I wouldn't be surprised if he knows where Evan is,' I threw out there, unable to keep my thoughts to myself any longer. I instantly wished I could take it back. My disregard for the fact that Tony was wrongly accused of the same thing, was regrettable.

'That's not fair, Caroline,' he replied.

14
CAROLINE

Eventually we were settled and back to our research. It was 1.30am and I did not have enough brain power left to concentrate. Tony was showing signs of two black eyes and the gash on his head wasn't as bad as I first thought, held together sufficiently with butterfly stitches. I had to remind myself that I was doing this for Rebecca, and Evan of course, because the thought of helping her husband in any way was going against my grain.

'Maybe we should leave this until the morning,' Tony suggested and I agreed by downing the rest of my wine and placing the glass on the table. Tony had already finished a large glass of wine and it had settled him. I was relieved because there is something quite disturbing about seeing Tony upset - despite being six feet tall, he blubbers a bit like a child.

'You know where everything is,' I said. 'Do you think she'll still want our help after this?'

'I really don't know. We'll need to wait and see if she gets in touch.'

'Are you sure you're ok? I'm worried about leaving you, you might have a concussion.' I stroked his hair.

'Stop worrying. I'm fine, honestly. I'll give you a shout if I need anything.'

'How can you shout if you're unconscious?' I asked.

'Shut up.' He laughed.

But that very thought was there now and this was enough for me to convince him that I needed to keep an eye on him. I suggested sleeping on the other sofa but we both agreed that it would make more sense if he slept in my bed beside me.

When we were both settled side by side I watched him trying to get comfortable. With a wound on one side of his head and bruising on the other, he settled for lying on his back, staring at the ceiling.

'I think you're going to have two black eyes,' I said before dimming the bedside lamp.

'Hopefully the press won't recognise me,' he joked.

'I just hope they don't find out what happened,' I said. 'That would just defeat the whole purpose of us trying to keep it quiet.'

He sighed before saying, 'I hate this place, Caroline. Do you ever feel like running away from here and never looking back?'

'That's the whole point of moving. I don't think I'll run too far though. But, if you left, I'd need to come with you.'

'If it wasn't for Mum, I'm sure I would have done it already,' he said. 'And yeah, I wouldn't leave you here of course.'

'Where would we go?' I asked, 'Tell me.' I closed my eyes ready to imagine us there together.

'Havana.'

'Havana?' This made me laugh, purely because I wasn't expecting it. Although I really had no idea what I was expecting.

'No? Ok, so where do you want to go?'

'I don't know, I don't think I'm ready for a culture shock like that though. What about Devon or Cornwall?'

'Mmm, I suppose it would be better than this.'

'A little cottage by the sea would be nice,' I said.

'It would,' he replied and at that I could tell he was already drifting off. I listened to the sound of his breathing change and took one last look at his beaten face. This was all my fault.

15
CAROLINE

25th March 2018

As the morning arrived, I could hear Tony clattering about downstairs. I lay in bed going over the events of the night before. I had no idea how Ray's attack on Tony would affect our search for Evan. If we were still to go ahead with it then we needed more to go on than 'a ruin.' The chances of finding and searching every single one in the area was far too time consuming. That was assuming it was in this area. I wasn't even sure if we'd hear from Rebecca again. Where would that leave us? Personally, I hoped we would carry on regardless but I doubted Tony would agree.

When I finally got up he was sat on the sofa drinking coffee. The curtains were still closed but there was enough light coming through to show that the bruising on his face was developing into different shades of purple and blue. His eyelids were pink and swollen.

'Oh my God, Tony. What a mess. How are you feeling?' I asked.

'I feel fine, just a bit tender,' he replied. 'How are you?'

'I'm fine. I managed to get a couple of hours at least.'

'Me too. Your cup's ready and the kettle's just boiled,' he informed me.

'Thanks.'

As I stood at the back door with my coffee and cigarette, I could hear the sound of footsteps crunching on the gravel at the side of the house. A police radio crackled intermittently with the sound of a muffled male voice as it got closer. A young male officer appeared from the side of the wall.

'Caroline Frank?'

'Yes. What is it?' I asked.

'I'm looking for Tony Delimonte. Is he here?' he asked.

'Eh, yes. Go back around and I'll let you in the front.'

'That's the police here to see you,' I informed Tony on the way to the front door.

'And so it begins.' He sighed.

'I doubt it. They'd have a hard neck.'

Mottled by the glass, the yellow high visibility vest wasn't at the door as I expected, it was further down the path conversing with another dark clothed body. I opened the door to hear Emma say 'It's ok, I've got this.' The officer turned and walked towards the van parked out on the street next to a couple of photographers. Retreating instantly, I left the door open so she could let herself in.

'Caroline, Tony.'

'What's up?' Tony asked as I quickly opened the curtains.

'Raymond Shelby has been charged with your assault. He's in custody at the moment,' she informed him. 'I'm going to need a statement?'

'I don't want to press charges,' Tony replied.

'It doesn't work like that in Scotland anymore, I'm afraid, Tony,' she said, confirming what I already knew.

'Do you want me to go upstairs?' I asked them both.

'No I don't mind, she'll probably want a statement from you too.'

'Did you see what happened, Caroline?' she asked.

'Yes I was in the car. How did you find out?' I asked.

'Ray told me when I was in this morning. You should have reported it,' she said. 'He's wondering what I'm going to do about you filling Rebecca's head with rubbish.'

76

'Rubbish? Come on Emma you know fine well it's not rubbish,' I snapped.

'Listen, all I want is for that boy to be found. So if you find anything before we do, I want to be the first to know. That's all I'm going to say on the matter. Just don't get the press involved, please,' she said. There she was, the Emma we knew and admired. I was beginning to wonder what was more important to her, finding Evan or her reputation.

'Ok,' I replied.

'You give your statement first,' Tony finally spoke, 'I'm going for a quick shower.'

While he was upstairs, I told Emma what I saw and about the ruin. Again, she told me not to involve the press. She would have known that Tony wouldn't have wanted them to know and wasn't out to cause trouble or jeopardise the investigation so her repetition was unnecessary.

When I had finished giving her my statement, I went in the shower while Tony gave his. Emma's words led me to think about the possible benefits of leaking the information about the ruin. There was a chance that we could find Evan so much quicker if the public were involved in searching ruins in their area; it would save so much time.

I have to admit: it's difficult not to think about money when you have none, but as soon as the thought of getting paid for it sprung to mind, I pushed the idea out again. *I'd never stoop that low,* I had to remind myself.

Emma was gone by the time I was finished getting ready. 'Should I phone Rebecca?' I asked Tony.

'No, I think we're going to have to wait on her getting in touch. We don't know what the situation is like between her and her husband. We could end up making things worse for her. In the meantime, I want to go here,' he said, holding out his tablet for me to look at. On the screen was an image similar to the one I had pictured in my head. Below it read *Renovation project- ruined barn- Crail.*

'Ok, let's go,' I replied, pleased that we were on the same wavelength.

16
CAROLINE

As we drove up the farm road towards the ruined cottage, juddering over the potholes made me squeamish. Either that or it was my nerves. The thought of not knowing what we might discover definitely wasn't helping.

'Isn't that it?' I asked as we turned around a bend. 'This can't be the place, Tony.' The old barn was certainly the one in the picture with its tin roof flaked with red paint, but it looked more like a tourist attraction. There were five cars and a group of more than a dozen people.

'They're maybe looking to buy it,' Tony said.

'Will we pretend to be interested and still have a look around?' I suggested.

'Ok. It must mean Evan isn't here but it's still worth taking a look.'

A large man with a tattoo on his neck approached as I stepped out the car. 'He's not here, love,' he said.

'Who?' I asked him, suddenly realising what the answer might be.

'The boy. Evan.' I looked at Tony in horror and for some sort of explanation. He gave me nothing.

'I'm sorry, what are you talking about?' I asked.

'The boy that's missing. Sorry love, I thought that's why you were here.'

'No, we're just looking to buy it. Why, what's happening?' I asked, pleading ignorance.

'It's all over Facebook,' he explained. 'Apparently that psychic guy who found the last bairn has said that Evan is alive and being kept in some kind of ruin.'

'Oh really,' I responded trying to keep up the pretence.

'Let's go. Caroline, we'll come back later,' Tony said, giving me the eye to get back in the car. So I did.

'Fuck! I don't fucking believe this,' he said. 'I don't believe it.'

We drove, both trying to figure out who had betrayed us.

'Check to see who the original post came from,' he said.

I tried to check Facebook on my phone but didn't have a signal. We were almost back at Blackbridge before my newsfeed finally loaded. It didn't take long to find the post, it was the second or third one to appear. It had been shared over 500 times and had been written by an Annabelle Whitaker.

'Annabelle Whitaker. Who the hell is she?' I asked.

'Never heard of her,' Tony replied.

'It's probably because she doesn't exist. The profile had been set up today by look of it; no friends list or photographs. She posted it on the Fife Mail's page.'

'It has to be Rebecca,' he said.

'Do you think?

'Well who else could it be? The only people that knew about the ruin were us, Rebecca and maybe Ray, but he's in a cell right now,' he said.

I decided not to tell him that Emma knew because after her going on about not getting the press involved, I was pretty certain it wouldn't have been her.

As we pulled into my driveway Tony decided that he would come in for a coffee but wasn't going to stay long. As we got out of the car a couple of reporters crossed the street and stopped at the gate, 'Tony, Tony, do you know where Evan is?' one of them shouted.

When I closed the front door behind us I could see that Tony was trembling as if he had been given a fright. 'Hey, come on, I'll put the kettle on,' I said.

'Tony, what are you so afraid of?' I asked as he sat down at the kitchen counter.

'Them,' he replied.

'Who? The reporters?'

'Forget it, I'm fine,' he said.

'You're not, you're shaking.'

'I hate them. This is exactly why I didn't want to get involved. This!' He waved his hand in the direction of the front of the house.

'Talk to me,' I said, knowing he was fighting back tears.

'It's the power they've got. Remember the article that said I befriended you to groom Jase. They made out like I was a paedophile.'

'Tony we didn't even know each other back then, we knew that, the police knew that, they even knew that.'

'I was still beaten up for it though.' He started to cry at the thought of the attack; three teenagers with a baseball bat, outside his flat. And here he was again, covered in bruises that he didn't deserve.

'I was bullied throughout high school for being lanky and ginger and this just feels like the exact same thing. There's never any escape from it, Caroline.'

'Why didn't you tell? You should have told me,' I said, embracing him as he cried into my shoulder. I felt a strong urge to protect him, not only was he vulnerable but once again, this was my fault.

Tony was quiet while we sipped away at our coffees. I checked my phone to see if there were any updates on the search for Evan. This was when I saw the breaking news on the Mail's Facebook page: *Evan Shelby- Forensics at Ruin after Psychic's tip-off.*

'They've found something.' I got up and stood beside Tony so we could read it together. In the photo, we could see the red tin roof of the ruined cottage we had visited earlier and the forensic team at work.

'I hope this means it'll all be over soon,' Tony sighed.

'I hope they've not found him there. Please Tony, tell me he's still alive.'

'Right now, Caroline, I really don't know.'

17
REBECCA

Ray was at the police station and because I didn't use social media, I had no idea about what was going on until Mum called to let me know. My initial thought was why would Caroline or Tony put it all over Facebook when they were so desperate to keep it quiet? I wondered if Tony had changed his mind and was willing to do whatever he could to help, even if it meant it would be all over the news. Maybe he was trying to prove to Ray that it wasn't all nonsense. Whatever the reason, it didn't really matter because it had worked. They had found something.

Pacing back and forward in the kitchen, I tried Emma's number but it was engaged. Mum had described exactly where the ruin was, so I had no option but to go there myself and find out what was going on.

The journey took about twenty minutes and by the time I arrived there were a line of cars and police vehicles pulled up along one side of the muddy single road track. Not caring if I would end up blocking the road, I passed the line of cars and abandoned my jeep as close as I could to the crowd of people that had gathered.

'What's happening?' I asked a group of bystanders as I reached the police tape. The cameras were already on me, snapping away.

'Somebody found a pair of boots and some rubbish,' answered a bearded man in camouflage clothing.

There was no sign of Evan. The forensics in their haunting white suits were hard at work with their cameras and brushes. Emma was there too, pointing and instructing two enthusiastic police officers. D.I. McCabe looked in my direction. Although I wasn't his biggest fan, I was grateful that he was at least now making his way towards me. He reminded me of a man I dated years ago, before I met Ray; tall and thin with poor posture. His hunched brow matching his shoulders leaving the resemblance of a tree on his forehead.

'Rebecca, D.S. Harper tried to call you. I'm sure you've already heard,' he said nodding towards the small crowd that I had just spoke to. 'A pair of men's boots have been found by a member of the public, we're going to send them to the lab.' He looked annoyed rather than pleased.

'Why would somebody leave their boots?' I asked, more of a thought slipping out that an actual question. I looked at the old cottage. It was nothing more than the rear and two sides that were left. The only shelter was part of a tin roof. I tried to fight the image of Evan being brought there, for whatever reason.

'We don't know but we're sending them in because they are the same size and make that match one of the set of footprints found down at High Gate. I think it'll be better for you to go home Rebecca. There's nothing else here. Do you want me to get an officer to come with you?' he asked.

'No, my mum's on her way from Dumfries,' I informed him.

'Ok, good. Get yourself home and we'll pop in later after we've finished up here.' His lips pursed together as he nodded slightly. I'm not quite sure what kind of look he was going for but it looked strange. *What is wrong with you?* I could hear myself screaming at him, inside my head. The only person that I can recall getting on my nerves as much as D.I. McCabe, is the man that he looked like.

Instead of trying to turn the jeep, I headed further down the farm road, unsure of where it would take me. As the crime scene faded in my rear view mirror, I couldn't help but look deep into the trees on each side of the road. I know it might sound a bit clichéd but I was looking for signs of a transit van. In all the scenarios that played over in my mind, the transit van was always there.

Why here? I wondered. The answer was obvious I suppose, on a normal day there wouldn't be a car or body in sight. But, why bring him here, only to move on? Surely the helicopters would have seen him? For all they knew, the boots might have been nothing more than a coincidence. They could have belonged to an innocent rambler who stopped to urinate and forgot to lift his spare boots, or left them behind because they were letting in water. But surely the same size and make was too much of a coincidence.

Tony was genuine and right once again. Had Evan been here last night when my Dad showed him this place? If only I had heard Ray leaving the house that night, there was a chance I could have stopped him. I wanted to contact Tony and beg him to find out where Evan was at that precise moment but I felt like I couldn't. I was embarrassed and ashamed of what Ray had done.

Given the circumstances, I was surprised when they took Ray to the station that morning. I don't think it was because he had assaulted Tony, it was because he threatened to go after him again. For everyone's sake, it was definitely for the best, including mine. My Mum was the person I needed by my side and she was now on her way.

18
REBECCA

There was no sign of mum's arrival as I pulled up outside the house. I knew she would take the journalists in her stride as she got out of her car but I couldn't bear the thought of her sitting outside the house with no escape from them.

Walking into an empty house was like a breath of fresh air. I had room to breathe without tension and the forever-suffocating atmosphere. Although, we spoke on the phone every day, this was only Mum's second visit since Evan had been gone. There would be no negative comments from Ray this time after she left or pretence while she was here. They were always civil to one another for my benefit but the awkwardness and knowing was still there. In her eyes I deserved better than Ray. In his, she needed to keep her opinions to herself. Ray's not a bad man by all means, his heart's in the right place, he just happens to have a complicated personality that takes a bit of effort to work out. My priority was Evan. I realised that Ray was becoming a burden.

I thought it was Mum calling to say she was running late when my phone rang, but it wasn't, it was my brother. Harry only ever phones when he wants something, so I quickly answered, thinking something had happened to Mum.

'What's wrong? Is mum ok?'

'What do you mean?' he replied.

'She's on her way here, didn't you know? I thought something was wrong.'

'Oh yeah, she mentioned it. No, that's not why I'm phoning. I'm sorry to ask, Becky, but is there any chance you could transfer a couple of hundred pounds into my account? I'll give you it back in a couple of weeks.'

'Are you being serious?' I replied. 'My son is missing, your nephew, and the first time you contact me is to ask for money?'

'I'm really sorry, Sis. I wouldn't ask if I wasn't desperate. I'm really sorry about Evan, how are you doing?'

'Do you know what Harry? Maybe I'd tell you if you genuinely cared.' I hung up, so angry that I burst into tears. Why does the world have to be filled with so many selfish people, I wondered. Some people are only out for what they can get: money, drugs, children, and it's the innocent ones that suffer. That's Harry for you- always me, me, me.

The sound of a car and the increased volume of the journalists let me know that Mum was here. I waited to hear her steps outside the door before I opened it. She dropped her bags at her feet and wrapped her arms around me. My diaphragm began to quiver as I tried to keep it together. There is no better comfort than the cushioning of her chest and smell of her perfume. I began to sob as she stroked my hair and squeezed me tighter.

'It's ok, I'm here. Mum's here,' she whispered. It took me back to my childhood, when she would rock me back and forth on her knee if I was hurt or upset. I felt her gently rocking now, like it was just a natural reaction for her. 'Come on, I'll put the kettle on.' She wiped the tears from my face and softly kissed my forehead.

'They found a pair of boots,' I told her on the way to the kitchen. 'Same size and make of the ones that left footprints near the underpass. The forensics are there now.'

'At least it's something, honey. What's Ray saying, have you heard from him?'

'No.'

'What a bloody idiot of a man, Rebecca. Like you need this right now. He should be here with you. '

'I know, Mum, leave it please.'

'I'm sorry. Have you heard from what's his name, Tony?' She asked as she turned on the tap to fill the kettle.

'No, I doubt he'll want to speak to me after what Ray did to him. He wanted it kept quiet too. I don't understand how everyone found out.'

'Come off it, what was he expecting, that you search every ruin on your own?'

'I know, maybe he changed his mind and told them himself,' I suggested.

'Well, if this Tony doesn't want to help you after finding out about that ruin, then maybe it's a good thing Ray did give him a slap. You won't know unless you ask so I suggest you phone him or go and see him. You've nothing to lose, except time, so go.' She waved the back of her hand at me to hurry me along.

'You're right.'

'Of course I'm right, I'm always right,' she chirped with a cheeky grin. This is why I needed her right then. She has a way of taking control, without overbearing me.

'I'll text Caroline,' I decided, knowing I wasn't mentally prepared enough to face the possible outcomes of a conversation. I stared at the flashing curser on my phone while considering how to approach it. I finally entered: *I'm sorry. How is Tony? x,* and sent it. The next few minutes were spent in silence, watching for some sign of life from my phone. A reply soon ended the anticipation.

He's ok. You have nothing to be sorry for, it wasn't your fault. I don't blame you for putting in on Facebook. I would've done the same. Are you ok? I see he was right about the ruin? Xx

I reply: *I'm ok, yes they found boots. I wouldn't blame him if he doesn't want to but I really need his help. I didn't tell anyone about the ruin. I thought it was you or Tony. Xx*

No it wasn't us. He's not here, but he will help you. I know he will. Do you want to come over? Xx, she replied.

I can't - my mum is here, but Ray isn't. Could you both come here if you can get a hold of him please? Xx

Yes I'll call him now, see you soon. Xx

'What did I tell you?' Mum said after reading the last text over my shoulder.

'I know, Mum, you're always right,' I smiled back at her before letting her hold me for another long while.

My mum spent the next hour or so, tidying up and scrubbing the areas I had been neglecting. I let her get on with it as I know it's how she copes at times like these. I found her cleaning out her kitchen cupboards a couple of hours after Dad died.

Be there in 5 mins x, a text read.

'Mum,' I yelled through to the kitchen. 'Come and sit down, they'll be here in a minute.'

The sight of Tony's face made me gasp. My hand was pressed firmly against my mouth preventing the air from escaping. It was a lot worse than I had imagined. The neat features of his face were almost unrecognisable.

'I'm so sorry,' I whispered as I reached up to hug him from my tip toes.

'It looks worse than it is, honestly,' he tried to reassure me.

'Come through, please. This is my mum, Margaret,' I introduced them.

'Nice to meet you, Margaret.' Caroline held out her hand. My mum took it and pulled her in for a hug.

'You must be Caroline,' she replied. I could see her looking up at Tony with a look that I knew was disgust towards Ray. 'Nice to meet you, son,' she said.

I pointed to the now spotless sofa. 'Take a seat. I'll put the kettle on.'

'You sit down too, I'll get it,' Mum insisted.

'I didn't think you would come,' I said to Tony. 'I wouldn't have blamed you.'

'I want to help,' he replied. He looked so dreadful that I could barely look at him.

'Can you do it again? Can you try to find out where he is now?' I begged.

'I'll try,' he replied.

Mum returned with a tray of tea and biscuits. Caroline and Tony smiled and thanked her politely.

'Should we make a start now?' Tony suggested and we all agreed. He wasn't as calm as he had been the previous night; I could see he was stressed and a little twitchy.

'What do you need?' I asked.

He looked at Mum. 'Could I use your wedding ring Margaret? Does it come off? I think there's a chance your husband will come through to help us again.'

'Yes,' she replied, easing it slowly over the strained protruding skin that gathered around her joint. She finally managed to get it off and handed it over. Again there was silence. Caroline closed her eyes and mum and I followed. I felt mum's warm hand wrap around my own.

A few minutes of silence was broken by Tony's voice. 'Hey Mig,' he said. My mum's grasp tightened. I opened my eyes to give her a look of reassurance but her eyes remained closed with silent tears forming in the corners. I've only ever heard my Dad calling her Meg, but with his Scottish accent it sounded more like Mig. 'Hey Mig, stick the kettle on,' he would shout.

'I have another gentleman here,' announced Tony. 'Harry.'

'That's my brother,' mum confirmed. I could tell this was not her first time. My uncle Harry is who my brother was named after. It's a pity there was no resemblance in their personality. Uncle Harry was a gentleman; our Harry, a selfish drunk who relied on mum to watch his kids when he was allowed to see them.

'One at a time please,' Tony instructed as I pictured my dad and Uncle Harry talking over one another. 'St. Mary's'

A sudden, loud knock on the door made us all jump.

'Ignore it,' mum said quietly.

'I can't - it'll be the police. Sorry.' I apologised as I stood up to answer it.

'Can we come in?' D.I. McCabe asked with Emma standing by his side.

'Yes.' They followed me through to what now looked like a relaxed get-together with tea and biscuits. D.I. McCabe held out his hand to introduce himself to Caroline and Tony.

'Hello again, Mrs Ritchie,' he acknowledged my Mum. Emma gave a brief nod. 'I'm afraid we have no further update, Rebecca. Potential evidence has been sent off to the lab so we won't know anything more until the results come through,' he informed me.

'Do you think they belong to whoever has Evan?' I asked.

'I'm afraid we can't say anymore at the minute... but it does look promising.' There was a pause before he turned to Tony. 'Mr Delimonte, would you mind coming down to the station? We have a few questions we would like you to answer.'

Tony quickly glanced at Caroline before she stood up. 'Why? This is ridiculous. Emma, come on.'

'Calm down Caroline, it's just procedure. You were bound to have known this would happen,' Emma replied.

'No I didn't. I thought the last time would have taught you a lesson,' Caroline threw back at her. 'You're within your rights to refuse, Tony.'

'It's ok, I don't mind.' Tony stood up.

'Thank you,' said D.I. McCabe. 'We'll give you a lift. In the meantime, we would appreciate it if you could all please leave us to do our job. Having the public handling evidence could jeopardise the case.'

'What case? If those are the boots you were looking for, then you should be thanking the public, and Tony. You never would have found them otherwise. What the hell have you came up with in the last fortnight?' I yelled at him.

'Rebecca,' mum scolded, embarrassed. 'Sorry, Detective, she's a little upset right now.'

'A little upset? I'm not upset Mum, I'm angry and no I won't leave you to do your so-called job. I will do whatever I need to.'

'Come on, let's go,' D.I. McCabe said to Tony.

'We'll leave you to calm down, Rebecca,' Emma added.

'It's ok, I'll settle her,' my mum told them. Every single word spoken was building up inside me and I felt a rage that I can't recall ever feeling before. In an attempt to get rid of it, I launched the mug in my hand across the room and yelled like a mad woman. 'Go.' Mum hurried them out.

Caroline took a hold of me in what felt like some kind of taught restraint that was forcing me to calm down.

'I've never seen her like this before,' Mum told her.

Caroline spoke incredibly calmly, 'Rebecca, this is your call. It might not be much but at least we have St. Mary's to go on.'

'St. Mary's. That could be anything or anywhere.' I'd almost forgotten the piece of information given by Tony before the room erupted.

'There are a lot of St. Mary's up in St. Andrews,' mum suggested as she gathered the last of the broken glass onto the dustpan. She laid it at the side of her and pulled her iPad from her bag. 'See, St. Mary's College, The chapel of St. Mary, St. Mary's church. It's a start.'

'I think I should tell the reporters outside, do you?' I asked, looking more for support than an answer, because my mind was already made up.

'That detective had a point, Rebecca,' said mum. 'We shouldn't jeopardise the investigation. We don't even know what we're looking for.'

'Evan,' I shot back in disbelief.

'Anything suspicious,' added Caroline. 'Do you want me to tell them?'

'Would you?'

'With the amount of students that will be roaming about St.Andrews, we could do with all the help we can get.'

'Thanks. We need to do this, Mum,' I said as I turned to face her.

'I know,' she replied.

19
CAROLINE

On the way to St. Andrews, Margaret made a list of all the possible links to St. Mary that she could find on Google maps. As we walked along St. Mary's Place, the sight of the Students' Association building in itself was overwhelming. We had still to reach St. Mary's College, St. Mary's library, St. Mary's Quad and St. Mary's Church on the Rock. I have to admit, I felt defeated before we'd even begun, and I don't think I was the only one.

After a couple of hours, everyone was running over the same ground, checking and rechecking, hoping to find that one thing that would bring us closer to Evan. There was no chance of *him* being here, that was for sure. Even to Rebecca this should've been obvious. She was questioning every piece of litter and every crumb as if she was sensing a story that didn't exist.

I was right about the students; it hadn't taken long before they were out in the hundreds and the police presence also picked up. Tourists were contributing ceremoniously although most appeared to be a little bewildered.

'Honey, I think we should go home,' Margaret suggested. 'We've been here for hours. We've checked here already.' She clasped her hand over Rebecca's shoulder and squeezed it gently. Rebecca tilted her head to lean towards it. Despite Margaret's despair, she had been trying to keep Rebecca's spirits up the whole time we were there. She was one of those mothers that made everything seem effortless, made everything alright. I can't imagine her ever complaining that being a mum was hard work or that she is too busy to be there for her children. I had only known her a few hours and already, I was envious that she wasn't my mum.

'Ok,' Rebecca replied.

As we walked down South Street towards the car park, I thought about my mum. She left my dad and me when I was seven, to live with George in his holiday home in France. It was obviously more appealing to her than our two bedroom flat in Eyemouth. So, I think it's fair to say that I've never really had a proper mum. We managed fine without her despite the effect it had on my dad's mental health. That's why I chose not to share any of my troubles with him in case I tipped him over the edge. We'd never relied on each other for comfort or affection; I guess my mum was the same. I couldn't remember her hugging or kissing me, telling me that she loved me or even apologising for abandoning us. Margaret would never have done that to her kids.

As I trailed behind, watching them link arms, Rebecca stopped suddenly and reached into her pocket. She brought out her mobile phone and examined the screen. 'Emma,' she announced. She took a couple of steps until she was under the stone archway before answering it, she covered her other ear with her finger.

'What, Tony?' I heard her say. 'Ok, thanks for letting me know.'

My heart sank.

'What did she say? Margaret asked.

'Tony's been detained, well she said a forty two year old male.'

'That's Tony. I need to go to the station. Could you take me to the station, Margaret?' I asked. All of a sudden, I was overcome with anger and felt the need to protect him once again.

'Of course,' she replied. 'What exactly does that mean?' I could see Rebecca's mind working overdrive.

'It means that they're clutching at straws. They're too narrow-minded to believe that Tony is psychic.' I said in his defence.

'There must be more to it than that?' Rebecca mumbled.

'No, there's not. He hasn't been charged with anything but they have the right to keep him in custody for up to twenty four hours. Then they have to let him go when they realise they've got nothing. They're bastards, the lot of them.'

'You better be right,' she retorted before marching off ahead.

'What's that supposed to mean?' I picked up my pace to catch up.

'It means that if I was wrong to trust him, and you for all I know. There's going to be hell to pay.'

The realisation that she thought I was involved in some kind of set-up, stopped me in my tracks.

'She doesn't mean it, honey,' Margaret said as she passed me, trying to catch up with Rebecca.

I sat down on the two feet high stone wall surrounding the car park, not knowing whether to cry or scream. All I knew was that I didn't want to be near her. What exactly was she accusing me of? I decided that I would have to get the bus back to Blackbridge.

As I headed in the direction of the bus station, I heard Margaret shouting my name. Tempted to keep walking, I couldn't. She was running towards me with her hands out, ready to take mine. 'Where are you going?' she asked.

'I'll get the bus,' I told her.

'No you won't, come on,' she said, tugging me in the direction of her car.

'Margaret, you heard her. What exactly does she think we've done?'

'She doesn't mean it. She's upset and doesn't know who to trust. You understand that, don't you?'

'I suppose,' I replied, trying to give her the benefit of the doubt.

Reluctantly, I followed her back to the car.

20
CAROLINE

The journey back to Blackbridge was awkward and silent. Even Margaret didn't know what to say. The only words that were spoken were from Rebecca when I was getting out at the Police Station- 'I'm sorry Caroline, but Tony's car can't be in my driveway when Ray gets home.' I ignored her and shut the door.

I realised that there would be nothing to achieve by going in, but I was ready to give it all that I had. My anger and frustration were fighting to get out.

As the Micra pulled away, I couldn't bring myself to turn and wave. I continued up the steps into the station and asked for D.S. Emma Harper. The girl at the front desk recognised me and told me to take a seat. I sat there tapping my feet and drumming my fingers on my knees until she appeared.

'Come through, Caroline,' she said before guiding me into an empty interview room on the right.

'Why have you detained him?' I asked. 'You've no idea what you put him through the last time. You can't do this.'

'We're just following procedure, Caroline,' she answered.

'No you're not. You've got nothing on him. It's just Max Watson all over again. Isn't it? Does McCabe not like gay men? Or is so embarrassed by his own incompetence that he's looking for a scapegoat?'

'That's enough. If he's done nothing wrong, like you say, then he has nothing to worry about, does he?' she replied. I took in a deep breath in the attempt to calm myself.

'Do you know who put that post on Face book for the world to see?'

'No, but we do intend to find out.' she replied.

'So it wasn't you? You were the only other person that knew about the ruin. It wasn't us and Rebecca didn't tell anyone. So that only leaves you,' I said.

'It wasn't me, I can assure you. I warned you against it for good reason. Now I suggest you go home.'

'I want to see Tony,' I demanded.

'Well that's not going to happen Caroline, so please just go.'

'What about Tony's car? Rebecca wants it moved before Ray gets home.'

'I'm afraid we can't touch it at the moment but leave it with me,' she replied.

'You know what? Forget it,' I said before storming out the door. They weren't going to touch his car in case they needed to search it for evidence and I knew it. I had heard enough.

By the time I left the main doors to the car park, I could see Margaret's Micra parked over by the gate. As I walked towards it I noticed that Rebecca was no longer with her as she stepped out the car. 'Come on, let's get you home,' she said. I allowed her to guide me, with her hand gently on my back like she did with Rebecca, into the passenger seat. As she walked around to the driver's side, I took more deep breaths in an attempt to stop myself from crying. Not that I was upset but I didn't want to lose it in front of Margaret and I know from experience that my anger could turn to tears the longer I tried to suppress it.

'You ok, love?' She put her hand on my arm and that was enough to start me off.

'It's not fair,' I cried. 'Why are they doing this to him? He's not as strong as people think he is,' I told her.

'I know sweetheart, but do you know what? They've got a job to do and he's got you. As you said, he'll be out tomorrow and you'll be there for him won't you?' she said and I nodded like a blubbering wreck. 'Let's get you home and get settled, tomorrow isn't that far away.'

21
CAROLINE

I managed to pull myself together by the time we pulled up my driveway. Margaret walked with me to the door, taking my keys from my hand to let us in.

'Get yourself a wee seat,' she said before heading to the kitchen. I heard her filling the kettle and searching for the cups.

Soon she returned with two cups on a tray with the sugar dish and spoon. 'I couldn't remember how many sugars,' she said.

'Thank you,' I replied, shovelling three spoonfuls into my cup.

'You need to look after yourself,' she said.

'Sometimes I feel there's no point,' I admitted. 'I'm just so angry. They go on about innocent until proven guilty but with Tony it's always the opposite. This happened after we found Jase, you should have seen what they put him through. It was me that had to pick up the pieces. He was a nervous wreck. I had to try and put my own shit aside to get him through it, I hardly even knew him back then.'

'But you know him now and if he got through it then, he'll get through it again. You're a good friend to him Caroline. Think about what you had both just been through, it's different this time.'

'Maybe you're right,' I said. 'Emma knows they've got it wrong. What is it with men being so narrow-minded?'

'Men can be a lot of things, I'm afraid.' She smiled and I couldn't help smiling back.

'Do you think I'm over reacting?' I asked.

'Not at all,' she replied. 'You care about your friend and prepared to fight his corner. There's nothing wrong with that.'

'You remind me of the lady that lived next door to us when I was young,' I told her. 'She was nice. She always had a great way of making sense of things. No matter how hard things got, she made it seem not so bad. If you know what I mean?'

'Let me tell you something - it's not what's going on in your life that matters, it's how you deal with it. My life hasn't been a bed of roses, believe me. When my husband died – the love of my life and childhood sweetheart, my son went off the rails and now my grandson who I love more than life itself, is missing. What good would it do if I let myself fall to pieces? There are people who need me to be strong and as long as that's the case, I will get up in the morning, put a face on it and do what needs to be done.'

'I don't know how you do it,' I said.

'Because there are more important people in the world than me,' she said.

'You're pretty special, Margaret, if you ask me.'

'Thanks, love, but that's debatable. Come here.' She opened her arms to welcome me in.

'Won't Rebecca be wondering where you are?' I asked.

'She knows where I am. I'll go and make something for her tea and then head home to Dumfries. You're welcome to join us for something to eat,' she said.

'Thanks but I'm not that hungry,' I said at the thought of Rebecca's coldness towards me in the car. 'I thought you'd be staying over, that's a long drive.'

'Three and a bit hours. I've driven it so often it doesn't faze me anymore,' she said.

'You better get going, I better not keep you any longer,' I said as she caught her glancing at the clock on the side unit.

'Do you have something in for tea?' she asked.

'I'll grab something out the freezer,' I replied, knowing full well it was empty.

'Ok, well make sure you do. I'll leave you to it then,' she said as she carried the cups and sugar back to the kitchen. I noticed how comfortable I was with her doing this; normally I wouldn't dream of letting a guests clean up behind themselves, except for Tony, of course.

Margaret had an effect on me that day. The next few hours were spent on the sofa considering how my life could have been so different if I had been mothered.

It was tough on both of us when my Mum walked out; Dad fell into a deep depression and I had no choice but to step up at eight years old and fill her role as best as I could. He didn't cook or clean. He didn't hug me when I was upset or scared. My childhood was taken from me the day she left.

On the contrary, Rebecca has been looked after and cared for her whole life. Margaret has wiped away her tears, cleaned up her cuts, made sure all her needs were met, guided and protected her and loved her. I was jealous.

Despite telling myself that I wasn't worthless, the thought of Rebecca accusing me of trying to deceive her, made me feel it.

22
REBECCA

I could smell the Chinese food as soon as Mum walked through the door. She didn't even make it to the kitchen before the door went behind her. It was Emma.

'Sorry, honey, I'm not going to have time to cook, I'll need to head back soon,' Mum said, holding up the white carrier bag. She went to get the plates out while I looked at Emma to see what information she had brought.

'How are you doing?' she asked to my disappointment. I shrugged in response.

'I was hoping you had some news. What's happening with Tony, or Ray, or the boots that were found?'

She pulled a chair out beside me at the table and sat down. 'They'll both be out by the morning, I'm sure of it. Tony's given us permission to search his car so I'm sure that'll happen sometime this evening. He may even be released tonight if all goes well. Ray will have to wait until he's appeared in court in the morning.'

'So why was Tony detained? He wouldn't have been detained for nothing.'

'The fact that Tony knew where those boots were, raises a red a flag for the likes of D.I. McCabe. There's no way he's going to let that go without investigating and I can't blame him to be honest.'

'And what do you think?' I asked.

'Would you like a bite, Emma?' Mum interrupted as she lay down our plates and nodded towards the leftovers on the worktop.

'No thanks, Margaret. I've just eaten.' She smiled politely and turned to me to answer my question. 'I've witnessed Tony's gift first hand, Rebecca. I can't explain how he does it, but I don't doubt it. When Max believed that Tony was involved in Jase's death, I had to agree. It was too much of a coincidence. Even when the truth came out about Mark Patterson, I still had my doubts. Tony gave me a private reading about a month later and I wanted him to fail. I wanted to catch him out because those doubts still niggled away. I had done my research and knew what to look out for – cold reading, it's called - the kind of general claims that anyone can relate to, pauses that allow time to read body language, stuff like that. Tony told me things during that reading that were far too personal and accurate, and not just once, he was consistent. I shouldn't be telling you all this Rebecca, but I'm pretty sure it's messing with your head, not knowing if he's involved or not. Just wait and see, he'll be released in the morning.'

'Caroline's not involved either, sweetheart,' Mum added.

'Caroline?' Emma looked puzzled.

'She was upset this afternoon and sort of accused Caroline of having something to do with it. It's understandable honey but I agree with Emma. They want to help, that's all.'

'Rebecca, you've nothing to fear when it comes to Caroline, I can assure you,' Emma said.

'I just don't know who to trust. It's doing my head in. Mum, I can't eat this.' I pushed my plate away.

The truth is, I was terrified that they were wrong; the fear of being betrayed and humiliated, stupid and desperate enough to be manipulated into believing a couple that - according to Ray - had already gotten away with murdering one innocent teenager. At the back of my mind I could hear his opinion of them both, *I don't care what anyone says, they're both involved,* is what he kept saying when they found Jase's body. But, not once did I doubt Caroline at that time. It was only ever pity that I felt. I knew I should never have spoken to her the way I did, but it was done now, I couldn't take it back. I regretted it but deep down I also felt like it was now out there as a form of protection in case it turned out to be true.

As for Tony, I was confused. I was more than aware how it must have looked to Ray, McCabe and the rest of his team. But, they weren't there that night. They were all thinking- *How else could he have known about the ruin?* But, if Tony was a liar, then it meant my Dad hadn't been there that night. I didn't want that to be true. I was relying on him to help us – the man I trusted more than anyone.

'Do you want me to stay with you tonight?' Mum asked. 'I could leave first thing.'

'I don't need you to but I'd rather you did so that you're not driving home in the dark.'

'Ok, I'll go and give Harry a call to let him know.' She grabbed her bag and headed through to the living room.

'When will the results be back about those boots?' I asked Emma.

'First thing in the morning, we hope. Listen, I know you've got your doubts about Caroline and Tony but you don't need to worry about them. You've got enough going on without turning against the people that are trying to help.'

'You really do trust them, don't you?'

'Rebecca, if they were involved in Evan's disappearance then we would know about it, trust me.'

'I want to, I really do.'

106

She put her hand on my shoulder as she stood up. 'I'll pop in, in the morning. As I said – there'll be a team out to search Tony's car but they'll have no reason to disturb you.'

After she left, we settled in front of the TV after Mum had tidied up and poured us both a gin and tonic. Mum got out her tablet as well as putting it on STV to watch her soaps. My first thought was of Ray sitting alone in a cell with nothing to occupy him. He would be struggling. It was the first time that day that I had given him much thought and I felt a sense of guilt. If it was the other way around, I'm sure I would never be far from his thoughts.

'What you thinking about?' Mum asked, snapping me out of the daze that had me staring at the clock on the wall.

'Ray.'

'He'll be fine. Some thinking time might do him some good.'

'Maybe,' I sighed. 'I'm going up to change the bed sheets; you could sleep in beside me tonight, if that's ok?'

'Of course, do you want me to do it?'

'No, it's fine. I'm looking for something to do anyway.'

When Mum had stayed over in the past, Evan had always given up his bed for her and slept on the sofa. Stupid really, but it just didn't seem right, having her sleeping in his room under the circumstances.

I climbed the stairs to sound of Emmerdale's theme tune and then closed the bedroom door behind me when I went. Standing at the window, staring down at Tony's car, I downed the G & T that was still in my hand. I was exhausted.

I grabbed the neatly ironed spare bedding from the bottom drawer before starting to rip off the bedding that was overdue to be changed. Pulling at the elasticated edges of the black fitted sheets, Ray's corner pinged off, and with it came a folded up letter. I couldn't image for the life of me why a letter would be in between the sheet and the mattress, given that all our mail was always opened and either shredded or filed down the stairs.

As I was just about to open there was a knock on my bedroom door, so I threw it down on the bedside table.

'That's the forensics started working on Tony's car, I just thought I'd let you know.' Mum made her way to the window to peer out.

'I don't know whether to wish that they'll find something or not,' I said, making a start on the bed. The folded A4 letter sat patiently waiting on me.

'I know what you mean, but it's only because you want progress, honey. You don't really want them to find anything, and they won't. Let's face it, only an innocent man would agree to let the police to search his car, surely? I watch those police custody programs - judges don't just authorise warrants willy-nilly, so it would be pretty stupid to agree to it if you were hiding something.'

'Yeah, if that was the car you used to commit the crime, Mum.'

'True. But, I still don't believe he's involved and deep down I don't think you do either.'

'Well, we'll soon find out,' I replied. I didn't even want to think about all that anymore. I just wanted to know what was in that letter. 'Could you pour me another drink, please? I'll be down in a minute.'

'Of course,' she said.

As I heard her descending the stairs, I sat on Ray's side of the bed and picked up the letter:

Dear Raymond Shelby,

We regret to inform you that we are unable to approve your application for a loan of £100,000. The reason for this decline is that due to your annual income, you do not meet the required criteria. If however, you would consider making an application for a smaller loan, our loan officer, Michael Halliday, will be glad to be of assistance.

The letter was dated three days ago. I felt sick with betrayal. Ray had never gone behind my back with anything and yet here he was applying for a loan that was worth more than our mortgage. Why on earth did he need £100,000? And why was he hiding it from me?

23
EVAN

I shone the torch on the clock that was ticking away in my ear. I couldn't make my mind up - what was worse? When I didn't know what time it was, not knowing whether it was day or night, or, the constant tick, tock, tick, tock, every second of every day. It made me think of that Chinese torture thing, when they get blind-folded, and water is dripped onto their heads until they go insane and confess. I suppose it was my own fault, though, I did ask for it. Why hadn't I asked for a watch?

It was 10.25am. In another three hours, I would have been alone for two whole days. The longest so far had been one and a half. All I had left in my carrier bag was a packet of beef Monster Munch crisps. But, even though I hadn't eaten since the Mars Bar the night before, I couldn't give in. If he decided not to come back, then I was going to starve to death.

It was weird because the black mask he wore used to freak me out. He'd come in, all covered up and hardly say a word, but after a few days, I looked forward to him coming because he'd bring me a bag of munchies: sandwiches, chocolate, crisps, nuts and a big bottle of Irn Bru. I didn't want to push my luck, but everything I asked for, he gave me. He was obviously given the job to look after me. I don't know why, but I had the feeling he wasn't supposed to be helping me.

He'd swear and boke when he had to carry my toilet bucket up the stairs but he wasn't mad with me. So, when he said, 'Do you need anything?'

I replied that I needed to go home.

'Sorry but that's not going to happen.'

Even though I kind of knew this, when I heard it from him, I burst out crying and begged him to tell me why he was keeping me here.

'I'm going to get you something to lie on, and a light. Do you need anything else?' He kneeled down beside me.

'A clock, a book, maybe? I need something to do.'

'What kind of book?' he asked.

'I don't know. Computer Science, anything to do with computers.'

'I'll see what I can do,' he replied.

And he did. He brought me a couple of thick textbooks and all the computer magazines he could find in whatever shop it is he goes to. He also brought me a colouring book and pens. I was tempted to say, 'I'm not six,' but now I'm glad he did.

I opened the packet of Monster Munch and counted them. There were eleven. I looked at the clock again. *I'll eat one crisp every hour,* I thought. *Then I'll sleep.*

As the crisp melted away in my mouth, I wished that someone was with me, because I didn't like my own company. I prayed for Mask Man to come back. I had never felt lonely before. Of course, I knew what it meant, but I had never really felt it. Whenever I went to school, there were always people about, and Mum and Dad were always in the house with me. They'd sometimes do my head in, but I'd happily put up with that again. I'd do anything to hear them moaning at me to 'switch that bloody X-Box off.' I knew Mum would be going out of her mind with worry, but there was nothing I could do to make her feel better. I prayed for her too.

24
REBECCA

26th March 2018

Mentioning the letter to mum didn't seem like a good idea so I had made the excuse of needing an early night and headed off to bed. I didn't get much sleep at all, so when mum left first thing in the morning, I lay on the sofa and prepared myself for confronting Ray. I knew he'd be home soon.

He'd only been home five minutes and once again the tension was building. He hadn't questioned me about Tony's car in the driveway and I hadn't asked him about his night in the cell. I didn't have the energy to argue about Tony and neither did Ray, by the look of him. Not only did I not have the energy, but with Tony being detained, I knew I didn't have the argument either.

I decided to give him time before questioning him about the loan, rather than pouncing on him as soon as he walked through the door. He looked shattered and was walking around looking lost. I bided my time, sitting quietly on the sofa with a cup of coffee.

Stopping in front of me, I knew something outside the window had caught his eye, because his gaze became fixed in the direction of Tony's car. Whatever it was didn't hold his attention long, because he turned around and disappeared into the kitchen. I stood up to take a look. Tony's car was gone and Emma and D.I. McCabe were approaching the front door, it would have to wait. Spotting me through the window she signalled for permission to let herself in. I nodded.

'Hi Rebecca,' she said. 'Where's Ray? We need to speak to both of you.' He must have heard this from the kitchen because he returned and began to hover at the back of the room.

D.I. McCabe checked to see that he had our attention before informing us that there had been a development.

'What is it?' I asked impatiently.

'We arrested a fifty-five year old male, named Billy McIvor in the early hours of this morning. His DNA was found on the boots that were sent to forensics yesterday and they match the prints that were found near the underpass. We're afraid that Evan's DNA was also found. There was an empty water bottle in a carrier bag that was lying close by.'

'I swear I'll kill him. See if he's laid one finger on Evan, I'll fucking kill him,' Ray said marching back and forth. I was expecting his fist to go through the plasterboard at any moment.

'I understand you feel like that, Ray, but the last thing any of you need, is for you to be locked up again,' he said.

'So, what now?' I demanded.

'We'll be interviewing him as soon as his solicitor turns up,' Emma answered.

'Who is he? What is he? Do you know anything?' I asked.

'He does have a criminal record, but it's mostly petty crimes. He's not a registered sex offender or known to be linked to any gang organisations. His mobile phone and computer have been seized so we'll know more when the specialists are finished with them,' McCabe informed us.

'We can't stay, apparently his solicitor is on his way,' Emma said trying to hurry them along.

'I know this must be difficult but we will keep you updated at every opportunity. The interview could take a while, or not depending on how much he's prepared to tell us. But at least we've got him now.'

'What about Tony?' I interrupted.

'He was released without charge,' Emma said confidently.

Ray was sitting down by this point and I purposely didn't look to see his reaction.

When they both left, I was shocked and confused. To have confirmation that a man had taken Evan that day and the thought of him taking him to that ruined cottage, for what? For sex was my first thought and I couldn't bear it, not my boy, not our Evan. I literally tried to shake the thoughts from my head, before trying to beat them out with the palm of my hand.

Ray got up, grabbed my wrist and put his arms around me. I broke right there and then. I knew that it was going to be over soon, that Evan was going to be found, but it was the first time that I had pictured him dead.

As soon as the front door closed behind Emma and McCabe, I asked Ray why the hell he needed £100.000. He looked surprised.

'In case we have the chance to pay off whoever has him,' he said, as if it should have been obvious.

'Do you know who has him?'

'Are you kidding me? You better be fucking kidding me, Becky!'

'So why the big secret?'

'I don't know. I don't even know. Maybe because we don't feel like a team anymore. You're treating me like we're strangers, Becky.'

I didn't say another word because I knew what he was saying was the truth.

Within a second or two after closing the kitchen door behind him, I flinched at the sound of the dirty dishes flying off the worktop and crashing against everything in their path. I considered going in after him but I knew that's not what he would have wanted. A man had just been arrested and all I had done was accuse Ray, my own husband of somehow being involved in our son's disappearance, just like I had done with Caroline.

I knew I had to wind myself in before I hurt anyone else. Tony had been released and that was a relief - Emma and Mum had been right. This reminded me that I had to let her know what was happening. And, I was due Caroline an apology.

All the built-up emotion inside me was bursting to be released. As my blunt fingernails failed to pierce the skin on my neck, I regretted cutting them back. Instead, I bent those stupid, useless fingers back until they almost dislocated. The release then came as a series of tears and wails as I lay on my bed. I cried until I had no more tears.

Pulling myself together, I picked up the phone to call Mum, but instead it started ringing in my hand. She was phoning me because Billy McIvor's arrest had just been on the news.

'Does anyone know who he is?' she asked.

'We've never heard of him,' I told her. I then went over what McCabe had told us about his petty crimes and not being a known sex offender or gang member.

'Oh, honey, I don't know what to say,' she replied and I couldn't blame her because I didn't know what else to say either.

'It's ok, Mum, I'll phone you as soon as we hear anything. I'm glad you got home ok.'

'Ok. They also said that Tony had been released without charge - well, the 42 year old male. Have you spoken to him, or Caroline?'

'Not yet,' I replied.

'Ok. You should maybe apologise for yesterday, I think she'd appreciate it.'

'I know, Mum, I'll call you later.' I was annoyed at her reminder but it was more so because I felt bad enough about it already without her highlighting it.

It took me a while to pluck up the courage to phone Caroline. How could I have been so heartless to accuse her of... having a hidden agenda, I suppose. I, for one, hated being accused of something I hadn't done, but this was on another level. If I was accusing her of being involved in Evan's disappearance, was I also accusing her of being involved in her own son's? I managed to convince myself that it was unforgivable.

'I want to apologise for the way I spoke to you yesterday,' I said, closing my eyes, waiting on a reply.

'Don't worry about it,' she said. 'You were upset.'

'I know but that's no excuse, what I said to you was awful, and I really am sorry.'

'If I'm being honest, it did hurt but you didn't mean it, that's the main thing.'

'I didn't mean it. I'm struggling to trust anyone right now. I feel so messed up.'

'Let's forget you even said it, how about that?'

'Thank you.'

'You haven't heard anything about Tony, have you? My wi-fi isn't working,' she asked.

'He was released without charge, this morning, I think. It could have been last night. I don't know,' I replied.

She sighed with relief. 'I hope he's ok.'

'They've arrested a man called Billy McIvor. They found his DNA on the boots and also DNA belonging to Evan.'

'That's good, Rebecca,' she reassured me as she heard my voice breaking.

'Is it?'

She didn't answer straight away. I'm guessing she was thinking it through and probably came to the same conclusion I had.

'Anything could come from this, Rebecca, so don't presume the worst.'

'I can't help it. It doesn't look good, does it?'

'What did you say his name was?' she asked.

'Billy McIvor.'

'I know that name. Damn it, I can't even look him up, bloody wi-fi. I've definitely heard that name before.'

'I'm sure we're going to find out who he is soon enough,' I replied.

'Let me know if there's anything I can do,' she said.

'Thanks, I will.'

Half an hour had passed and I hoped that was enough time for Ray to calm down. When I opened the kitchen door, Ray was sitting at the table with his new tablet in his hand.

'The man looks like a fuckin' half-wit,' he said as he threw it down. He walked over to the worktop and leaned against it to look out the window.

I went over to where it had landed and looked at the screen. On it, was the name Billy McIvor and a photo of a scrawny man with bad skin and tattoos, wearing a Celtic top and holding a beer. Below, it said: Self-employed at *none of your business*. Lives in Blackbridge. I scrolled the page to see if there was any other information but all I could see were images of half naked women, sectarian nonsense and bad jokes. The man was clearly a small-minded, sexist bigot. Not the criminal mastermind that we had suspected. But then again sometimes the dumber people are, the more dangerous they are.

No matter how useless McCabe and his team had been, surely they would be able to get the answers from him that we needed?

Ray was still standing in the same position so I tip-toed over, avoiding the broken mugs that were spread out in bits on the grey tiles. I gently put my arms around him and rested my head between his shoulder blades. Unsure of how he'd react, I was relieved when he placed one of his hands over mine.

'I'm going to do time for him, Becky. I'm going to kill that scrawny little fucker.

25
CAROLINE

There was no point in staying home; I knew Tony wouldn't come straight to me when he was released. He would have to check on his mum and go home for a shower and sleep. The main reason though, was that for the second month running I hadn't paid my Virgin Media bill so they cut me off; phone, wi-fi and TV package. It had finally reached the stage that I had nothing left with no income. Nobody knew I was broke and I suppose it was all about saving face.

I knew I could post things to sell on Facebay, that would have the quickest and easiest way of making some money, enough to eat at least. But, that would be no different than putting 'I don't have a penny to my name,' as my status. People do it all the time and there's nothing wrong with it, but when you have a house as big as mine, you'd expect the owner to have enough money to just give stuff away to charity. For some reason, I felt that there would be somebody somewhere judging me and I couldn't bear it. I couldn't bury my head in the sand any longer though and I knew the first thing I had to do was phone an estate agent.

'I can come out to valuate the property this afternoon at 3pm if that's any good?' said the overenthusiastic lady from Fife Properties.

'That would be perfect,' I replied, the anxiety of the whole process already flooding my thoughts.

It was 12pm and my next priority was to find a wi-fi connection. I had to find out who this Billy McIvor was. I needed a face to the name.

The most promising of places would be the town centre, so that's where I headed. On the way there, I figured that most pubs would have wi-fi, and the first one I came to was The Windsor.

The bar was almost empty, as you would expect at that time of day. Standing tall behind the bar, polishing glasses was a middle aged man who clearly thought he was something, his bar and all that. Perched on the other side was a couple around the same age, looking like it was probably their second home.

'Just a glass of water, please,' I said as I took a seat on one of the bar stools.

'Certainly.' They all recognised me, the not so discreet woman attempting to whisper had said my name as soon as I had walked through the door, but I didn't really care. Some days I would, some days I wouldn't.

'I heard they arrested someone,' I said, nodding at the low sounding TV on the wall. Having spent months in a pub when Jase was missing, I knew that everyone has an opinion on everything, and everyone knows each other - or so they like to think.

'Billy McIvor from Hamilton Crescent. They're searching his house just now. My mate that works on the taxis had a drop off, says it's a bit gruesome with all the police tape and forensics.'

'Do you know him?' I asked.

'Kind of, he's been in here a few times; plays pool for the Lister. I always thought there was something weird about him. Did you no think so, Tam?' He turned towards the couple that were listening to every word.

'Oh aye, something no quite right there,' Tam replied.

I sipped my water and realised that this is where I must have heard his name before. I spent every night in that pub for months, so the chances of bumping into him were pretty high. I took my phone out of my pocket.

'Have you got wi-fi?' I asked. 'I've got a feeling I'll recognise him.'

'Sure, capital W,' he relied, pointing behind me to an A4 sheet of paper pinned to the notice board. *Wi-fi Password-Whiskey01*, written in black marker.

'Thanks.' My mission complete. I quickly searched for him on Facebook. The first profile I clicked on, was a man wearing a Celtic football top and I recognised him immediately.

'Is this him?' I asked, while holding my phone up for all of them to see.

The woman stepped down from her stool and came over for a close look. 'Aye, that's him, hen, the sick bastard.'

But that's not how I recalled him. From what I could remember, he seemed genuine; harmless. Where everyone else in the Lister avoided the subject of Jase's disappearance, he approached the subject with concern and empathy. He was what I would call - a people person and a decent enough guy. He wasn't a drunk or weird, he was just your average bloke who enjoyed a pint.

I sat for a while longer, reading comments on some of his posts, trying to find a hint of something 'off' about him but I couldn't. Some of his posts could be classed as offensive if you had the inability to see the humour in them, but that was all it was, sarcastic humour.

I thanked the barman or owner, whoever he was, for his service and made a quick exit.

Tony hadn't called yet but he could possibly have been still sleeping. I hoped this was the case because as time was ticking by, the more I thought about what state he would be in when I finally did see him. It was time to call it a day. I headed home to wait for him getting in touch, and get ready for the estate agent.

Running over the house with a duster, my thoughts turned to Rebecca. Arresting Billy McIvor meant that Evan was going to be found soon, and the likelihood of him being alive was unlikely. Rebecca was finally going to know what it felt like and despite the fact she had pissed me off and I pretended to be fine about it, this was the last thing I wanted. None of them deserved to experience the kind of pain that I'd been through.

I wracked my brains trying to bring back memories of the conversations I had with Billy McIvor. Although most of them were short, drunken acknowledgements – a quick *hi, how are you doing?* I did remember him telling me that he had a teenage daughter that he wasn't in contact with. The freshest memory was him telling me that he had received a pay-off from the council; it was some kind of compensation for the abuse he had received as a child when he was in the care of the local authorities. I don't remember him coming straight out and saying it, but somehow I knew he had been sexually abused. I guess that's why I remember the conversation – it's not the kind of conversation you forget in a hurry, even after a good few drinks.

Was he an abuse victim that had become an abuser? I've heard about this often but never understood it. I guess that's why I've always had an interest in Psychology. How could someone that has experienced something so terrible, go on to put other children through the exact same thing? Even though this does happen often, and maybe had done in Billy McIvor's case, but murder – that's a whole different ball game, surely?

I cursed the non-existent wi-fi signal for preventing me to carry out further research on him. I'd have to go back out later, after the estate agent had been.

26
REBECCA

It was after 5pm, and although only a few hours had passed since they left, it felt like days. I had done nothing but watch the hands going around on a clock because waiting was all there was to do. Around me, the press outside seemed to multiply by the hour and the phone never to let up – I left that to Ray and he didn't seem to mind. One of the calls was from his sister in Australia, who had only ever emailed up until now. I'm glad it wasn't me that answered. She's a bit like my brother Harry- you only hear from her when she wants something. We've never really gotten on that well and I had no interest in starting now.

'Could you let them in, please?' I said to Ray as McCabe's car pulled into the driveway. I sat on the sofa, legs curled up by my side, holding a cushion in front of me, the way I did when watching a horror movie.

'How are you doing?' Emma sat next to me at an angle so she was facing me.

'Please just tell us what's happened,' I said. Emma looked at McCabe, who was still standing, waiting to do the honours.

'I'm afraid we still don't know where Evan is,' McCabe began.

Ray let out a groan full of frustration. 'So what do you know?'

'Billy McIvor has provided us with an alibi for his whereabouts at the time when Evan is believed to have gone missing,' said D.I. McCabe. 'It's being checked out as we speak.'

'So what exactly does that mean?' I asked. 'He's been with Evan, but he wasn't the one who abducted him?'

'Possibly, if his alibi is confirmed, then it means there has to be more than one person involved,' Emma replied. 'As we said, Billy McIvor is not known to be a gang member so anything like that is unlikely. All we are saying is that there could be someone else involved.'

'Just because you don't know that he's a gang member doesn't mean that he isn't. What about that Tony?' Ray questioned. 'You didn't have much luck there did you?'

'No Ray, we have no reason to believe that Tony is involved. He was released without charge and I suggest you accept that,' Emma advised.

Before anyone could say anymore, D. I. McCabe's mobile phone started to ring in his pocket. 'I'm going to take this in the kitchen,' he said while holding it up in the air. He closed the door behind him.

'This Billy must know where Evan is,' Ray said to Emma.

'That is what we plan to find out, trust me. He's denying all knowledge at the moment,' she replied.

'This is where your justice system's messed up. Give me five minutes with him and we'd know exactly where to find Evan.'

'Trust me, Ray, it's times like these I wish I could turn a blind eye.'

'Where did he say he was when Evan was taken?' I asked.

Instead of answering, she turned her gaze towards the kitchen door. D.I. McCabe had something to say as he stood in the doorway- I could tell from his sigh. Instead of saying it, he nodded at Emma, she sighed, and then nodded back.

'What? What does that mean?' Ray asked in annoyance.

'Billy McIvor's alibi is solid. Emma, we need to go.'

And that was that. Once again, we were left waiting. 'I can't bear this much longer, Ray.'

'I know,' he replied as he sat down next to me. 'Just when you think they're getting somewhere, then you're back to feeling like they're never going to find him.'

I stared at the clock, considering the possibility of watching it again until they returned with some sort of new information. Ray reached for his tablet that lay on the coffee table and sat back shoulder to shoulder with me so that I could see the screen. This gesture was his way of showing me that he was sorry about going behind my back about the loan and that he didn't want to hide anything from me. He was so transparent sometimes.

In return, I made an effort to pay attention to what he was up to. I watched as he searched Billy McIvor's Facebook profile. There was a friends list of over 300 people – both men and women.

'I'm going to search through each of these profiles to see if there's any clues to what their relationships are to him. It's going to take a while and will probably be useless. But this is what I do, Becky. I search the internet and social media, looking for something that might lead us to him. I know it annoys you, but this is me, feeling that I'm doing something. You get that, don't you?'

'I suppose. I'm not going to complain but I can't sit here and watch you doing it though. You get that, don't you?'

He smiled and I felt a warmth towards him for the first time since Evan went missing.

27
REBECCA

27th March 2018

The next morning, I woke up to the sound of Ray's muffled voice coming from downstairs. It was the aggression in his tone that made me wonder who he was talking to. It carried on for a few minutes before he shouted, 'I don't care. You should have told us.'

Should have told us what? I wondered. My eyelids were heavy and I felt groggy. Forcing myself out of bed, I threw on my housecoat and rushed down to see what was wrong.

Ray was perched on the edge of the sofa with his face in his hands. The length of time it took for him to look up was concerning. Ray's a man's man, who thinks crying is a sign of weakness but I could tell that's what he was doing. In the sixteen years we had been together I had never seen him shed a tear and the shock of it caused a panic to rise within me.

'Ray, what is it?' I placed my hand on his bare shoulder. His skin was cold and clammy. Shaking his head, I knew he was giving himself time to compose himself. He took a deep breath.

'Billy McIvor...his alibi,' he stood up and walked to the window. He couldn't even look at me. 'He was visiting Mark Patterson in prison.'

'Who's Mark Patterson?'

'The one who killed Jase Frank,' he answered.

But I already knew the answer before I finished asking the question.

'No,' I cried. I didn't know exactly what this meant but the thought of that same man being involved made me think that it was too late. It also meant that there was no way he could have taken Evan that day, as he was serving a life sentence in prison – there were three of them involved. I started to run towards the doorway but before I even made it out of the room, I threw up all over the carpet. I kept running up the stairs towards the bathroom. I just made the toilet this time. The bile was burning my throat. My whole body trembled as the sight of the toilet seat faded into a white haze.

'Becky. Becky.' I heard Ray's voice as I began to come round. My head hurt and was throbbing like a giant pulse. I opened my eyes to see that my face was resting on the pink bobbles of the bath mat. The feeling of a cold compress against my forehead is what sobered me to the point where I finally felt that I could get up. Ray told me that I must have hit my head on the corner of the bath on the way down and was now bleeding. Taking my hand, while placing his other hand on the small of my back, he guided me back to bed.

I felt awful but the coolness of the pillow and bed sheets prevented me from throwing up again. As I tried to focus on my breathing, in through the nose, out through the mouth, I heard a knock at the door.

'It's not a good time,' I heard Ray telling whoever it was. There was a pause before he said. 'Look, why don't you come in, I'll tell her you're here...I'm sorry I need to clean that up.' I imagined some poor soul stepping over my vomit. I tried to sit up but my head only throbbed harder. I had to lie back down.

'Becky?' Ray whispered into the bedroom.

'Who is it?' I asked.

'Caroline Frank. I told her it's not a good time but I've had to tell her to come in, she's in a bit of a state.'

'Tell her to come up.'

'Are you sure?'

'Yes.'

'Here,' he said covering me with my housecoat that I must have thrown off at some point.

'Can I have some water?' I asked as he opened the window to let air in. Aware of my breath, I rummaged around for chewing gum in the drawer of my bedside table. To my relief there was a near finished packet of polo mints, the empty end twisted to a point. I was still unravelling it when Caroline walked in. My head was hurting too much to care about the awkwardness between her and Ray.

'Oh, Rebecca,' she said as she sat down next to me. 'Are you ok?' She looked as bad as I felt.

'I'm fine, I passed out,' I replied. She softly parted my hair to get a closer look. Slowly removing her fingers from my hair, she looked me in the eye and said, 'Did he do this to you?' Initially I was puzzled by this but when she turned to check there was nobody in the doorway, I knew she meant Ray.

'No, of course not,' I snapped, insulted on Ray's behalf. At that moment he returned with two glasses of water, thankfully unaware of what she had just accused him of.

'I wasn't sure if you would want one too,' he said to Caroline before placing them both on the bedside table.

'Thanks,' she replied.

'Sorry about the other night, and I'm sorry you had to see it,' Ray apologised.

I was surprised by this. Ray very rarely apologises.

'It's done now,' she replied, giving a hint of a smile to put him at ease. I couldn't make out whether it was genuine or not.

Ray didn't leave, but headed to the window instead. He must have felt the need to be there and I didn't blame him for not wanting to be alone at a time like this. Maybe partly it was because he didn't trust her. It was the first time he had met her so I couldn't really blame him for that either.

'I can't believe it, Rebecca, I honestly can't,' she said. 'Have they said anymore, other than what was said in the paper about Patterson?'

'They didn't even tell us that much. I had to read about it too,' Ray said with his back to us, his fingers clasped together behind his head. I hadn't put two and two together, but it made sense to me now. *You should have told us*, is what Ray had said earlier.

'What do you think this means?' I asked in the hope that one of them could correct me in my thinking. Neither of them answered. 'Why do you think he was visiting him? I'm sorry but I need to know what somebody else is thinking.' I pleaded.

'I'm sorry but I don't know,' Caroline answered. 'Hopefully it's just a strange coincidence. Patterson is one evil bastard though, Rebecca.'

'It's no coincidence,' Ray mumbled.

'I really shouldn't be saying this and I hate myself for even thinking it, Rebecca, but maybe you should start preparing yourself for the worst,' she said before standing up, unsure of where to look or what to do.

'I agree,' Ray said, choking on his words. 'It sounds like a paedophile ring to me. He'd probably be better off dead.'

'Don't say that,' I demanded.

'How could they not have fucking known this, Becky?' He was crying now and I couldn't bear it. It was definitely some kind of organised crime but a paedophile ring was my worst nightmare. Caroline didn't say a word and I wondered if this had ever crossed her mind too. Was there more than Patterson involved in Jase's abduction?

'I'm going to clean that mess up on the carpet,' Ray said before crossing the room without looking at either of us.

'Do you agree with him, Caroline?' I asked.

'I'm like you, Rebecca, I don't know what to think.'

'Wouldn't Tony have known this, if it was true?' I asked.

'Maybe, I don't know. He's not been in touch. I'm getting worried, to be honest.'

The sound of the front door closing caught our attention. The sound of Emma's voice was a relief as my initial thought was that Ray had gone out in that state.

'Why the fuck did you not tell us?' Ray yelled at her.

'I'm sorry, Ray, I got here as soon as I could. We didn't know about the press report, it wasn't our doing,' she answered. 'Is Rebecca ok?' She must have seen the vomit.

'No, she was sick and passed out. How the hell do you think she is after hearing that?'

'Where is she?'

'Upstairs with Caroline.'

I'm presuming she wanted to avoid anymore confrontation with Ray, because she came straight up without another word to him.

'Oh, Rebecca,' she said as she noticed the mark on my forehead. 'I'm so sorry.'

'You had the chance to tell us yesterday when I asked you about his alibi, you knew then, didn't you?'

'I'm sorry, I didn't want to cause you both any unnecessary worry, in case it proved to be false.'

'But you knew before you left.'

'I really am sorry, Rebecca,' she said, and I left it at that. What was the point of arguing about it now anyway, it wasn't going to change anything.

'Rebecca, I'm going to get going,' Caroline announced, and I couldn't blame her. The air was tense and morbid. If I could have escaped, I would have too.

'Thanks for coming,' I said as she leaned over the bed to hug me.

'You know where I am,' she replied softly.

Emma helped me down the stairs, then made us all coffee. Sitting around the kitchen table, we were all quiet and didn't know what to say to each other.

'When is this all going to end?' I said to break the silence. I didn't know how much more I could take.

'Patterson and McIvor are both refusing to give us information and denying their involvement. There is a thorough investigation going on at McIvor's property and his computer and phone records are being examined. It hopefully won't be long now,' Emma replied.

'But don't hold your breath,' Ray mumbled, as I thought the exact same thing.

28
CAROLINE

When I got home from Rebecca's, I knew it was time. It wasn't just about the money, I wanted to run away from Blackbridge and all the pain that still lingered. The estate agent valued the house at £290,000, photos would be taken when I was ready, a home report had to be done and then I'd be good to go.

The reality of it all, filled me with sorrow. Standing in the doorway to the lounge, I looked around the room and pictured Jase sitting watching the TV and more often than not, playing his games console. I could see him as a toddler, running around with his action figures. A more vivid memory sprung to mind – of the day that I left him cruising around the furniture after his dad Ronnie summoned me into the hallway. I was greeted with a knee to the stomach and punches around the head. I can't remember the reason, not that there had to be a reason. I'm just grateful that he stopped when Jase appeared at the baby gate, having taken his first steps from the centre of the room. His smile was a picture; only two bottom teeth protruding from his gums.

'Clever boy.' Ronnie beamed as he leaned over to pick him up to celebrate. 'Come and see this, Mum,' he continued as if nothing had happened. We went into the lounge and sat at opposite ends while Jase walked unsteadily between us. I'll never forget that little cheeky face- it was like watching a butterfly in the midst of a storm.

That's what life was like back then. It was as if a switch would come on in Jase's presence that would protect him from what was going on outside his little world.

I wished I could unravel all the memories, gathering all the good ones and packing them in a box to take with me. Blackbridge was welcome to keep the violence and pain that it seemed to breed on.

It had been Ronnie's idea to move to Blackbridge. 'It'd be good for business,' he said. I'm from the Borders originally and although I felt a long way from home here, I didn't care because I had him- the love of my life, my best friend and protector.

We first met when I was a student at Edinburgh University. It was 1997 and I was in my second year. Sharing a flat with three other girls who liked to party as much I did, meant that studying had made its way down on my list of priorities. Ecstasy and amphetamine were as common as alcohol, and Faithless and The Prodigy were an essential part of the buzz. As the nightclubs closed their doors in the early hours of the morning, the house parties began. I first met Ronnie in a smoke-filled room in a student's flat somewhere down Lothian Road.

Ronnie had the respect and charisma that was common in drug dealers; they were worshipped at house parties. I was wary of him at first, everyone knows that you should never trust a dealer. But, he had a smile that made my stomach do flips. The more pills that I popped, the more I was convinced I had found my soul-mate.

Around that same time, maybe it was that same night, my flatmate Maria started dating Ronnie's friend Greggs so it was inevitable that we would end up spending more time together. Marie and Greggs only lasted a few weeks but by that time Ronnie and I were inseparable. I was in love and he soon persuaded me that there was more to life than books. Cocaine was going to be the answer to all our prayers.

Back in those days, cocaine was a rich man's drug. Having dabbled in other drugs, I couldn't see the attraction to begin with. It was too expensive to buy and the high was barely a touch on the rest. But, Ronnie was convinced it would make him a millionaire, and who was I to try and stand in his way? The thought of spending the rest of our lives together living a life of luxury was enough for me. *Party Central forever,* he would say. Nothing lasts forever though, does it? Within a year, I was a cocaine addict without the party.

We rented the house initially. Ronnie and I were good together and I didn't mind playing the housewife role because I needed to focus my energy on something – the house was pristine and I must have been the only woman in Blackbridge polishing windows at 3 o'clock in the morning. Business was booming and within four years we were in a position to buy. For me, that's was around the time that things took a turn for the worst - the customers seemed to get younger and younger and I soon realised that it was me that was getting older, too old for that lifestyle.

The first couple of times I suggested that we settle down and get married, Ronnie laughed it off. I even managed to get myself off the drugs to prove to him that I was serious and begged him to do the same. I put it down to a clash of our backgrounds. I wanted to settle down, get married and start a family, like my parents had done and failed at. I wanted to be the kind of Mum that I missed out on. Ronnie had grown up in a care home, so I presumed he didn't get it the whole family thing. It wasn't until I threatened to leave him that he finally agreed to marry me. That in itself should have been a warning, it was far from the romantic gesture I had dreamed of.

He changed after that. I knew he felt betrayed and must have felt some kind of resentment towards me but I thought it would pass. It didn't. We had a small wedding at Gretna Green with only a few of Ronnie's friends present. Exactly one week later, he broke two of my ribs.

It's easy to make excuses for someone who has had a troubled background, and that's exactly what I did. There were tears and apologies after my first few beatings and I often wonder where I would be now if I left him then. The only thing I could be sure of though, is that I would never have had Jase. And although it was tough, it was worth putting up with in exchange for the short few years that I had him in my life.

It was definitely time to move on; leaving that house meant leaving that life behind for good. I hated the place more than ever. Finding out that Patterson was involved in Evan's disappearance was so unexpected that I was on the verge of a panic attack. Despite being locked up in a cell fifty miles away, it felt like he was still here, haunting me. I couldn't help wondering if Billy McIvor had managed to slip through the net and if he had a role to play in Jase's murder too. Maybe that's why he paid such an interest in me in the Lister – that thing where criminals feel the need to be helpful in the aftermath. And they were saying that McIvor was not working alone, so could the other man that abducted Evan, also have played a part in Jase's death? It all felt too personal.

I was convinced it was Patterson that was pulling the strings and that was why I had felt the need to warn Rebecca. I couldn't even face him during the trial. The images that I had created in my mind were bad enough without his face being in them too. Having never admitted to the crimes he committed and pleading not guilty, the truth about what he had done to Jase never came out. And as far as I know, despite the efforts of the detectives and reporters, he's never disclosed any of the details.

I'm not stupid, I know that grief is different for everyone, but I had been monitoring myself through the stages; the denial, the anger, the depression and although there was a long way to go, I knew I would never accept what happened to Jase until I had some form of closure. But I also knew I would never get that closure unless Patterson told me how and for how long he made my boy suffer.

The not knowing was the only thing that was holding me back. I had battled against the possibilities in my head over and over, so no matter how horrific, I'm sure it would be nothing new for me to process. Yes, it would be another set-back, but at least it would all be there, waiting on me to accept it, no matter how long it would take.

Jason was only thirteen, just like Evan, when he...or they, took him from me, and thinking back to that night, felt like it happened yesterday. The community hall was offering football training on a trial basis, and I encouraged him to go. He would never have gone otherwise. I was concerned about him, that's all. When you see that your child doesn't want to go out or invite friends over, it's a worry. He told me he preferred his own company but I didn't believe it. Children don't choose not to have friends, do they? Now that he was the '*man of the house,*' he felt it was his duty to protect me. 'I'll look after you, Mum,' he would say. I told him over and over that it was my job to protect him, not the other way around. 'Well what about if we just protect each other,' he said. I agreed and then did the very opposite.

The coach said that he had scored a goal that night, the pride showed in his little exerted face. His team mates praised him (I imagined high fives and hugs like they do on TV). When he left the centre that night, one of the boys saw him walking through the pen that leads to the park. That boy was the last person to see him alive, before Patterson got his hands on him. Or so I was led to believe. Could McIvor have been involved?

Football finished at 8pm and he promised he would come straight home. By 8.30pm I was around at the community centre. There were no cars in the car park and the shutters were down. I walked through that very pen where he was last seen and didn't see a soul. A mixture of fear and anger washed over me. Fear because I had no idea where he could be and angry because I thought he was probably doing something completely innocent and had no idea how worried I was.

Having kept myself to myself all those years, I didn't have friends to call. I didn't know the coach's surname; I had spoken to him but knew him only as Jim. I gave him until 9pm to come home before I phoned the police. Because it had only been an hour they didn't share my panic.

Another couple of hours had passed when they finally called for the coastguard, police dogs and helicopter. They had managed to get a hold of Jim. I now know his surname is Thomson.

Initially I felt relieved that they were finally taking me seriously but the moment I heard the helicopter flying over the house, the reality hit home. Watching the coastguard searching the waters from the upstairs window was when I experienced my first ever panic attack. One of the officers who had been with me all night, one of the first on the scene was doing her best to calm me down but, as soon as it passed, along came another. They ended up calling the doctor to give me some kind of sedative.

The next morning everyone in Blackbridge and further afield knew that Jase was missing. Hundreds of people volunteered to help with the police-controlled line searches. It was all too surreal. The community spirit was incredible and got me through the first few months. Old ladies brought me meals, and cards from strangers arrived in the post.

As the months went by nothing came of the investigation, I saw D.I.Watson and Emma less frequently and people had simply lost interest. After each appeal, things would spark up again for a week or so and then fizzle out again. I began drinking more and more in the hope it would ease the nightmare of it all, but it only got worse.

When I met Tony and he helped me to find Jase's body in that field, I refused to believe it was his. I was in denial right up to the point when D.I. Watson confirmed that it was indeed my boy's skeleton.

Now, I knew I had to pack up Jase's room sooner rather than later. We were a team, Jase and I, we had shared dreams; we were going to see the northern lights one day; we were going to travel across Europe in a campervan and live off beans and Pot Noodles. Now all I had were memories, a mind full of uncertainties and a few cardboard boxes that would soon contain the life he left behind.

29
CAROLINE

As I began transferring his things into boxes, I had to remind myself that I was simply taking him with me; I had no intention of throwing anything out. I was going to make a fresh start away from Blackbridge and in order to do that, I had to clear his room.

It wasn't easy and I shed many tears. Every single thing I picked up had a memory attached to it; the Christmas he unwrapped his Star Wars figures; the Karate grading that he won his one and only trophy; the holiday in Ibiza when he insisted on wearing his new Harry Potter glasses every day instead of his sunglasses, and came home with a tanned face and white circles around his eyes. I missed him so much.

When I finally finished, I tried Tony's number again. I had already left him six voicemails. 'Hi Tony, it's me again. Please get in touch, I'm worried about you. I just need to know you're ok, and if you're not, come over and we can talk about it. Please Tony. Hopefully speak to you soon. Oh, and you'll be glad to hear I've finally packed up Jase's room. Speak to you soon.'

I hated the thought of Tony shutting himself away from the world in some kind of deep depression. He wasn't strong enough to deal with all this again and I should have known.

I remember when he had to pop out one day when we were at his Mum' house for a little visit. He was away longer than he had anticipated and it was summer, so I sat chatting to Mrs Delimonte out in her garden. I learned more about Tony in that hour than I had from him the whole time I had known him.

'I'm so glad you two are friends, my dear, you've no idea how happy that makes me. It's just a pity you didn't meet under happier circumstances,' she said.

'I'm glad we're friends too,' I replied.

'Do you know, he's just like his father? He's a lot more responsible than his father ever was, but they have the exact same nature. Tony senior was a gambler. Do you know he lost his first ever car that he had worked hard for over a game of poker? And it just goes to show what his so-called friends were really like. You see, if I was playing cards with my friends and one of them bet their car that they adored and I won, I'd never take it from her. I don't think any true friend would do that, do you? No, me neither,' she said. Tony's Mum didn't stop for a breath when she was telling a story, so you just had to nod or shake your head quickly to answer her.

'You see, that's where they're similar. Tony senior had a heart of gold but he was credulous. As a result people would take a loan of him left, right and centre and he would let it happen because he was weak, he didn't know how to stick up for himself or god forbid, fight. Tony's the exact same. He's a good boy, Caroline. He's not a man's man though, if that's what you're looking for. Well... I guess he is a man's man,' she laughed. 'Oh you know what I mean.'

'I know what you mean,' I laughed. 'I'm not looking for anything. I just want a good friend and that's what he is.'

'I quite believe it. I bet you didn't know he used to shout the bingo numbers at the bowling club for all the old dears.'

'No, I didn't,' I smiled, knowing I'd be able to tease him later.

140

'He didn't really want to do it, but did it anyway, just to keep them all happy. He used to do the chemo runs too.'

'Chemo runs?' I asked puzzled.

'Anytime there was news that one of the members had cancer, which was often unfortunately, Tony would offer to run them to Edinburgh or sometimes Dundee. It could be every day for weeks, but he wouldn't complain. He'd drive them there, then hang around all day until it was time for them to come home. Mrs Henderson said he was like an angel. She would come out feeling hellish and Tony would make sure she was comfortable and always managed to cheer her up; he's a good boy, Caroline. That's why people find it so easy to take advantage of him.'

I always knew that the point of her telling me all this, was a plea for me to be good to him and treat him right.

I questioned what kind of friend I had been to Tony. Had I taken advantage of his gift, and his good nature? I had, hadn't I? And now, he had once again been accused of abducting a child. I hadn't been a good friend at all.

To my relief, my phone started ringing and it was him.

'Tony, how are you?'

'I'm ok. I'll be round in five.'

***

'Can I have a coffee? I can't stay long,' Tony said after letting himself in. He looked like shit. I didn't answer I just headed to the kitchen and he followed.

'I shouldn't have got involved, Caroline,' he said.

'Why? What happened?'

'Just what you would expect. Where was I when Evan went missing? Who was I with? What was I doing? How did I know about the ruin?'

'What did you say?'

'I couldn't remember where I was. You're talking about two weeks ago. It's not like one of those flash bulb moments, or whatever you call it. Like, where were you when John Lennon got shot or when you heard about the plane flying into the first tower. They checked my phone and there was a text to my mum that morning saying I would be over for lunch. My mum then had to confirm that I was there all afternoon, luckily my Auntie was there too.'

'What about the ruin?' I asked.

'I told them the truth. I can't prove that I'm psychic. I can't provide scientific evidence, but obviously they can't prove that I'm not.'

'Why did they keep you so long?'

'That D.I. McCabe is another Max Watson. He's an arsehole, he really is,' he said.

We sat together. As he sighed he sank himself further into the sofa. He hadn't shaved in a couple days and isn't really a man who can pull off a bit of stubble. He didn't smell too fresh either.

'I'm done, Caroline, I can't do it anymore. I don't want to be involved. I'm sorry,' he said albeit with reluctance.

'I'm sorry,' I said. 'I shouldn't have talked you into it.' It was the guilt talking obviously, because deep down I was gutted that he was giving up.

'Really, is that it? I thought you were going to give me a hard time. That was why it's taken me so long to get in touch, I thought you'd try and convince me to keep going.'

'You've done more than enough already,' I said, trying to be a good friend. 'If it wasn't for you, they would never have arrested McIvor or found out that Patterson was involved. You did know that, didn't you?'

142

'I heard.' He shook his head before putting his face in his hands. 'I thought that when they made that arrest that it would all be over, and now this. I'm not sure he's going to come out alive, Caroline. I'm really scared for him. How's Rebecca?'

He was clearly upset so I gently placed my arms around his shoulders. 'She's not good. Nobody is at the moment.'

I finally got around to pouring the boiling water into the mugs and we went through to the lounge for a comfy seat.

'Are you going to be ok?' I asked, concerned about his mental state.

'I'll be fine. I just need to keep my head down until everything blows over. Did you read what they wrote about me?'

'No, my connection is playing up and I haven't had any wi-fi.'

'I'm sure you'll read it at some point. I just hope that they give up now that there's more important things to be reporting.'

'I'm sure they will.' I got the hint that he didn't really want to talk about it anyway.

'So, you finally packed Jase's room up? Are you ok?' he asked.

'It was hard, but I'm fine. I'm going to sell the house. I've had the estate agent out.'

'It's about time,' he replied. 'The further away from here the better.'

'Oh, thanks.'

He smiled. 'You know what I mean.' And I did. He was feeling the exact same way about Blackbridge as I was. 'If you need any help, let me know.'

'I'm sure I'll need a hand tackling that overgrowth out the front.'

'Then I'm your man. But right now, I need to get going.'
'Will you give me call if there's any updates on the news? I don't know how long the wi-fi will be off.'

30
REBECCA

28th March 2018

I had to do something. The waiting and lack of information from McCabe and Emma was driving me insane. Yes, Evan could be dead, I knew that, but dead or alive I needed to know where he was. Two days had passed and Emma and McCabe had nothing more to say, and according to Caroline, Tony didn't want to help me, so it was down to me. My only regret is that I couldn't confide in Ray. I knew he would have stopped me.

Somebody knew where Evan was and I believed that someone was Mark Patterson. I have no idea where my courage came from but I was on my way to look him in the eye and ask him where my son was. I told Ray I needed to get out of the house, so was going to stay at my mum's for the night. He didn't want me to go, and on reflection it sounds absurd that I would leave at a time like this, but I couldn't tell him the truth, could I?

Arranging the visit was easier than I thought it would be. Having never been near a prison in my life, I had no idea where to begin. I went on the Scottish Prison Service website and dialled the number that was given. The cheerful man who answered informed me that because I was not on Patterson's list of visitors they would need to ask his permission for me to be added. The sound of this made me anxious and I couldn't help wondering if being on a child killer's friend list would be a permanent thing. Nevertheless, a phone call came two hours later, giving me the go ahead and a visit was arranged for 3pm .

I was sick with nerves and had to keep reminding myself that I would be safe. There would be guards there if anything were to happen. I've never needed to defend myself in my whole life but I was trying to convince myself that if it came to it, all the pain and anger and frustration inside me would erupt and be enough to deter anyone.

On my many visits to Dumfries, I had not given the prison much thought. It had always been there in the background, towering over and filling in gaps between houses, but I had never been this close. My legs were not taking me any further than the sign that read H.M.P. DUMFRIES. The entrance was only six steps in front of me but my feet would not budge. The building itself was actually quite nice. The gate house entrance was a red sand-stone arch, like one you would see on a castle. ONLY ONE VEHICLE INTO VEHICLE LOCK AT A TIME, the sign read. I wondered if it was the prisoners who used this entrance, in the big white vans with the blacked out windows that you see on TV. Was this their gateway to hell or luxury in some cases?

I felt like I would shatter into a million pieces if someone said 'boo' to me at that moment. I was beginning to realise how crazy the whole thing was. This was the man who murdered Caroline's son. He burned him in acid, and buried his bones in a field. I thought of Evan and inhaled until my lungs couldn't take anymore of the bitter cold air. I had to do this. I had come too far to turn back now.

My hand was trembling as I handed over my two forms of identification; my driver licence and council tax bill. After reading the rules on the website, I was expecting to be searched so it didn't come as a surprise. The woman behind me was looking antsy and informed me that she hates this bit. My instinct was to study her to see if she might be hiding something. I stopped myself and instead, found myself saying, 'me too.'

The visiting room was quiet. Prisoners with their bright yellow vests sat waiting at their empty tables. The ones who had already arrived were greeted with subtle hugs and kisses with a close eye from the guards. I focused on the half empty tables, the ones where the prisoners were facing an empty seat. There were five. I didn't recognise any of them. My whole body was trembling now and I felt like I was going to throw up. People were looking and whispering.

'Is that not that missing boy's mum?' I heard someone say. I wanted to turn back and run out the door. One of the men caught my eye as he raised his finger in front of him and nodded his head. He was definitely looking at me. It was him. I could see that now. He had changed drastically from his photos in the papers. His face was now gaunt and grey, and older looking. I walked towards him and took a seat. Thankfully, he didn't want to shake my hand. I focused all my attention on him and tried to shut out the rest of the room as if I had tunnel vision but I didn't know what to say. Hi? Pleased to meet you? Thanks for letting me come? All the normal niceties just didn't seem to fit. Clearly, I hadn't been thinking straight because if I had, I wouldn't have been there. I must have been out of my mind to think that he was going to give a full confession.

'I shouldn't have come, I'm sorry,' I said, getting ready to leave.

'So why did you?' he asked, his voice deep and quiet.

'I want to know where my son is.' I didn't mean to whisper but it was all that came out.

He gave a slight snigger and shook his head. 'I've no idea where your son is. I did know that's why you would be here though.' He leaned forward, elbows on the table. 'Let me guess. Bill's been arrested, even although he was here, in that very seat you are sitting in now when Evan went missing.' He raised his eyebrows to display how ridiculous he found it. 'So, that must mean I'm involved. I'm the mastermind behind the whole thing. Am I right?'

'Yes. How do you know his name?' I asked.

'Fuck sake, the same way every other fucker in the country knows.'

The vastness of broadcasting was not something I had considered before. Near enough everyone in the country would have read, watched or heard about Evan one way or another. Tears gathered in the corners of my eyes and I wanted them to dry up. I didn't want to break down. Not now.

'Look,' he said, 'I'm sorry about your boy, I really am, but it's nothing to do with me.'

I stayed silent until I had myself under control. 'Do you know who is?' I asked, and felt pathetic. I was pleading with a child killer to put a crying woman out of her misery.

'Look, I'm going to tell you the truth. You won't believe it but it's all I've got.'

'Ok.' I nodded.

'I have been locked up in this shit hole for ten months for something I didn't do. And they'll lock someone else up for...whatever has happened to your son. It's going to be Billy by the looks of it. Now don't get me wrong, Billy's no angel, but this? No way. They'll lock someone up so that you and the rest of the world will think he's guilty and deserves to rot in hell. And the arsehole who really done it will be out there, moving on to his next victim.'

I stared at him, searching for a hint that he was lying, but he was so convincing.

148

'So you are saying that you didn't murder Jase?'

'Exactly. I knew his dad, for fuck sake. I watched the wee boy cry at his funeral, and so did Billy. And I'm betting that whoever did do it wasn't there. Anyone in their right mind would not have made that kid suffer any more.'

Mark Patterson knew Caroline's husband? Why hadn't she mentioned this? I now wondered what the hell was going on. Was he playing mind games with me? Was this something he had rehearsed? Believed? My mind was exhausted.

'I don't believe you,' I said.

'You don't have to believe me but if you want to believe what they're telling you, well that's up to you too. But just you wait and see and remember this conversation when the next boy goes missing, 'cause my bet is that whoever killed Jase has now got Evan.'

'I don't understand. So you're saying someone has set you both up?' I asked. I was somewhat intrigued by what was going on in his head, like all of a sudden I was Clarice Starling, trying to suss out Hannibal Lecter.

'Exactly, and believe me, I want answers as much as you do.'

My thoughts turned to Caroline. What would she say if she knew I was there? What would she do, if she was sitting face to face with the man who killed her son? As if reading my mind he asked, 'How's Caroline?'

'I can't answer that,' I said, feeling more and more uncomfortable.

'Fair enough.'

'How do you know Billy McIvor?' I asked.

'Same way that I knew Ronnie Frank. St. Margaret's...School for boys,' he said with infliction.

'And you've stayed in touch this whole time?'

'On and off,' he said.

'And he believes you didn't do it?'

'He knows I didn't do it, poor bastard that he is.'

'So, who do you think set you up then?' I asked.

'I'm not sure, definitely someone that has it in for us St. Maggie's boys. It would explain Ronnie Frank's death as well, suicide my arse. Not one person that I spoke to at his funeral believed that either. What does Caroline think about that one? Does she believe that the man who had it all, was suicidal?'

'The man was a thug and a bully, he clearly had issues,' I informed him.

'Don't we all, love, and as shit as this place is, not once have I thought I'd be better off dead.'

'I think I'm going to go now,' I announced. As short as the visit was, I had heard enough and had nothing more to ask.

He nodded and waved his hand slightly. He was finished with me too.

31
REBECCA

I couldn't go straight to Mum's, I needed to clear my head. Devorgilla Bridge isn't far from the prison, so that's where I headed first.

Standing on the bridge, I rested my chin on my folded arms and stared at the water below. The last time I was there, Evan had been about eight years old. He read us the history of the bridge straight from the tourist brochure. It was built in the thirteenth century and something to do with a flood was about all I could remember. I could hear his eight year old voice and see his blonde curls. I wished he was there. 'Come on, Mum, it's only a bridge,' he'd be saying, and I would ruffle his hair and tell him, 'You used to love this bridge.' And he'd tell me, 'Don't mess the hair.'

I couldn't control my tears. I leaned over and let them fall into the river below. I cried until I was numb. The conversation I had just had with Patterson was replaying over and over in my mind and I wondered if all criminals say that they're innocent.

And the connection between Patterson, Billy McIvor and Caroline's husband took me by surprise. Why hadn't she mentioned this?

My mobile was ringing and when I looked at it, I could see it was Ray so I answered. 'Hey, did you get to your mum's ok?' he asked.

'I'm...I'm not there yet. I've stopped over a few times for coffee. I'm at Devorgilla bridge trying to clear my head. I think I'm going to come home. I'll stay at Mum's for dinner then head back tonight.'

'Are you sure? It's a long drive,' he said.

I could hear the distant sound of our front door bell.

'Who's that?' I asked.

'It's no-one,' he replied and told me to wait a minute. Ray is a terrible liar. He can't seem to grasp the concept that it's not just the words you say, it's the way you say them. He was at the door but hadn't taken the phone with him, but I could still hear him telling whoever it was to come in.

'Yeah, it feels strange, you not being here,' he said as he put the phone back to his ear. 'I'm glad you're coming home.' He sounded sincere again.

'Who have you just let in the house?' I asked.

'No-one, it was the post man,' he answered and I knew he was lying.

'Ok, well I'll be home around nine or ten o'clock,' I said before hanging up. I couldn't believe he lied so blatantly to me, like I was stupid. I instantly regretted not challenging him there and then. Hiding the loan application from me was one thing. He even managed to make me feel guilty about overreacting about it. But at that very moment, there was someone in my house that Ray did not want me to know about.

I had lied to him too and tried to rationalise my reasons for doing so. There was going to be a reasonable explanation, or at least, I owed him the chance to explain himself. I forced it to the back of my mind as I prepared myself to spend the next few hours with Mum. She didn't need to know where I had been either.

32
REBECCA

Mum's house was a lovely Victorian semi in Nunholm Road. As I pulled up, Mum must have seen my jeep because she came to the window to welcome me with a smile. I wondered if Harry had made an effort to stay at home to finally acknowledge that his nephew was missing – I doubted it.

'I was getting worried,' she said as we reached the front door at the same time.

'Sorry, I stopped a few times on the way,' I replied. Lying to my mum didn't come easy because it's something I've never done as an adult.

'You ok? I knew it would be too much for you driving this distance when your head's all over the place. Come and get a seat,' she said, taking my coat from my shoulders.

'I'm fine, Mum, honestly. I just stopped for a drink whenever I got the chance. In fact, I hope you don't mind but I'm just going to stay for tea then I'm going to head back tonight. I just feel too far away here,' I said.

'Maybe have a little nap first then if you're sure. I was surprised when you suggested it to be honest,' she replied. 'Come on, I'll put the kettle on.'

I took a seat in her show house lounge. 'Where's Harry?' I shouted through to her.

'Oh he had to pop out, I'm sure he won't be long,' she replied.

'To the pub, by any chance?' I said loud enough for her to hear.

'I'm sorry, honey, you know what's he's like,' she said and I soon wished I hadn't said it. He's thirty eight and my mum still feels responsible for his behaviour. You would think he was eighteen by the way he acts.

Harry had always been a drinker, but it definitely got worse when Dad died. Losing him made me appreciate Mum even more but Harry was the opposite. His wife, Tracey, separated but not divorced, was the best thing that could have happened to him especially when the kids came along but he blew it. I couldn't really blame her for kicking him out. I'm sure he only got access to the kids because she knew it was really my mum that took care of them.

'He hasn't been drinking that much,' mum said as she returned with our tea.

'Has he got a job yet?'

'Sort of. He sometimes gets a phone call in the morning to help out one of the local window cleaners,' she said.

'I hope they breathalyse him before letting him up a ladder.'

'Oh Rebecca, stop it, please,' she begged.

'I'm sorry, I'm just annoyed with him that's all.'

'Right, well, forget about Harry, you're here to see me, are you not?'

'Yes,' I replied.

'Well, I want to know how you really are? I've been reading the papers and you haven't been saying much on the phone.'

'Oh, I don't know, Mum. My head's all over the place with it all. I'd rather not talk about it.' I was worried she would see right through me.

Half an hour later we sat with trays on our laps in front of the T.V. My head was bursting with questions and I was aware that my mum kept looking over and every time I returned the glance she smiled and looked back to the T.V. Her head would have been working overdrive too but I didn't have it in me to try and put her at ease.

'Are you going to have a nap before you head home?' she asked.

'No, I'll be fine. I wouldn't mind a coffee though,' I replied.

As she headed to the kitchen with our trays, I heard the front door. It was Harry. After taking a minute or so to remove his coat and shoes, he appeared in the doorway with his dirty blonde curls like a mop on his head, his bright blue eyes and baby face. Harry certainly got the looks when it came to dishing out the gene pool. Unfortunately for him, I think I got all his brain cells.

'Hey, sis, how are you?' He came towards me and gave me an awkward hug. I could smell the drink. 'I'm so sorry.' I didn't return his attempt at affection.

'For what?' I asked bitterly.

'I'm sorry I've not been there for you. I just don't know what to say or that. You know what I'm like.'

'Yes, I do, Harry. It's ok. You've clearly got more important things to think about.'

'Please, not now,' Mum said, carrying in a tray of coffees. 'Here, drink this.' She gave Harry a sharp look.

Harry slumped into his seat - Dad's seat. I didn't want to upset my Mum but the sight of him brought up years full of resentment.

'So did you manage to get a hold of the money that you so desperately needed, Harry?' I asked.

'What money?' asked Mum.

'The money that he needed so badly, that he had the nerve to phone and ask for when his nephew had been missing for over a week. I didn't get a genuine *how are you*

155

then, did I? There was no- *is there anything I can do?* Or *Rebecca, I'm here for you.* No, it's was the usual; Rebecca, do you have a loan? I'm desperate.'

'You didn't?' Mum looked at Harry in disgust.

'I'm not listening to this.' He stood up and walked out. No doubt, he needed another drink after that.

'I'm sorry, Mum. I couldn't help it.'

'It's ok. I'm sorry about that, I really am. He should have come to me,' she replied.

'That's not the point, Mum. Stop apologising for him, he's a grown man.'

'I know. I've just got more to worry about than him at the moment, that's all.' She was upset and her mask was cracking. I've always admired the way she puts a face on and keeps everyone going, despite her own suffering. Unfortunately it's was also something I had come to rely on.

'Mum, I'm going to get going. Go and pour yourself a glass of wine and put your feet up.' I wrapped her in my arms.

'Oh, honey.'

I would have invited her to come home with me, but until I figured out what Ray was up to, I didn't think it was wise. I also had to get my head around my visit with Patterson and decide what my next move would be.

33
CAROLINE

I spent the day packing more boxes. Tony had text earlier to let me know there was no further updates so I continued to keep myself busy by cracking on. I came across a packet of microwave rice in the cupboard and frozen mixed veg in the freezer so at least I didn't starve. This also set me up nicely for the dusty bottle of red wine that I found in the garage.

I was half pissed when *Rebecca calling* appeared on my mobile.

'Hello,' I said, as I topped up my glass.

'Caroline, I'm sorry but I need to speak to someone,' she said. 'I wasn't planning on telling anyone. I don't even know what I was thinking or if I should even be mentioning it.'

'What is it? Are you ok?' I asked.

'Wait, I'm going to pull over,' she said. I waited a minute or two until she did. 'I went to see him in prison.'

'Who?'

'Mark Patterson.'

'You didn't? Oh, Rebecca.'

'I know. I was hoping he would tell me where to find Evan,' she said.

'Are you sure you're ok? What happened?' I asked, not quite believing what I was hearing. A strange need to protect her came over me. The image of Rebecca with her petite frame and innocence, in the same room as that monster, made me wish I had been there.

'He said that Billy McIvor is being set up.'

'Of course he's going to say that. I suppose he told you that he was set up too?'

'He did.'

'You shouldn't have gone, Rebecca.'

'I know. There's something I need to ask you.'

'Go ahead.'

'Did you know Mark Patterson before he killed Jase.'

'No, is that what he said?' I asked.

'Well, not really, but he said he was at your husband's funeral and that they grew up together.'

'Apparently they did,' I replied, slightly embarrassed that I hadn't mentioned it before. 'It was brought up around the time of the trial, but I don't recall seeing him at the funeral.'

'Billy McIvor was there too,' she said.

'What, Billy McIvor knew Ronnie?' I asked in disbelief.

'That's what he said. They were all in a care home together.'

'St.Margaret's?'

'Yes.'

'Rebecca, I know Billy McIvor from the pub, remember I said I recognised his name? I've had a few conversations with him but I'm pretty certain he never mentioned that he knew Ronnie.'

The fact that Mark Patterson and Ronnie grew up together could have been a coincidence. As I sort of accepted this, I put it to the back of mind. It made no sense, even if he did have it in for Ronnie, why would anyone kill a child to get revenge on someone after they were dead? It's not like Ronnie would be here to suffer. Do people still want revenge on people after they are dead? Of course they don't. I told Rebecca this, and that it was just a coincidence but she wasn't convinced.

'So if you believe there is a connection, then where does Evan come into it?'

'I don't know,' she said. 'I don't know.'

'What else did he say?' I asked.

'That Ronnie didn't commit suicide.'

'He's full of shit. You shouldn't believe anything he said, Rebecca.'

'I don't know what to believe anymore.'

'The only person that I ever met from Ronnie's childhood was Greggs. They were best friends and business partners – drug dealing was their business if you didn't already know that.' I then started rambling on about Greggs and how he must have known them all too. The more wine I was drinking, the more it was pouring out and I ended up going off on a tangent that was totally irrelevant to what we were even talking about.

'Could you not speak to this Greggs that you mentioned, see if he knows anything that we don't?' she asked, reminding me that I had gone way off course.

Even with alcohol in my system, the thought of revisiting my past was making me anxious. It was a different world and I was glad I had left it behind. Ronnie never spoke much about his upbringing and I respected that it was in the past. Greggs was his *brother from another mother*, he would say. He was the only person Ronnie trusted. He was the one that inherited all of the drug money because it went into a bank account that only the two of them had access to. After Ronnie's funeral, the police came to the house looking for Greggs and I told them that I had no idea where he was and I didn't want to know either. I never heard from Greggs again and I was glad because I wanted that life to die with Ronnie.

'I could,' I finally answered. Jase wasn't here anymore so it wasn't like it could affect him in any way. I had nothing to lose. If this was all I had in the way of helping, then I knew I couldn't refuse, it was nothing compared to what Rebecca had just done.

'You don't sound sure. Maybe we should tell Emma and let her look into it?' she suggested.

'Emma will know all this,' I told her. 'People like Greggs don't speak to the police. There's a chance I'll be able to find out more than Emma.'

'He's not dangerous, is he?'

'I won't be in any danger,' I reassured her, although I couldn't be sure. 'I'll be in touch.'

After downing the rest of the bottle, I decided to phone Tony. Even if he didn't want to help, I was still going to need his support. He wouldn't deny me that.

'Hey,' he answered.

'Hey.'

'Are you ok?'

'I'm fine. Did you manage to get a good night's sleep, then?'

'I did. There's still no news, if that's what you're phoning for. I take it your wi-fi's still playing up?'

'It is, but that's not why I phoned. Do you want to come over?'

'It's ten o'clock, have you been drinking?'

'I've just finished a bottle of wine. Can you tell?'

'I can always tell,' he said.

I told him about the conversation I just had with Rebecca and my plans to go and see Greggs. 'Do you think I should?' I asked.

'Caroline, I'll phone you in the morning,' he said, trying to avoid the subject.

'Don't be like that, I don't mean get involved. I just mean, do you have any advice?'

'I know you were nice about it, Caroline, but I also know that you probably think I'm being selfish for not wanting to help. But if I knew where Evan was I would tell you, or Rebecca, or the police, but I don't.' He paused. 'And as for this Greggs, no I don't think it's a good idea.'

'But we don't know what else to do.'

'I'm only going to tell you this because I feel I have to; I don't know what it means and I don't plan to try and find out, ok?'

'What is it?'

'Twins. It's something that keeps coming to me. Nothing more, nothing less, just twins. And it didn't come from me, ok?'

'Ok, I promise. Do you think Evan could have been a twin at birth?'

'I don't know, Caroline. I just told you that.'

'Ok, sorry.'

'Get yourself to bed. Take a glass of water and some painkillers with you,' he said before hanging up. Even though it had just left ten, I did what was I was told.

Lying in bed, my thoughts were making me dizzy. I thought about all the possible scenarios where a twin could be placed. The best I could come up with was that somebody's twin knew where Evan was. Either that, or Evan was a twin. I was going to have to ask Rebecca.

34
REBECCA

Ray was waiting up for me when I got home from Dumfries and didn't suspect a thing. I let him hug me while I wondered if the affection was a reaction to his guilt. Even though I knew that someone had been in my house, I hadn't come as far as working out how I should approach it. I've suspected Ray of having an affair before, but it was during the times that my hormones were erratic- during and after pregnancy. My behaviour towards him over the last couple of weeks could have been enough to push him elsewhere if I had kept it up, but not now; not when we were softening to each other again. Not while our son was missing.

This didn't stop me discreetly searching the house for clues, and smells. I even sniffed our bedding, but that's when I sat down and told myself to get a grip. I clearly wasn't thinking straight, and paranoia was creeping in; all I needed to do was confront him. I know what I heard and he wouldn't dare to look me in the eye and lie.

I sat awake propped up against the pillows on our bed while he locked up and brushed his teeth.

'Who did you have in the house earlier? And don't even think about lying to me,' I said, as soon as he walked in.

He sighed. 'We need to do something Becky,' he said. 'We need all the help we can get.'

'I agree. And?'

'I think we should hire a private detective.'

'You've hired a private detective?'

'No, not exactly. You know Max Watson? He worked with Emma on the Jase Frank case.'

'I don't know him, but yes I know who you mean. He was also an arsehole apparently.'

'Who told you that? Let me guess... Caroline told you that he was mean to Tony Deli-scumbag.'

'Is that who was in our house when you told me it was the postman?'

'I'm sorry about that but I didn't think it was a good time to discuss it over the phone.'

'Why didn't you tell me before you invited him here, before I went to Dumfries?'

'I was going to but your mind was elsewhere. I tried to speak to you a couple of times this morning but you were too distracted. Then, I just figured it would maybe be better for me to meet him first anyway.'

I thought back to the morning, when I was rushing around trying to get a bag packed. I was going over in my mind all the possible scenarios that could occur at the prison. I was having conversations with Mark Patterson in my mind, and Ray was right, I dismissed him so he couldn't distract me from my thoughts.

'Why him, though? If you had come to me before now to ask me what I thought, I would have told you that it had crossed my mind too. But you can't just jump right in there without us even discussing it.'

'What's your feeling about Emma and McCabe? Now be honest,' he said.

'I can't stand him, I've no idea how he ever made D.I. He's brought absolutely nothing to the investigation and is getting paid a fortune to turn up and look the part. And what's with making us call him D.I. McCabe. We don't even know his first name.'

'Michael.'

'I like Emma, but as a person and liaison officer, I'm not quite sure about her as a detective either, if I'm being honest.'

'A bit harsh.' He smirked. 'But I agree with everything you just said. We need someone that knows what they're doing.'

'But why Max? What makes you think he's any better? He wasn't the one who found Jase. Caroline said he was out his depth too.'

'Emma. I've quizzed her about him so many times and I'm convinced he's the right man for the job. He's professional, easy to talk to. I'm confident that if you met him, you'd want him to help us. He certainly comes across as somebody that knows what he's talking about.'

'Are you sure it's not because you hate Tony and have that in common? Because, that would be pretty lame and stupid, Ray.'

'It's nothing to do with Tony. When I asked Emma about the cases he had worked on and solved, she rattled them off until I had to say I had heard enough. All sorts of cases – child abduction, murders, rapes, human trafficking, drugs. He has a lot of connections and is well respected. I know for a fact that Emma wishes Max was in charge of our case. She may be good at reading other people but she's no poker player. Her face says it all, Becky, don't tell me you haven't noticed. Professionalism definitely isn't one of her strong points.'

'I have noticed,' I replied. 'I'll sleep on it. I agree that hiring a private investigator or detective, whatever you call them, is a good idea but I'm not happy about jumping straight in with the first one that comes along. '

'That's good enough for me.' He kissed my cheek and turned out the light.

I appreciated that he was giving me the chance to call the shots because I had a feeling that if we had still been at war with each other, he wouldn't have hesitated to go ahead regardless of how I felt - a bit like what I had just done to him by visiting Mark Patterson. All I needed now was for him not to find out how shameless I had been.

35
REBECCA

29th March 2018

When I woke up to the sound of the familiar voices coming from the kitchen, I decided I wasn't in a hurry to get out of bed. I didn't hear Ray getting up or the door going. My concern was that Emma and McCabe were downstairs and it had only occurred to me after waking up in a sweat during the night, that they were likely to be monitoring Patterson's visitors. If that was the case then I was sure that Ray was going to find out very soon. I lay another twenty minutes.

Emma was handing out coffee as I reluctantly entered the kitchen. 'Morning, Rebecca. That's your cup there.' She pointed at the purple mug Evan had given me for Christmas.

'Thanks.' I pulled out a chair and joined them at the table. To my relief the air wasn't tense.

'How's your mum, Rebecca?' McCabe asked. It was the sarcastic way in which he said it that made me wonder if he was being facetious or if I was just being paranoid.

'Fine, how's yours?' I asked, surprising myself more than them. Ray and Emma both cast their shocked eyes on me.

'My mum died five years ago, but thanks for asking,' he replied.

'I'm sorry.' I meant it, I really did, but I wouldn't have been surprised if he was lying just to make me look even more ridiculous.

'What's going on?' Ray looked at each of us in turn.

'Nothing,' I replied. 'I'm sorry, I didn't sleep well.'

'I think it's better that he knows, Rebecca,' Emma whispered, loud enough that there was no point in even lowering her voice.

'Knows what?' Ray demanded.

'Your wife went to visit Mark Patterson in prison yesterday afternoon,' McCabe announced.

'You better be joking. Becky?' He looked at me and knew fine that it wasn't a joke.

'Seriously? What is going on in that fucking head of yours?' he ranted while tapping his skull with his forefinger.

'I'm sorry, I knew you would try to stop me,' I said.

'Of course I would stop you. First Tony and now this, Why? What exactly have I done to deserve this? You make out like I'm the bad one.' He thumped his fist down hard enough on the table to spill Emma's coffee. She jumped up as the spill ran in her direction.

'Wow there, calm down,' McCabe said as he got to his feet.

'It's not about you,' I yelled back. 'And what have you done? You applied for a massive loan without me knowing and hired a private investigator, so don't make out like you're the victim here!'

'Well what am I supposed to do? Go to a psychic? Ask him to look into his crystal fucking ball? Oh, or I know, visit some psycho in prison and risk getting myself killed while I'm at it?'

'Enough. You both need to calm down,' Emma yelled at the same volume as us. 'Come on,' she said as she guided Ray out of the kitchen.

'Are you happy now?' I said, directing my anger back towards McCabe.

'No, I'm not. Sit down.' He shut the kitchen door and sat down opposite me. 'I'm not sorry. He needed to know.'

I said nothing. Instead, I clenched my teeth and breathed in deep through my nose.

'We don't want another investigation on our hands, Rebecca. These men are dangerous.'

'What evidence was there against him?' I asked.

'Against Patterson?'

'Yes.'

'He told you he's innocent and you believed him?'

'I don't believe him, I just want to know.'

'Rebecca, all psychopaths are innocent in their own minds. They don't take responsibility for their crimes. It's always someone else's fault. Most of the time it's their victim's.'

'I just want to know,' I repeated.

'OK,' he said then stopped as Emma returned. He waited on her taking a seat. 'I won't bother with the circumstantial evidence. Let's just say there was a lot. But the barrel of acid used in the attempt to decompose Jase's body was found in his lock up. He used a false name when signing the lease. The clothes that he wore during...his procedure, were found in a bag found in the lockup. DNA matching Patterson and Jase Frank were found on each article of clothing; Jase's DNA was found in his car and there was proof that he purchased the acid online using his credit card. So is that enough evidence for you? I can go on,' he said.

'No, that's enough.'

'Please Rebecca, leave the detective work to us. There are people out there who use vulnerable people like yourself for their own advantage,' Emma said.

Vulnerable is not a word I would have used to describe myself. Maybe I'm a bit naive at times, but certainly not vulnerable.

'Is there anything we should know about your visit with Patterson before we go?' asked McCabe.

'He thinks that someone has it in for the boys that went to St. Margaret's Boys' home or school, whatever it was - him, Billy McIvor and Ronnie Frank. He doesn't believe that Ronnie committed suicide and apparently he's not the only one.'

'What else did he say?' McCabe asked.

'That was about it.'

'I know it's difficult for you but staying at home really is for the best,' Emma added.

'So, Ray has hired a private investigator?' McCabe asked. I imagined that to be the biggest insult he could receive but I didn't sympathise. He was the one that was proving himself useless.

'Not exactly but we're planning to. He's been in contact with Max Watson.'

Emma's eyes widened and her jaw tensed as she tried to hide what looked like a hint of amusement.

'We need to go but we'll need to discuss it this afternoon. You're within your rights do so but I don't agree that it's a good idea.' There was no goodbye as he walked away and I wish I could have been a fly in his car when they got in it, because I had a feeling that Emma was about to witness an outburst.

36
REBECCA

I heard Ray in the shower and thought back to him crying when he found out that Patterson was involved. Now that I had calmed down, I felt even more regretful about going to the prison. At least Ray was honest with me afterwards about the loan and inviting Max around.

I sat on the bed and waited on him coming out of the shower. Things hadn't always been like this between us. In fact, it had never been like this at all before Evan went missing. I had gone too far this time. Just when we were making progress, I threw it back in his face. I had to restore all the damage I was causing and get us back to how it used to be.

It was never love at first sight, or any other kind of soppy love story for us. We knew each other for a while before we started going out; I worked in accounts for our local council and Ray worked in I.T maintenance. Anytime there was a problem with one of our computers, Ray would appear to sort it out. Because I was in a relationship at the time, I didn't take any notice.

When I say relationship, looking back I think it was the idea of being in a relationship that appealed to me more than the boy himself. Although he was twenty four years old, 'man' is not a word I could use to describe him. He was tall but insecure, childish and extremely needy. Finding out that he stalked me whenever I wasn't with him was the final straw. And that's when I started noticing Ray.

His smile is what I noticed first of all. Followed by his fresh scent, confidence and toned body that could be made out under his white shirt after careful observation. He soon noticed that I was paying more attention to him and things just went from there. Three years later, we were married and I was pregnant with Evan.

Our marriage had always been solid; based on love and trust. Both our laid back attitudes meant we never really argued, if something had to be said, it was said and done with. There was no resentment or grudges held (not for long anyway).

It was definitely me that was causing all this tension between us, he had just been retaliating to my awful behaviour; my digs, my snide remarks, my fury, my pain and my need to take it out on someone else. I wasn't giving him credit for the pain that he was also experiencing.

Wrapped in a towel from the waist down, he walked past without a glance in my direction and opened the door to his wardrobe.

'I'm sorry,' I said but he didn't react. 'I shouldn't have gone to the prison. I should have told you and let you stop me.' He remained facing the wardrobe but stopped what he was doing. 'I just felt like I had to do something.'

'Because it's better than doing nothing, like me,' he said.

'No, that's not what I'm saying. We're just dealing with things differently that's all.'

'We should be a team, Becky. We should be sticking together. You weren't even planning on telling me that you had been.'

'I know. I'm sorry.'

'I've never been the possessive type and you know that. I've always trusted you. Have you any idea how that felt, knowing you were there with him and I wasn't there to protect you? If something happened to you, I wouldn't have known until it was too late.'

I stood up and put my arms around him. I wanted to reassure him that nothing would have happened, because the reality was that it wouldn't have, but there was no point. 'I'm sorry,' I said. 'I wasn't thinking about you and I should've been.'

'From now on, we stick together,' he said, and I nodded in agreement.

While Ray got dressed and I sat on the bed feeling grateful for having one less thing to worry about, I received a text message from Caroline. *Was Evan a twin? xx*

The puzzled look on my face was probably why Ray asked who it was from.

'It's from Caroline, asking if Evan was a twin,' I told him.

'Why would she ask that?' he said.

'I think she probably means at birth or before he was born,' I said. 'It's maybe something to do with Tony,' I said, trying to be honest with him.

As I sent a reply saying *No x*, her choice of words caught my attention. *Was* he a twin? I thought about this for second and wondered if she was now referring to Evan as being dead, like it was confirmed. If she thought he was alive and had lost a twin, he'd still be a twin, right? You don't lose that status because you're sibling is gone. That's like saying I would no longer be a mother if I lost Evan.

'I thought he was going to keep his nose out?' Ray interrupted my train of thought.

'I know how you feel about him but you can't deny the fact that without him, McIvor would never have been caught,' I said.

'I don't trust him. All that psychic crap, I don't buy it. I don't want you near him.'

I was tempted to react and tell him that he couldn't control who I saw, but stopped myself. Arguing had obviously just become a habit.

'Ok. But if he knows stuff, do you not think it's better to find out, regardless of whether you trust him or not?' I suggested.

'Maybe. I still don't want you near him though.'

'Ok, so should I phone her to find out what this is about?' I asked.

'If you want but promise me you'll stay away from him, Becky. I need your word.'

'I promise.'

37
CAROLINE

After searching through Facebook for Greggs, the closest I could find was his sister, Angela – a harmless but mouthy woman. From her profile pictures, I could tell that she still lived in the same house, and had a handful of kids with ridiculous names.

Adamson Street hadn't changed much. The council houses had improved, with their new orange roof tiles and off-white roughcasting, but the place was still a shit hole. Gardens were full of rubbish, windows were boarded up and kids as young as three or four were running about without an adult in sight. How long would it take their parents to notice if one of them went missing? I shuddered at the thought.

I hadn't messaged Angela, so she had no idea I was coming. I thought that giving her notice of our reunion would only give her the opportunity to refuse or make up some excuse not to see me. It was going to be awkward for both of us but she was my only hope of tracking down Greggs. *I'm doing this for Rebecca*, I kept telling myself.

My heart was thumping against my chest as I struggled to undo the latch on her gate, while hoping I wasn't being watched through the window. The sound of children running riot told me that there had to be an adult at home so I rattled on the letterbox.

'Mum, the door,' I heard coming from the hallway. She still didn't answer so I rattled it again.

'What?' she said as she opened it. She looked at me as if I was a nuisance caller, waiting to find out what I was selling.

'Hi Angela,' I said. Her eyes widened and mouth opened as she recognised me.

'Oh my God, Caroline. I didn't recognise you. I thought it was the police with that knock. How are you?'

'Fine, thanks. Sorry for turning up like this, I was just wondering if we could have a little chat?' She was reluctant, I could tell - the pause made me feel inadequate; not quite sure if I was coming or going.

'Eh, what about? Is it about Gregory?' she asked.

'Yes.'

'You better come in,' she said, 'Excuse the mess. I haven't had the chance to do any housework today.'

'Don't worry about it. I'm not here to see your house,' I said trying to put her at ease, while the sight and stench of dirty nappies piled up in the corner of the room made me gag. There were clothes everywhere, on the sofa, the floor, the door handles.

'Do you want something to drink? She asked as she lifted a pile of laundry to make room for me to sit down. I could only imagine what her glasses and mugs looked like so I had to refuse.

'No, thanks. I won't keep you long. You look like you have your hands full,' I said with a raised voice so she would be able to hear me above the TV and the little ones screeching.

'Yeah they keep me busy,' she laughed. 'Right, through to your rooms,' she yelled. The older boy sitting in front of the TV got up. The two little ones that were running around in vests and nappies, didn't pay her any attention. One was a boy and the other a girl, not identical but too similar in age not to be twins. I quickly passed on the thought that they could be the twins Tony that had been referring to.

175

'Right, the pair of you, go,' she said guiding them out of the room. She closed the door behind them and sat on the arm of the chair.

'Sorry for turning up like this out of the blue, it must be a bit of a surprise,' I said.

'That's ok, it's good to see you. It's a nice surprise,' she replied but I knew she didn't mean it. 'Have you heard from Gregory?'

'No, that's why I'm here. I'm hoping you could tell me where to find him. I need to speak to him about something,' I told her.

'You'll be lucky.'

'Why, where is he?' I asked.

'I've no idea. We haven't heard from him in years, coming up three. I thought that's why you were here,' she said.

'No, sorry. I had no idea. Three years?' I was surprised because that's how long it had been since Ronnie's suicide. I thought about the visit I had from the police.

'He went AWOL a few days after your Ronnie's funeral. The police said that it's likely he had some kind of breakdown. We reported him missing, but the scummy bastards weren't interested. Some people don't want to be found apparently.'

I was stunned by this news and stayed quiet while I tried to think it through. Ronnie and Greggs were like brothers so a breakdown was understandable. But I couldn't help wondering if he was simply living it large somewhere exotic without a second thought for Angela and the kids. He did inherit Ronnie's fortune after all. With the age of her kids it would mean he didn't even know about half of them. Maybe I was wrong. I had heard of people having breakdowns to the point that they didn't even know what

176

day of the week it was. All that drug money could have been sitting in a bank account somewhere, untouched.

'Fucked up, eh?' she said.

'It is Angela, it sure is. So he's never met the twins?' I asked.

'Nope. Our own flesh and blood and he doesn't even know they exist,' she answered. There was hurt in her voice and I wondered if part of the reason she had so many kids was to make up for the fact that Gregory had been her only other blood relative. Although, I'm sure all the Benefits were coming in handy.

'I'm so sorry, Angela.'

'Don't be daft. Here's me complaining about my shit when you've been through a lot worse. I'm sorry about your lad, that was awful. And Ronnie of course. He was a good one Caroline,' she said.

'Thanks,' I replied. If only she knew. Ronnie was like another brother to her, always there to protect her and bail her out. She wouldn't have believed me if I were to tell her what he was really like. 'That's how I understand what it feels like to lose someone. You must be devastated,' I said.

'It's the not knowing,' she said. 'I fear that he's dead. He would phone, Caroline, no matter how fucked up in the head he was. Wouldn't he? Breakdowns can't make you forget who you are, could they?' she asked.

'I really don't know.' I wasn't sure what answer she'd prefer.

'What did you want to see him about?'

'It was just about some of the boys he grew up with,' I said.

'Maybe I could help?' she suggested.

I was in two minds whether to tell her or not, she's hardly Miss Discreet. But without Greggs I had nothing.

177

There was a chance that she could be of some use so I decided to take the risk.

'Do you know Evan? The boy that's missing,' I began.

'I don't know him personally but yeah I've heard all about it.'

'Well apparently Mark Patterson who killed my Jase, and Billy McIvor, that's the guy who's just been arrested, were in St. Margaret's together. I was hoping Greggs might know something about them. Or, anything else that might be relevant. Do you know anybody else that was brought up with them that I could maybe track down?'

'Fucking hell. Really? Do you think all this could have anything to do with Gregory going missing?' she asked.

'I don't think so, I really don't know.' And the truth is I hadn't even considered it until then, and to my dismay, Angela had just made herself a part of it. Regret was already creeping in.

'Right, let's think about it,' she said. 'I've got letters. When Gregory was in St.Margaret's, I was in foster care. We wrote to each other once a week. I've still got them.' She finished her sentence as she disappeared out of the room.

While she was away, I worked out that I could have her living room spotless in less than five minutes. With a pair of rubber gloves and a bin bag, it would take around one minute to collect the rubbish, another to throw the washing in a washing basket and the toys in the toy box, one to dust and one to hoover.

She finally returned with four shoeboxes piled up in her arms. 'Found them,' she smiled.

'Great.'

'I haven't read them in years. Gregory would kill me if he knew I was letting you read them,' she said.

I smiled at the thought. 'You were kids, they can't be that bad.'

'They're bad, trust me. I can't even bring myself to read these ones again,' she replied. Two of the boxes had sad faces, drawn on with a blue colouring pen. The other two had smiley faces and were covered in girly stickers. 'People have no idea how bad children's homes were back then. I suppose Ronnie would have told you all about what went on in that place.'

'He didn't. He wouldn't speak about it at all.'

'Really? He must have tried to shut it all out then. That makes sense, I suppose. Oh Caroline, those poor boys.'

She handed me a happy box, moved a pile of newspapers onto the floor and sat down next to me. The sad boxes were pushed around the side of the sofa, out of sight.

Opening the box, the smell of the old yellow folded paper, scattered like a raffle draw, took me back to my own childhood when writing letters was the done thing. A time when receiving letters in the post was exciting, unlike the final reminder letters I had been receiving lately.

I picked one from the top, unfolded it and instantly felt the sentiment from the child's handwriting. I now imagined Greggs sitting in front of a large window in a minimalistic dormitory with metal framed beds, neatly made. It read:

Dear Angela,

I reseeved your letter. I hope you are feeling better. David had a soar throte wonse and had to get his tonsels out. I hope that dosn't happin to you. He said that they cut a bit out your throte and make you eat jaggy cornflakes. David beat me up again yesterday but I didn't cry... I stopped reading. 'I'm not sure this is a good idea, Angela,' I said. 'It's like reading someone else's diary.' When I looked at her for a response, her hand was over her mouth, her face red and soaked with tears.

'Oh God, Caroline, I miss him so much.'

'Of course you do,' I said and placed my hand on her arm. 'It's no wonder.'

We decided to continue. It took the best part of an hour to read all the letters in one box. Nothing stood out as being relevant, there were names, but no surnames.

'It was worth a try,' Angela said, blowing her nose. 'I need to get the dinner on, do you want to stay?'

'No thanks, I better get going. But thanks anyway and thanks for your help,' I said.

'I haven't been any help. Wouldn't there be records somewhere?' she suggested.

'Maybe, I'm not sure if they would be confidential or not.' I replied.

'True. Wait a minute.' She started typing into her phone and I stood while she found what she was looking for. 'You could check the local authority archives. It says here that sometimes the institutes themselves hold records but it's not there now is it? I think they made it into flats.'

'Where would I need to go for that?' I asked, and waited patiently on her finding out for me. While she was tapping away, I looked down at the two sad boxes and felt an urge to know what was in them. All I needed was one full name. Not only that, but I wondered if they would give me an insight into that part of my husband I knew nothing about. What caused him to become the monster he did?

'Bankhead, Glenrothes, I think. You need an appointment. You'd be better explaining what you're looking for first, in case that's the wrong place. I'm sure they'd point you in the right direction though.'

'Thanks. I really appreciate it.'

'It's funny,' Angela said as her two little ones ran past her. 'Twinnies, I haven't heard that word in years, I remember when all twins got called, *the twinnies.*'

'What makes you say that?'

'Gregory mentioned them in a couple of letters, seeing the twins reminded me,' she said.

'Why didn't you say?' I asked, wondering what else she had failed to mention.

'He didn't say what their names were, just referred to them as the twinnies. I thought you were looking for names.'

'I am. It's ok. They weren't mentioned in any of the ones I read, that's all,' I said. 'I'll leave you to get on. I really hope you hear from Greggs soon.' I looked once again at the two forbidden boxes.

'Yeah me too,' she replied. 'I'll let you know if I hear anything. It was good to see you again. Listen, I'd offer to help with the whole archive thing but it's not easy to get out alone when you've got kids.'

'Don't worry about it, I'll be fine. Do you know what might help though? I couldn't borrow those boxes could I?'

She considered this for a second. 'Are you sure you want to? I've never read them as an adult but I cried my eyes out when they first arrived in the post.'

'Maybe they're not as bad as you remember,' I suggested. 'I'm sure it would be different reading them as an adult.'

'I suppose. Take them, as long as you bring them back,' she said.

'I promise, I will. As soon as I'm finished with them.'

'Ok. I guess I'll see you again soon,' she said. She gave me hug and then headed to the kitchen, leaving me to let myself out.

On the way home, I thought about the upbringing they must have had, and couldn't help comparing it to my own. Maybe I was lucky after all, having a Mum until I was eight and allowed to stay in my own home with my screwed up Dad until I was old enough to leave. Angela, by the sound of it, was better off than Greggs. The thought of those poor boys being brought up in that Care home - if it was as bad as Angela made it out back then, it was no wonder they were all messed up in the head. I thought about Billy McIvor's pay-out from the local authorities and found myself hoping that the same thing hadn't happened to Ronnie and Greggs.

Ronnie never laid a finger on me until after we were married. One night after a concoction of whiskey, Valium and cocaine, I was curled in the foetal position while he punched and kicked me over and over. He was so out of it he had no idea what he was saying or doing. *How do you like that, you little shit,* he kept repeating. When he finally stopped, I could tell he was crying and I knew then, that he had experienced the same thing as a child. We never spoke about his past so I couldn't say if this is what happened in care or before, but after reading those letters, even the 'happy' ones, I wouldn't be surprised if he had been on the receiving end of it in St.Margaret's.

It made me wonder about the whole nature/nurture debate. Was Ronnie a product of his environment? There's no doubt he had anger issues that were taken out on me. He wasn't just violent though, he had a real wicked streak.

I recall one night that we were both high and he wanted to tie me up. He had never been violent during sex, I was never raped. But, this one night, he was frustrated because he couldn't ejaculate due to the amount of cocaine he had taken. He lit a cigarette and after a few puffs, he held it

182

against the skin on my stomach. I protested and he pulled it away immediately. Presuming he was just having some kind of absence in his drug-fuelled state, I relaxed when he got up and stumbled out the room. He returned with duct tape.

I had no control because of the ties around my wrists and soon I would have no way to vocalise my pain. He lit another cigarette and held it in place, watching carefully as it burned its way through the layers of skin. The look on his face was one of fascination. Despite my crying, wriggling and wincing, he repeated the process until I had thirteen burns.

The next day, I confided in one of Ronnie's friends that had been coming about the house. His name was Charlie and he was a good guy. Ronnie was oblivious to the fact that he had become more of a friend to me, than him. Charlie was disgusted when I showed him the water-filled blisters on my stomach. Hurting women wasn't something he or his friends would tolerate, apparently. I didn't expect him to go to the police though, that was not the done thing. I guess in a way it showed Charlie's innocence, he was a boy in a man's world.

Fortunately for Ronnie, it happened before the law was changed, meaning I would have to press charges for him to face them, rather than it being in the hands of the procurator fiscal. That wasn't going to happen; for my own safety I had to deny that it happened. Ronnie backed off for a while, but it certainly wasn't an end to the violence.

Ronnie, Patterson and McIvor had all turned bad. Greggs seemed to be the only exception. And now, from what I had just learned, they also grew up with twins. I was pretty certain that this was no coincidence, surely they had to be the twins that Tony had mentioned. I didn't know what this meant in terms of Evan's abduction, or if the rest of the letters would shed any light on the issue but I was eager to get home and find out.

38
CAROLINE

Sitting at the kitchen table with a fresh cup of coffee and the shoeboxes full of letters, I lit a cigarette without a care that the smell would linger through the rest of the house; it was my last packet. As I removed the lid from one of the boxes, I felt an odd sense of betrayal as I was about to read about the childhood that Ronnie hid from me. It was strange seeing his name in the ones I read earlier, but I didn't really have time to take it in.

I had grown to hate Ronnie, but what I hated more was the fact that I was still looking for a reason to excuse his behaviour towards me. Maybe it was a reason to help me forgive him that I was looking for.

I lifted out the folded letter that was on top of the pile. It read:

Dear Angela,
I got your letter and it was good to here about your holiday, but you didn't say if you asked Tom and Ella if I could come and stay with them to. Pleese ask them but don't tell them it's becos I hate it here in case they phone Father, I don't want him to punish me again.

Things are getting a lot wors. Remember I told you about that man that we need to call Uncle. Well he lives with us now. Every night, Father thinks he takes us out to the garden to do sports but he dosn't. He makes us fight until we're hurt and crying.

He made me fight Ronnie and you know how small he is. He kept telling me to punch him harder. If I didn't do it he was going to hurt both of us. Ronnie stopped speaking to

*me and I'm scared that he'll look for a new best friend,
probably Billy and Eddie becos they like him to. Ronnie
closed his eyes when they two had to fight each other and
put his fingers in his ears.*

*I've seen them fighting before but mostly just rolling
around the grownd giving little punches. They had to really
hurt each other and were both crying the hole time.*

*Maybe if I give Ronnie one of my comics he will forgive
me.*

Yours sinseerly
Gregory
P.S. Don't forget to ask Tom and Ella.

I could have cried at thought of them both, so young and
vulnerable. To think they would have been ten years old
with nobody to wipe away their tears.

What sort of grown man would get pleasure from
watching young boys fight until they cried? I looked at the
date on the letter- 21.04.1983. I opened each letter from the
box and tried to find the next one. I remembered Angela
saying they wrote to each other once a week so I searched
until I found the 28th of April. It read:

Dear Angela,
*I'm sorry to here that Ella and Tom don't want me and I
don't blaim them. Maybe I could run away and you could
hide me somewhere. Didn't you say they had a large coal
shed out the back? I would live there if you brought me
food. Then we could be together all the time. I'll ask Ronnie
to see if he wants to come with me. He wasn't angry he was
just sad but the comic cheered him up.*

*Things are still bad here. I was at a hospital yesterday
becos my thumb is broken. Have you ever been to a*

hospital? It has lots of nice nurses and I got a lollipop but it stinks. Do you no how I was telling you about the fights, well Uncle didn't think it was fair that Ronnie coodn't hurt me so he helped him. I put my hand out to stop his kick and it broke. It's the sorest thing that's ever happened to me but I got out of fighting so I'm kind of glad. I'm kind of glad I'm fat too becos Timmy Boylen's rib got broke. Timmy's 14 and really strong but he's skinny and that's why it broke.

Uncle's latest thing is having us kicking and using our knees and elbows too but we're not allowed to hit faces. All our marks are covered by our clothes. He deminstrated on Eddie and we thought he was dead. He nocked him unconshis. We all hate him Angela. Mark can hardly walk and he had to tell Father he fell down the stairs. Father thinks Eddie has the flu. Billy has asked some of the older boys if they would kill Uncle. I hope they do.

I'm so glad you live in a nice house. I'll speak to Ronnie about running away, I'm sure we can come up with a plan.

Yours Sinseerely
Gregory

I lit another cigarette. I knew care homes were bad back then, but not on this scale. Was the man who abused Billy McIvor that Father or Uncle, or some other Uncle that was allowed to get his hands on him? How many of the boys mentioned had been sexually abused? Had Ronnie? I felt sick at the thought. But, now I had a surname – Timmy Boylen. I had to get the wi-fi sorted in order to find out the answers to all my questions. I was positive that if I searched for him, I'd find him. I was also sure that if I searched for articles on St. Margaret's, I would be able to find out who these scum-bags were. I hoped to read that they had been locked up for what they had done to those kids.

The next letter, I read with a sense of relief:

Dear Angela,

We're going to do it! We're going to run away! I have your plan here and I think it's perfect. We don't have money for the bus but we're going to walk. We will meet you at the river (where we had a picnic) next Sunday at 6pm.

I have news for you. We got rid of Uncle. He went away for a couple of days and when he was away we planned to get our own back. Billy gathered all the boys that hated him- Me, Ronnie, Mark, Timmy, Eddie and the hardest boy here, his name is James.

We convinced Uncle that we wanted to practice what we had learnt and wanted to team up and have one big massive fight and that we would have to go into the woods so that Father would not hear us as it was sure to be noisier than our usual one to ones with everyone sitting around watching. I can't believe he fell for it.

When we got into the woods, James took the first punch and we all just laid into him, elbows, knees, everything. He tried to fight us off, he broke Billy's nose but we kept going. Everything he taught us we used against him. We stopped when he stopped fighting back. He lay still under a tree and we thought he was dead. We didn't know what to do so we left him there.

James went back to check but he was gone. We haven't seen him since and we're just hoping he doesn't come back. I really don't think he will. So, things have been better for most of us and I think we have a better chance of running away now.

I love you Angela and we will be together soon. Remember, next Sunday 6pm by the river.

Your Sinseerly

Gregory.

I continued to read the letters. They didn't run away and Uncle didn't return. I was grateful that I wasn't getting to hear the full extent of what was happening in that building. I had read enough. I at least, had enough information to go forward.

Billy and Eddie were always mentioned as if they were a duo, so my bet was that they were the twins, and I could try to find Timmy Boylen. I didn't try to excuse Ronnie's behaviour but I came to the conclusion that he felt an empathy that Billy lacked. Billy had obviously turned into a child abuser, but I believe that the reason Ronnie never laid a finger on Jase, was because he didn't want him to suffer in the same way he did. I was simply irrelevant, obviously.

Not only did I need wi-fi, but I needed cigarettes, petrol, coffee, milk and sugar. I had an idea; there was a box containing Ronnie's jewellery in the loft, which I had put away to give to Jase when he was older. There were plenty of pawn shops around here, and if it made enough I would get something to eat - it had to be worth enough money to do me a couple of days at least.

39
REBECCA

30th March 2018

Given that Ray and I were both making an effort to remain on side, I agreed that hiring a private detective could be a good idea, but I suggested that we research thoroughly first. He was happy to oblige although it wasn't as easy as we first thought; there were so many of them.

It's not like searching for a plumber or electrician where you go with the one with the cheapest call out charge. It's like trying to work out who would do a better job, regardless of the price - I agreed to apply for a smaller loan if need be. Some sites offered profiles of their detectives and others provided an email address for further information. After two hours or so of reading as many profiles as we could, we were no further forward.

'This looks promising,' he said. 'If they're a member of this, then it surely means they're the real deal.' He had come across *The Association of British Investigators*. We searched their member database for investigators in and around our area. Needless to say, *Max. J. Watson* popped up.

There was no denying that the tag under his personal information displayed a longer list of skills than the rest. Surveillance, specialist and forensic services, tracing and status reports, fraud investigation, undercover investigations, general investigation.

'Are you sure you're not just being stubborn Becky?' he asked, and I had to admit it that I think he was right.

'Keep looking, if we can't find anyone else then maybe we don't have much option,' I replied.

'You shouldn't judge someone based on someone else's opinion,' he mocked.

I had said these words to him more often than I could remember, so I had to take this on board.

'Ok, maybe I'll see what he has to say for himself. But I'm not making any promises.'

***

Max Watson agreed to meet us at the Dakota Hotel on the other side of the Forth Road Bridge. He was based in Edinburgh so it was near enough half way. This was my chance to suss him out, especially given the opposing views from Emma and Ray vs Caroline and Tony - it was going to be interesting if nothing else. I figured that he could come to the house later to face Tweedledee and Tweedledum, if we decided to go ahead with it. McCabe had gone over his concerns with us, but basically it all came down to him being afraid that his toes were going to get stepped on.

Regardless of all the doubts that Caroline had placed in my head, as I stepped out the car, I was leaning towards hopeful. It was an extra pair of hands that I was certain would be more useful than the ones we already had. When we walked through the entrance to reception, we were pointed in the direction of the lounge.

Ray pointed in Max's direction to let me know it was him. He stood up from his seat at the bar and walked towards us. He looked around sixty, with neatly styled silvery white hair. The lines on his face were fine and I could tell he had been handsome in his day. Being slightly taller than Ray, put him around the six foot mark.

'Mrs Shelby, I'm Private Investigator, Max Watson. Please call me Max.' He held out his hand for me to shake.

His voice was gentle and friendly, unlike the deep, coarse sound I was expecting.

'Call me Rebecca,' I replied.

We sat down at a small table overlooking the Firth of Forth and a waiter came over to ask what we would like to drink. Max ordered a black coffee and Ray and I opted for the latte. Looking around, there was only one other couple in the dining area and one waitress preparing the tables for lunch.

'I'm sorry for what you're going through. I can't even begin to imagine how you must be feeling right now,' he said with a look of sincerity.

'Thanks,' I tried to say, but it came out mute. I had to cough to clear my throat.

'As you know, I've already spoke to Ray but I'm happy to answer any questions that you might have, Rebecca,' he said.

I thought for a second about the kind of questions you might ask in this situation: *What do you have to offer?* Or, *Why do you think it would be worth our while hiring you?* Maybe I was wrong though since it was Ray that approached him. So, instead I asked the first thing that came to mind. 'Why did you resign?'

Ray was clearly embarrassed as his hand reached up to cover his eyes and then tried to disguise it as a temple rub.

'Fair question,' he said. 'It was something I had been considering for a while - you have a lot more freedom as a private investigator. But I have to admit, that the deciding factor for me was when I had a disagreement with my superior and felt I was wrongly undermined.'

'Was it to do with falsely accusing Tony?' I asked.

'You could say that,' he admitted.

'How do you feel about it all now?' I asked, feeling confident that I had every right to know what we could be working with.

He paused while he considered the question. 'My only regret is how I handled the situation.' He sighed. 'I could have been more professional when dealing with Tony, I admit. But, I have to say I would follow that same line of enquiry if I felt it was necessary. I have no regrets there.'

'It sounds a bit like you have it in for him. Is that the case?' I asked. He was making it easy for me to continue with the questions, so I did.

'I don't have it in for him. You make it sound like it's personal and I can assure you, that's not the case. For starters, at the time, I was accused of being homophobic. That's absurd. I am no more homophobic than I am heterophobic. I have a number of gay friends. As for the psychic stuff, I'm not a believer but I respect that if people want to believe then that's their choice.'

'There had to be some reason you suspected him,' I said. Ray had now removed his hand from his face and was now listening with interest.

'Yeah, what was the reason?' Ray asked.

'Tony Delimonte has a history of fraud,' Max announced.

'I knew it, I fucking knew it,' Ray said aggressively while managing to keep his voice not much more than a whisper. We all looked towards the barman in recognition that we were trying to be discreet. He continued to stack his glasses without a glance in our direction. I instantly thought about Caroline and considered the fact that there are always two sides to a story. I had only heard Caroline's side up until now.

'Why haven't we been told this before?' I asked.

'I'm not sure. Maybe you should ask D.I. McCabe that,' Max replied.

'Does Caroline know?

'I doubt it,' he replied.

'If we were to hire you, what would be your plan?' I asked.

'My main objective is obviously to find Evan, but in order for me to do that, it would be useful to find out, why Evan?' he answered. 'There was an article printed in the newspaper not that long ago, saying that I apparently said there was no connection. Did you read that?'

'Yes,' Ray and I replied.

'I have never given an interview to any newspaper, let's just make that clear. Now I'm not saying there is or there isn't connection, but given that Mark Patterson is supposed to be involved, the chances are greater now. I have ways of finding out if Evan's routine was consistent enough for it to be planned or not, or if he just happened to be in the wrong place at the wrong time. That's presuming it hasn't been looked into before now.' He raised his eyebrows looking for an answer.

'It's never been mentioned. They must have though, surely,' I replied.

'I've been following the investigation but obviously not everything is reported, so a chat with D.I. Watson and D.S. Harper would be helpful. I'd have to take it from there. If there's a reason for Evan's abduction then I'm confident that I could get to the bottom of it. I'm fast and thorough and have had time to run through the facts and possibilities, so I feel like I have a bit of a head start.'

'What if there's not a reason, though?' Ray asked.

'It might be opportunistic, Ray. But if that was the case, then I'm pretty certain he would have been found by now.

194

Opportunists make silly mistakes and usually leave a trail of evidence.'

'So what about Jase? Was there a reason for what they did to him?' I asked.

'There were too many coincidences for there not to be, in my opinion, but unfortunately, whoever took over the case didn't reach a conclusion.'

There was a silence as we all seemed lost in our own thoughts.

'Please excuse me.' Max stood up. 'I hope you don't mind but I'm going to go out for some fresh air. It'll give you two a chance to talk.' He removed a packet of cigarettes and a lighter from his pocket before leaving the table.

Ray sat forward in order to face me directly. 'We've nothing to lose, Becky. He sounds a lot more competent than McCabe, do you not agree?' he said.

'That wouldn't be difficult,' I replied, unable to resist the dig. I stared out the window, while Ray waited on a proper answer.

Instead of thinking about Max I wondered if Caroline knew about Tony's history of fraud. She had had a colourful past too, so maybe she did. There was no way she would doubt his psychic abilities, but then I'm not sure I would either. Max had said enough to convince me that he'd be worth a shot and the feeling of possibly being closer to the truth was frightening.

'Becky, at least give me an answer. What are you thinking?' Ray asked.

'We've nothing to lose.'

'I agree.' He squeezed my hand in triumph.

When Max returned, I told him that we wanted to hire him. He smiled and nodded in response. 'I promise, I'll do everything in my power to find him.'

Looking at Ray, it was clear he had every confidence in Max, and I have to admit - I felt it too.

'So, what now?' I asked.

'I'll get a contract drawn up, I'll speak to D.I. McCabe and D.S. Harper, and I'll need to come to your house to take a look around and ask you both some questions,' he replied.

'Perfect.' Ray stood up to shake Max's hand.

'There's one thing I'd like to know before we go, and I'm sure you've been asked this before, but it's really important. That's the only reason I'm asking. Have either of you been involved in any kind of illegal activity? Ever had any dealings with...let's say, shady characters,' he asked. 'Anything at all?'

I looked at Ray and he looked a little uncomfortable. 'I've met a few shady characters but not recently,' he finally admitted. I remained seated while both of them sat back down.

'Who?' Max asked.

'I smoked weed when I was young, just the usual teenage stuff. I came across a few dodgy folk in dealer's houses but never associated with them. It was always just a case of in and out as quick as you could.'

'Well if anything more specific comes to mind, please let me know. What about you Rebecca?' he asked.

'Me? No.'

'You're an accountant, right?' he said.

'Yes.'

'Ever been asked to do anything illegal? Tax evasion, money laundering, stuff like that?' he asked.

'No. No, I don't think so.'

'You don't think so? I'm sure you would remember if you had,' he said.

'No I haven't, definitely not,' I replied.

196

'Well, same to you, if you think of anything let me know.'

'Ok,' I said before we all stood up.

'I promise I'll do my best to find him,' Max said. 'You have my word.'

'Thanks,' Ray replied. 'We just want him home.'

***

'It's weird having to tell a detective you used to be a stoner. I was worried he was going to arrest me,' Ray said on the way home.

'He couldn't arrest you, he would need to provide evidence to the police and they would arrest you. Isn't that how it works?' I said.

'Yeah I think so. It was still weird though,' he replied.

We sat in silence the rest of the way home. I had a sinking feeling, thinking back to the time that I was asked to do something illegal. It had happened a long time ago and as I was certain it was unrelated, I forced it to the back of my mind where it had been buried before.

40
CAROLINE

'Caroline, is there something you want to speak about?' Tony asked from the doorway to the kitchen. Usually when people ask this, they already know exactly what the subject is.

'Like what?' I asked, wondering what he was getting at.

'Like why there's nothing in your fridge and your cupboards are empty,' he said.

I had considered telling Tony how bad things were because he really had no idea. My finances have always been a personal matter and the thought of being pitied, was enough to stop me from mentioning it. I had managed to pawn Ronnie's jewellery and make all my necessary purchases, but it didn't help the fact that direct debits were coming out my account every other day.

I received another reminder that morning, in the form of a text message, saying that I have gone over my agreed limit on Account ending 268, and that to minimise fees, I must pay in cleared funds by 3pm today. I wasn't sure how much longer I could ignore them. It just seemed ironic that my bank account was below empty when there could be an account sitting somewhere with Ronnie's fortune in it.

'I'm having financial trouble,' I said.

'What bad enough that you can't afford food? How bad are you talking?' he asked.

'It's bad,' I replied. 'I don't have a penny left to buy something for lunch, let alone fill my cupboards.'

'Oh for goodness sake Caroline, you should have told me. Right, get your coat,' he said.

'Why?' I asked.

'We're going for something to eat,' he replied. 'And we'll stop at the shop on the way back.' I felt an instant relief, knowing that I was no longer alone with my secret.

As we left Blackbridge, he took a right, so it was safe to presume that we were going along the coast for a fish supper – something we used to do together regularly.

'I went to see Greggs,' I told him, feeling a tad guilty after him advising me not to. He looked back at me shocked, or disappointed, one of the two.

'And?'

'Well, I didn't actually go to see Greggs, I went to his sister Angela's. Greggs has been missing for three years.'

'What do you mean missing?' he asked.

'Missing, as in nobody knows where he is. Nobody has seen him since Ronnie's funeral.'

'That's a bit strange, don't you think?' he asked.

'I would say.'

'Do you think he could have something to do with Ronnie's death?'

'No. They were like brothers,' I replied.

'Yes, but didn't you say that they had a joint bank account? You'd be surprised how far some folk will go when there's money involved. I remember having a feeling when you told me that there was something not quite right about it,' he said.

'What, you think he could have pushed him for the money?' I asked.

'It would make sense.'

'No way. Not Greggs. I'm presuming I was drunk when I told you about it,' I asked, vaguely remembering the conversation.

'I can't remember, to be honest. You just said they were drug dealers and shared an account. You wanted nothing to do with the money and couldn't access it even if you wanted to.'

'That's right. No, I know it sounds like a strange coincidence but Greggs was a softy compared to the rest of them. The least likely to kill someone,' I said.

'Yeah and their wives would probably say the same about Ronnie,' he remarked.

I considered this, and it was so true. Ronnie presented himself as a kind, doting husband to everyone, except me. Maybe Greggs was no different. Maybe his experience at St. Margaret's had turned him into a thug too.

'There were twins at St. Margaret's at the same time as the rest of them,' I said, while we were on the subject of Greggs.

'I think it's Billy McIvor,' he replied.

'Really? So do I.'

'Yip, and it would explain a few things, don't you think?'

'Like what?'

'Like, maybe it was his twin visiting Patterson in prison, or maybe it's his twin's DNA on the boots,' he answered.

'Is twins DNA identical?' I asked.

'I think so, I'm sure forensic science would be advanced enough these days to tell the difference, but maybe not if they don't know what they're looking for,' he said.

'Well, if it is Billy that has a twin, then his name's Eddie.'

'How the hell do you know that?' He glanced over at me with surprise and held his gaze long enough that I had to remind him to keep his eyes on the road.

'Angela has boxes full of letters that Greggs wrote to her when they were kids. I brought a couple of them home with me and I noticed that Billy was hardly mentioned without

Eddie. They all read Billy and Eddie as if they came as a pair.'

'What else did they say?'

'There was a boy mentioned called Timothy Boylen, I tried to find him on social media just before you arrived but didn't have any luck. I thought that if I could track him down he might know something about the boys in the home that would explain what's going on. Rebecca said that Patterson told her someone has it in for the St.Margaret's boys but I don't believe that for a minute. There must be something, though. Do you not think?'

'Like what?'

'I don't know. I've read a lot about how bad they were treated and how they beat up a man they called Uncle, because he was a horrible bastard and deserved it. Who knows what else went on it that place, it could be anything. But then again, it might be nothing. Maybe you're right about it being Billy's twin Eddie that's the other person involved. Maybe they formed their own little perverted group and...' I stopped there, I couldn't even bring myself to finish the sentence.

'You need to stay out of all that shit, Caroline. Don't be tracking anyone down, you never know what you might get caught up in. Leave it to the police.'

'Do you think I should tell Emma?'

'If Billy does have a twin, I'm sure they'll know about it already.'

He was right. They would have known and if they had any sense they would have checked the records themselves and contacted boys from the home. They wouldn't have known about Uncle though and I knew I couldn't let that lie. Men like him would just move on to the next set of kids he could get his hands on.

We were both quiet until we reached our destination. The sign above the door read: *Anstruther Fish Bar,* and the queue as always was out the door and trailing around the corner, despite the rain.

'Come on there's an umbrella in the boot,' said Tony. We joined the queue and huddled underneath the green and white golf brolly.

'Where do you think you'll move to?' he asked. 'I could imagine you in a nice little cottage somewhere.'

'Me too. Anywhere along this coast would be nice. I suppose it depends on what I get for the house.'

'You should get a fair bit, I would imagine. Oh and don't worry about money, I'll give you a loan until the sale goes through or however long it takes, it doesn't matter, just don't be worrying about it, ok?' he whispered in my ear so that people around us couldn't hear. His volume returned to normal to suggest that we tackle the weeds and ivy on our return.

'Ok,' I replied. 'I think it's about time I tried to get a job; one that pays.'

'We can look into that too, if you want.' He pulled me in tighter for a hug and I wished once again that I had told him sooner.

'You do realise that this is the reason I have to sell the house? Don't get me wrong, I was always going to move, you know that. I just didn't realise it would have to happen this soon.'

'Well you know I'm a great believer that everything happens for a reason. What's my favourite saying?'

'What's meant to be, will be,' we said together, and I smiled because it had been about the millionth time I had heard him say those words.

'Things might seem shitty now but it will all work out for the best.'

'I hope you're right.'

'Anyway, what you having?'

'Fish supper of course, everything on it,' I answered, and the thought of it, along with the smell lingering out the door made my stomach do a little dance.

'Same here. Pickle?'

'And Irn Bru.' I smiled back at him.

***

We got back to the house about an hour later. Neither of us had mentioned anything else about Evan's case and it made me realise the extent to which it had taken over. The break from it was just what I needed. Instead we spoke about what my new house might be like and what I still had to do to prepare the old one for selling.

We headed straight out to the shed. I grabbed everything I could find; sheers, hedge cutter, chainsaw, ladders, gardening gloves and tools that I had no idea how to use.

'Where do we start?' I looked around the overwhelming mess that had become of my house and driveway.

'You start weeding and I'll tidy up the ivy.'

'Ok.' So that's what we did. Surprisingly, I found it quite therapeutic. I've never been green fingered but that feeling of getting a job done while your mind is free to wander, was quite liberating. The sun had come out and with the sound of the waves, there was a calmness that I hadn't felt in a long time.

On our second coffee, we sat on the doorstep. It was far from finished but we had made good headway.

'I think we should take the chainsaw right along the bottom,' I suggested, drawing a line with my hand along the bottom of the eight feet conifers.

'No way, you're not serious?' Tony replied.

'I think I am. You know how much I hate the conifers in Blackbridge. The less there is to hide behind, the better, if you ask me.'

'I'll do it if you want,' he smiled. He obviously liked the idea too. We were like two rebellious teenagers. Cutting down hedges in Blackbridge was frowned upon for some reason, but I no longer cared.

'Fuck it, let's do it. Let's start a revolution.' We both laughed as I held up the chainsaw.

41
REBECCA

31ˢᵗ March 2018

Max Watson didn't hang about. I got the impression he was a no-nonsense kind of man and that was fine with us. 'Is it ok if I have a look around,' he asked, moments after walking through the door. Ray and I sat together in the lounge, waiting on his return. I didn't ask if he wanted me to go with him because he gave me the impression he didn't need me to. He was in Evan's room for a while and my eyes were fixed on the ceiling- I could tell by the creaks in the floorboards, exactly where he was at each moment until he left the room.

'Raith Rovers supporter?' he smiled as he joined us.

'Sure is,' Ray answered proudly.

'The boy's got taste,' he said.

I felt it unnecessary to mention that Evan had no real interest in football, despite Ray's persistent encouragement. He's always made an effort for Ray's sake and happy to accept the latest strips when they came out but that was as far as his interest went.

'Now if you don't mind, what I would like to do is speak to you both individually. It's nothing to worry about, it's just the way I like to do things.'

Ray's glare turned into a *fair enough* shrug. But I knew what this was all about. I had gone over the moment several times when he asked me if I had ever been asked to do anything illegal. He knew I was lying. He's a detective for goodness sake, an expert in body language.

'Ladies first?' he said.

'Would you mind if we went for a walk?' I asked, 'I could do with some fresh air.' I wasn't lying, a rush of nausea washed over me and the air in the room had suddenly gone muggy. Ray's paranoid eyes burned a hole in me. 'I'm sure we won't be long, will we?' I looked from Max to Ray and shook my head dismissively.

'No, I'll try to make it quick,' Max replied.

The chill in the air as I stepped outside, quickly got rid of the sick feeling that I was sure was going to floor me. We headed off down the street and I caught Mrs McCutcheon next door peering from behind the blinds. She had been the only one in the street to remove her conifers and there was no questioning why. Our casual pace should've been enough for her to realise that there was nothing exciting going on. We were simply out for a chat, heading nowhere in particular, or at least that's how I hoped it looked.

'Rebecca, if this is going to work, you need to be completely honest with me,' he said. He paused for a second to look at me. I nodded in agreement. 'When I asked you about having any dealings with criminals, you said no. Now I'm not sure if that's because Ray doesn't know or you thought you might get into trouble.' He looked me in the eye and waited for a reaction.

'I don't know what you're talking about,' I replied.

'I think you do. Come on Rebecca, I'm no fool. What is it that you didn't want to say in front of Ray?'

I said nothing. I couldn't bring myself to admit to something that I could potentially be arrested for. Did Max have a duty to go straight to the police? It wasn't something I had looked into. I knew I could get struck off but whether or not it was illegal, I had no idea. My guess was that it was.

'Listen, I'm here to find Evan, ok, I'm not here to get you in trouble. I give you my word,' he said as if reading my thoughts.

I was certain that what I had done, could be nothing to do with Evan going missing, so it seemed ridiculous to bring it up and risk the aftermath.

'Rebecca, what if I promise you that I won't tell a soul if it turns out to be unrelated. I have a feeling that's why you're holding back. I'm here to find Evan, that's all.' He looked me in the eye and gave me a reassuring half-smile.

'What exactly do you need to know?' I asked.

'Whatever it is you don't want me to know,' he replied.

'I need to sit down,' I told him, so we made our way towards the park.

The park is surrounded by a railing with one of the benches on the outside, overlooking a valley of trees. We both sat down and I fixed my eyes on the tree tops.

'I met a man a good few years ago,' I told him. 'He was running a car dealership. I know I should have sent a suspicious activity report to the NCA, but I didn't. He let it slip about his other income but I turned a blind eye. I continued to do his tax returns regardless. He came to me about three years ago desperate for a large sum of money to be moved out of his account. He offered me money and I stupidly agreed to help him.' I stopped to take a deep breath, Max was watching me intently.

'How did you help him?' he asked.

'I have an offshore account that I opened years ago. It was sitting empty so that's where I wired the money to. It was then transferred into another account that he said he had access to. I suggested that he simply transfer between the two accounts himself but he said he couldn't. I even trusted that he would leave my payment in the account, that's how stupid the whole thing was.'

'What was his name?' Max asked.

I paused. 'Fisher. Gregory Fisher.'

Max then looked like he was searching the treetops for an answer.

'You must have wondered at some point if there is a connection between Jase Frank and Evan's disappearance. Assuming there is one of course,' he said.

'Yes.'

'Well, Gregory Fisher was Ronnie Frank's business partner and I'm presuming that was drug money. Possibly blood money too. You see the thing is, Gregory went missing after Ronnie's funeral and nobody has seen him since.'

'Greggs? Gregory Fisher is Greggs?'

'Yes. Has Caroline mentioned him?'

'She said she was going to speak to him. I guess she didn't know he was missing. But, I don't understand - What does this have to do with Evan?'

'Off the top of my head…it might be a case of using Evan to get to you and that money?' he suggested.

The sudden realisation that this could somehow be my fault turned my stomach; a shame like I had never felt before. 'But I don't know where it is,' I was pleading as I got to my feet.

'Do you still have access to that account?'

'Yes, but it's empty. It was transferred out the same day.'

'But you should have the account details for the one the money was transferred into,' he said.

'I don't know. What good would that do?'

'It would possibly lead us to Gregory Fisher for starters,' he said. 'Or if someone is after that money then it might be helpful to know where it went.'

'This is ridiculous. What you are saying is that Evan could be alive and all we need to do is hand over money. This isn't America, for fuck sake. It's not a movie. Nobody does that.'

'I agree, but I'm going to have to follow this up,' he said. 'You understand that, don't you?'

'So what now?' I asked.

'We go back,' he said. 'You've done the right thing by telling me the truth.'

'I don't believe this. So what, I need to go home and tell Ray that our son might be missing because I'm a criminal and could end up in prison?'

'I promise you, it won't come to that. It's a lead that I need to follow up, that's all.'

'I can't tell him,' I said.

'Do you want me look into it first? I'm not comfortable keeping secrets, Rebecca, let's make that clear. But, I can see how distraught you are and I don't want to make things worse for you than they already are.'

'I'd appreciate that,' I replied.

'The details of the account that the money was transferred into would help, though. If you have a way of tracing them, then it could speed things up a bit.'

'I'll have a look,' I said, but I already felt defeated - especially knowing that what I was looking for was an old piece of paper containing my hand scribbled note of either Gregory's bank account number or my login details for my overseas account; the chances were next to none.

'It could be something or nothing,' he said, 'but it's definitely worth checking out. You've hired me to find

Evan and that's exactly what I plan to do. I aim to follow every possible lead until my job is done. And, the benefit of being a private investigator is that it gives you a lot more freedom to investigate than the police.

'I need a minute,' I said.

He walked away and waited at the railing. I thought back to the first time I met Gregory Fisher. It must have been 2009 or 2010 because it was around the same time that I was offered the job in London.

He was mannerable and what my mum would call pleasantly plump. Like a million other clients in their first year of trade, he didn't have a clue where to start on his tax return. I have no excuse for the way I handled the meeting and I'll admit there was a little harmless flirting going on. He wasn't attractive by all means but he was confident and cocky in a way that was both charming and harmless.

Having recently purchased one of the local pubs as well as starting up his own taxi firm, I saw straight through his attempts at overstating the incomes of both. He knew I saw through it but managed to charm his way into getting me to go along with it, to turn a blind eye, if you like. When I left that firm to go self-employed, he was one of the many clients that came with me.

He was happy to meet up every quarter to ensure his accounts were running smoothly. We didn't ever discuss anything other than his finances so I couldn't say we really got to know each other better, but he obviously trusted me. Enough so, that I was the person he came to when he was in some kind of trouble.

My office in the county buildings was where we met the last time I saw him. I knew right away that something was up, stress was radiating from him. It scared me a little. Not for me, I never felt threatened by him, but I was afraid for him.

What he needed was pretty straightforward. All he had to do was to go down to the bank and transfer his money into a different account.

'Look, I can't explain,' he said. 'But you have to trust me on this. I'll make it worth your while. Fifty grand?'

Fifty grand is more than a year's wages for me. After considering what would be involved, the risk was small so it was a no brainer. Too many questions would be asked if I used my business or current account but overseas accounts aren't regulated as thoroughly.

That evening, I used my personal laptop to transfer the funds from his account to my offshore one then back to the one he wanted it in. No questions were asked and I never heard from him again. Every now and again, I wondered what happened to Gregory and why the urgency for this to happen. I never for the life of me thought it would come back to haunt me like this. I prayed that this was not the lead that Max was looking for.

'McCabe's here,' I panicked as we turned into the drive and I saw his car.

Max stopped and gently held me by the elbows. 'Rebecca, as far as anyone else is concerned, you've done nothing wrong. Please don't worry about this, it could be nothing. Relax.' His calming tone was reassuring so I took a deep breath and prepared to act normal.

Emma and McCabe were sitting with Ray. Emma's face softened when she saw Max- I'm sure she would've given him a hug if we hadn't been there. McCabe rose to shake his hand.

'It's a pleasure to meet you,' Max said. 'I was hoping to have a quick chat with you at some point.'

'Of course,' McCabe replied.

'What's going on?' I asked, noticing that Ray and Emma's eyes were cast on me as if waiting on the chance to speak.

'Our officers are in the process of tracking down Billy McIvor's twin brother, Eddie. We believe that he could be the other person that's involved in Evan's abduction.' Emma informed me.

'That would explain a few things,' Max commented. 'Do you have CCTV for McIvor's prison visit?'

'Yes, we do,' McCabe answered dismissively, making it clear that he felt that Max had spoken out of turn and that he wouldn't be elaborating. Max gave a respectful nod. All that was missing were his hands up in surrender. *Awkward* was the word that sprung to mind. I just wanted out of there,

there was so many things running around in my head and I needed to try and think them through.

'We can have that chat now, if you have time,' McCabe announced, giving me the opportunity I needed to escape. He had made it clear to Ray and I that he would not be sharing information with Max unless one of us was there to agree to it.

'I need to lie down,' I said to Ray. He nodded back to let me know that he would take care of McCabe's requirements. 'I'll switch the kettle on before I head up.'

Closing the living-room door behind me, I made my way to the kitchen, filled the kettle and leaned on the worktop. I hadn't self harmed for over a week and my awareness of the block of knives next to me was fighting for my attention. I thought about the blade slicing my skin and forced myself to look at the marks on my arms. *It won't help*, I told myself.

The turmoil and shame was building up inside me and I had to release it before it came out as a scream that I imagined would have the ability to shatter windows. If I were to contain this, I needed a silent release; a painful shock to my system. I reached for a glass, opened the top drawer of the freezer and half-filled it with ice-cubes.

I made my way past the closed living-room door, without an interest in what was being said, up the stairs and locked myself in the bathroom. I looked in the mirror at my withered reflection, the glass of ice resting between the taps of the sink.

It was a magazine article that came back to me, that must have been stored in the recesses of my mind because I can't say I had ever given it a second thought. I remember reading about a teenage girl who self-harmed. I don't remember the details, only that her mum was advised to

213

offer her an ice-cube whenever she felt the urge to hurt herself. The pain caused by holding an ice-cube against the skin for a length of time was enough to satisfy that relief she required, but it didn't cause any lasting damage.

Removing an ice-cube from the glass, I searched my skin for the most sensitive looking area. Deciding on the soft skin on my inner arm, above my wrist, I held it in place. The initial sensation was shock from the cold, but was soon replaced with that piercing pain that I wanted to feel. I held my breath as the dull burning sensation intensified to the point that I could feel nothing else; no guilt, no shame; no heartbreak; nothing. I continued to hold it until I couldn't take anymore.

For the minutes that followed, I felt satisfied. Laying on my bed, I listened to the voices below but couldn't make out what was being said, until the door opened.

'Right, we'll leave you to it. It was nice meeting you Mr Watson.'

'And you,' replied Max – I'm sure the 'Mr' remark I'm sure didn't go unnoticed.

After they left, Max asked for another coffee and suggested that they now have that chat. It was Ray's turn for a confession. Not that he would have much to say. Not like I had.

I knew I had to get to my office to see if I could trace that account number but what I really needed to do was talk to someone. Now that Emma and McCabe were away, I had the perfect opportunity to go downstairs and confess to Ray – that would be the right thing to do. I thought about what I could say – *Do you know how those St.Margaret's boys have abducted our son? Well, one of them used to be my client and I'm sorry, but it was my stupidity and greed that brought them into our lives.* I couldn't do it. I wouldn't have used those words but that was the truth of it - it was my fault our son was taken from us. If I couldn't speak to Ray, then it would have to be someone else. I couldn't bear the disappointment from my Mum. There was only one more person I could think of as I reached for my phone.

43
EVAN

The man wearing the black mask over his face, handed me his mobile phone. As soon as I heard the words, 'Hello, Evan,' I recognised the voice on the other end. It was him.

'Tell me, Evan, what do you know about the job that your Mum does? Rebecca, isn't it?' The sound of her name made me want to cry but I knew I couldn't. I had to be brave and do what I was told.

'Yes. She's an accountant, she does everything that accountants do,' I replied, trying to sound confident. *Never show weakness,* is something my Dad has always tried to teach me, even though that I'm not like him, I'm not strong. My Mum says I've got her nature, and I think she's right because all the times I try to act tough in front of my friends, I know deep down I'm not.

'Are you trying to be smart, Evan? Because nobody likes a smart arse.'

'No, I'm not, I'm sorry. I just meant she does accounts, tax returns, things like that.'

'Ok. Good. Does she work mostly from home or from her office?'

'She does both, but mostly her office.'

'Ok, so here's the problem. If, say for example, that I wanted to look over some of your Mum's paperwork, where might I find that?'

'I don't know, on her laptop probably. I'm sure she has everything saved on it.'

'And what kind of laptop does she have?'

'It's a Lenova Yoga Book.'

'Yoga?' he laughed and I knew this meant he had no idea how cool they actually are.

'It's more like a tablet that a laptop. The smart keyboard allows you to put paper down and when you write on it, it then saves it in digital form. I've seen her using it a few times when she's been working at home,' I told him. I didn't think he needed to know that she doesn't really have a clue how to use it properly. She's not really into computers like me and Dad but we thought she might like it because it was kind of girly.

'How long has she had it?'

'We gave her it for her birthday last year.'

He sighed and sounded a bit annoyed. I didn't want to annoy him and I didn't mean to. 'So, before that, what did she have?'

'A Macbook Air.'

'And where's that now?'

'Me and my Dad dismantled it,' I said reluctantly, knowing this probably wasn't what he wanted to hear. I couldn't help it. The more I tried to help the more he hated me for it.

'Right, let's try something else,' he sighed again. 'Does your Mum have any real paperwork anywhere? As in sheets of paper with information on them?'

'She has old filing cabinets full of paperwork in the lock-up. There's two or three of them, I think.'

'Finally. And where is the lock-up?' he asked. By this point the phone started shaking in my hand because I don't pay attention to street names and stuff.

'It's the ones that are shaped like a circle a few streets away from our house, we live in Duddingston Grove,' I said. I was so relieved when he accepted it, like he knew what I was talking about.

217

'Pass the phone back,' he replied, so I did. The man with the mask obviously heard him because he held out his hand before I even took it away from my ear. And because the room was so silent, I could still hear his voice.

'He sounds like a pain in the arse. Don't worry, another couple of days and you can get rid of him. I'm sure that won't be a problem for you. Will it?'

'No,' replied Mask man.

I sat back down on the mattress that I now had and couldn't be brave any longer. I couldn't understand what this had to do with my Mum. After thinking about it a lot, I thought I had been kidnapped because I had been caught out for the time I sent Ransomware to my friend's Dad. I presumed he had just deleted it and it had been forgotten about.

'What does he want?' I asked. My voice came out all squeaky. 'I should have asked him. Maybe I know how to help. Maybe you don't need to kill me.'

'I doubt it,' he replied. From the light that was shining from the lamp sitting in the corner, I could see that his eyes were all red and bloodshot. I don't know why but I had a feeling he didn't want to kill me.

'And, I'm afraid, I need to do what I'm told,' he said.

44
CAROLINE

The urgency in Rebecca's voice gave me the impression she had something important to tell me. The last time I spoke to her was the night she was on her way back from visiting Patterson in prison, and I was a little tipsy. The only thing that came from my visit with Angela was learning that Billy McIvor is likely to have a twin brother. I had decided I would tell her on the off chance that D.I. McCabe hadn't figured it out yet. I considered that I probably should have phoned her before now.

I parked at Ruby Bay car park next to the toilet block as instructed, purposely arriving early to spend time alone. Why she chose Elie Beach, I had no idea. But it just happened to be my favourite place in the whole world.

It's not the same having nobody to share it with and I knew that's why I had avoided the place for so long. Jase and I were sure we would buy one of those fancy houses overlooking the bay. We would have needed a lottery win, of course. The house prices in Elie are extortionate. Most are second homes and holiday lets; rich folk dodging council tax. Not that I blame them, it's certainly the perfect place to be when you want to escape the rest of the world. I vowed to come back another day, when Rebecca's car pulled up in the space next to mine.

'Thanks for coming,' she said.

'That's ok, it's good to see you. Why did you choose here?' I asked.

'It's sort of a special place for me, I used to come here with my mum when I was young and then Evan when he was young,' she said. 'And, everyone minds their own business.'

'I used to come here with Jase too,' I told her. 'We always said we would live here one day.' She gave an understanding smile and took my hand. The gesture was an odd one but she looked like she didn't care. Desperation was visible on her face.

Walking together, I took her lead down the track towards the lighthouse. 'Have they found the other person that's involved yet?' I asked her, taking a guess at what was wrong. Her quick steps were reflecting her nerves and I could tell there was going to be some sort of outpour on its way – she was definitely holding something inside that she had to let go of.

'Not yet, they are looking for Billy McIvor's twin, though' she answered.

'Are they? That's good,' I thought of Tony. I knew that wasn't why she brought me here so decided to avoid starting a new conversation about how I already figured out he had a twin. 'What's on your mind, Rebecca?' I asked.

She stopped dead and took me by the forearms. 'Can I trust you not to say anything to anyone?'

'Of course,' I replied. This was when I realised just how desperate she really was, because I knew deep down that she didn't trust me.

'I need someone to speak to that won't judge me,' she said.

'Well I'm hardly one to judge,' I replied.

She let out a sigh and said, 'There is a chance this is my fault. It could all be my fault.' We reached a bench, where she took a seat and smoothed the skin firmly on her face with her hands.

'Has something happened?' I asked.

'Evan could be anywhere, dead or alive because of one stupid mistake I made,' she announced.

'What makes you think that? I'm sure that can't be right.'

'I haven't even told you yet that we've hired Max Watson. I'm sorry, I know you don't like him, but he was the best we could find,' she said.

I bit my tongue, knowing that there must be more to come. 'It's nothing to do with me. You do what you need to do,' I said, while thinking, *Why? Why would you even consider him?*

'I got involved with Gregory Fisher...' She looked me in the eye as if seeking recognition.

It took me a minute. 'Greggs? You had an affair with Greggs?' I gasped.

'No, nothing like that, I did his accounts for him,' she replied quickly, 'It never occurred to me that Greggs was Gregory Fisher.' I was somewhat relieved but still shocked.

'I take it this was before he went missing?' I asked.

'I presume so,' she said.

'So what does this have to do with Evan?' I asked, struggling to make the connection.

'I wired a lot of money to an offshore account for him and Max thinks it could be something to do with that money,' she said. 'Patterson and the McIvor twins must think I have it, I don't know.'

'Rebecca, I don't know what to say. I don't know what this means,' I admitted.

'Neither do I,' she said. I presumed the long silence that followed was due to us both searching our heads for some logic.

'So you think they could be using Evan to get to you?' I asked.

'That's what Max said,' she answered. 'It doesn't make much sense. I don't know what to do. Oh Caroline, what if this is all my fault?'

'You can't think like that. You're talking like this is fact when it might be nothing to do with Evan,' I said, still struggling with the idea. Because, if this was the case then it would make sense that they had taken my Jase for the very same reason. After Ronnie's suicide, surely they would suspect that I had access to that money. They obviously knew that it was Greggs' money too, given that they'd gone after Rebecca. But, it didn't make sense that they would go after her when Greggs had clearly taken the money and ran.

The police had convinced me that Jase's abduction was random; it could have been any one of those boys that were taken that night. But it wasn't. Now I knew that my son was killed because of his own father's drug money. I felt sick.

'I don't know how much more I can take. I just want it to be over. I just want him back,' she said and I felt her pain – I was thinking the exact same thing. Her cry had turned into more of a wail and all I could do was hold her.

As the sea air nipped at my face, I suggested that we head back to the car park. She struggled to her feet and I could tell from the way she was moving that her energy had gone. She was defeated. Assisting her all the way, I then guided her to my passenger seat.

'I'll put the heaters on, you can't drive like this, give yourself time,' I said and she accepted this.

'I can't do this anymore, Caroline,' she said.

'Yes you can,' I told her. 'I'm here, you've got Ray, your mum, Emma, Tony and lots more, I'm sure. You're not alone.'

'I need to go to my lock-up to see if I can get some information for Max, will you come with me?' she asked.

'Of course, anything you need.' I replied, while realising that there was nothing much I wouldn't have done for her right then.

'I don't want Ray to know,' she said.

'Do you want to go now?' I asked.

'It's not that simple. I don't want Ray questioning why I'm there. I'm sick of lying and hiding stuff from him,' she said. She was being irrational but it was to be understood.

'He won't know,' I told her.

'He will. I have that phone tracker thing,' she informed me.

'I don't think he'll be checking up on you,' I said for further reassurance.

'He will be. I told him to. I went behind his back with Tony and again when I went to see Patterson. I promised I wouldn't do it again. God, this is even worse.'

I realised that she was telling the truth and not being irrational after all. I've heard of these phone tracker things but I didn't think people actually used them. 'I'm sorry, Rebecca, but you need to either tell him the truth or lie. I don't think there's a middle option here. It sounds to me like you would rather he didn't find out yet so let's just make up an excuse and go now. Phone him, tell him we're going to the lock-up to find something else.' I watched her as she considered this.

'I'll say I'm going to look for the USB stick with all Evan's photos on it. It's not a lie. I do need to find it,' she said.

'Ok. When you're feeling up to driving, I'll follow you there.'

I phoned Ray and he sounded pleased that I was keeping him in the loop. He didn't mind that I was looking for the USB stick but said that it wouldn't be a problem to get all the photos from some cloud on my laptop when I got it back. This got me thinking - our electrical devices were seized the day Evan went missing and if they had been thoroughly searched then shouldn't they have picked up on my dealings with Gregory Fisher? But then surely I would have been questioned about it? I knew I couldn't think about that now so I prepared myself for the task of searching through my archived paperwork that filled three filing cabinets. I was just glad Caroline was going to be there to help.

The lockup is a few streets away from the house. When we applied to the council, it was the closest one available. There are ten in total and merge together to form the best part of a circle. I've always refused to go there alone as the access is away from the housing estate, facing a dense line of trees. We rented it initially to keep Ray's old Mark 3 Escort in, then after he sold it, it became a place for us to hoard junk.

I parked the car on the main street around from the lock ups and Caroline pulled up beside me.

'Do you think the police could know about the money and not said anything?' I asked as soon as she got out.

'I doubt it. Greggs is a missing person though, so it's surprising that they've managed to miss it. They obviously haven't had a thorough check through your accounts,' she replied confirming my suspicions.

'It's this one here,' I said, pointing to number six; the outline of the rust marks revealing the different colours it has been painted over the years.

When I realised it was unlocked, I cursed Ray for not double checking - neither of us had mastered the knack for the old thing. I quickly scanned over the bags and furniture for the touch light we use for camping.

'Please tell me you keep your paperwork together,' Caroline said seriously. I managed a smile and told her it was all in the filing cabinets. I had three large filing cabinets because unlike any normal person, instead of sorting through them, when one was full, I simply bought another. When I finally got my head around trusting that electronic copies were enough, I stored them in the lock up with the intention of sorting through them one day.

'It's not in any alphabetical or chronological order though,' I admitted. It wasn't until I reached the back of the lock up that I noticed that they were not sitting in their usual place. I looked around in case I had walked past them, but sure enough, they were missing - all three of them.

Before Caroline had the time to ask what was wrong, I phoned Ray. 'Have you moved my filing cabinets?' I asked.

'No,' he replied. 'Why would I?'

I realised in my panic, the implications of my question. 'No wait, sorry, sorry my heads all over the place. It was me that moved them, there they are. Ignore me.'

'Is everything ok? Is Caroline with you?' he asked.

'Yes, everything's fine. I should be home soon. Well it depends on how long it takes me to find this stick,' I lied, once more.

'Ok, good luck, but don't stress over it. See you soon,' he said before hanging up.

225

'Somebody's been here,' I told Caroline. 'They're gone.'

'Are you sure?

'Yes, they were right there.'

'Is there anything else missing?'

I quickly glanced around but there wasn't anything obvious. Our old 42" plasma TV still sat firmly on its dusty glass table. 'No. My guess is that whoever took them, knew exactly what they were looking for. There are things in here that are more valuable than those cabinets – not that they're worth anything.'

'Unless they contain information that'll lead to that drug money. Rebecca, this is all getting a bit too much, don't you think? If I were you I'd phone Emma and McCabe and tell them everything. They need to know.'

I knew she was right. I sat down on edge of Evan's old gaming chair and rested my head in my hands. 'Oh shit, Caroline, what's going on? I'm going to have to tell them, and Ray.'

'I don't know. Max's theory sounds plausible though. I can come with you if you want,' she offered.

'Thanks, but I think I need to do this alone,' I replied. She gave me a hug and with it, I felt her concern.

46
REBECCA

I was going to hold my hands up and take what was coming, I had no choice. There were no other cars in the driveway when I got home so I knew I would have the chance to try and explain myself to Ray, before I phoned Emma.

'Can we talk?' I said to Ray as he stood peeling potatoes over the kitchen sink.

'Yes,' he replied with his eyebrows in that puzzled shape. *Can we talk?* He would have known from past experience that it has a silent *but you're not going to like it* on the end. He sliced the last potato in his hand and threw it in the pot. While he was drying his hands on the tea towel, I decided there was no easy or right way to say it, so forced myself to spit it out.

'I did something really stupid a couple of years back,' I began, but because my anxiety had opened the floodgates, the words continued to come out with short bursts of breath. 'I shouldn't have done it. I didn't think it would hurt anyone. I should have told someone before now but I didn't think-'

'Becky, stop rambling and tell me, it's ok,' he said, as he pulled out a seat for me to sit on.

'I'm sorry, I'm so sorry-'

'Becky, breathe. Whatever it is, we'll deal with it,' he said. He was being so nice to me and he had no idea what I had done. I took deep breaths until I felt able to speak again.

'I moved money for a drug dealer. I didn't know he was a drug dealer at the time. Max thinks it could be why Evan was taken, and now my files have been stolen from the lock up.'

'What?'

'The St. Margaret's boys, men, they're after that drug money and they must think I know where it is.'

'Fuuuuck. Fuuuuuuuck,' he yelled as he turned away from me. He reached to punch the wall but stopped himself in time. 'I don't fucking believe this, Becky.' Picking up his phone, he dialled before waiting for an answer. 'I need you to come over as soon as you can.'

'Who was that?' I asked.

'Max,' he replied. In search for somewhere to think, he headed to the hall and started pacing. He hadn't asked me to elaborate and the blame had yet to come so I stayed where I was.

Thirty five minutes later, Max arrived. After following Ray into the kitchen, he must have sensed the tension as he looked at each of us to see who was going to enlighten him on what was going on.

'I've told him,' I said. 'And my files have been stolen from the lock up.'

'It's better that he knows, Rebecca,' Max replied. 'Have you reported them missing?'

'Not yet.'

'Tell me what this has to do with Evan,' Ray demanded, his tone reflecting his anger towards me.

'It's not definite but a possible motive. If Patterson and the McIvor twins believe that Rebecca has information or access to that money, then they might be using Evan as a decoy,' Max told him.

'So how do they intend to get information from Becky? If all this shit is true then why didn't they take her instead?' he asked and I could tell that he wished they had.

'I'm going to be completely honest and I know it's not what you want to hear, but, Tony Delimonte's involvement with you, is concerning me. How well do you know him?' Max asked but directed his look more towards me.

'I've only met him a couple of times,' I told him. 'He gave me a reading where he spoke to my dad, that's how he found out about the ruin. He gave my mum one too.'

'I don't trust him,' Ray added.

'Right, well don't, because I have a feeling he's involved,' Max replied. 'Ask yourself, Rebecca, think about the things he said that were apparently from your dad. What did he say that convinced you he was genuine?'

'He knew about the job I turned down in London, about the ring he gave to Evan and that Harry wasn't happy about it. He knew that he called my mum Meg.'

'Who else knows this stuff?'

'Nobody, just our family. Mum, dad, Harry, that's about it,' I said.

'Harry is your brother?' he asked.

'Yes.'

'Well there's my first suspicion.'

'That's ridiculous. So you think Harry could have told Tony all this stuff?' I asked, realising how absurd the idea actually was.

'I wouldn't rule it out. I wouldn't underestimate Tony if I were you. Does anyone else know about the money, that account?' he asked, and I wanted to say no.

'I told Caroline,' I said.

'Caroline Frank?'

'Yes.'

'You trust her and she trusts Tony,' he said.

'I only told her a couple of hours ago so that makes no sense whatsoever. This is outrageous. And there's no way that Tony has managed to get all that information from

Harry. I can't even listen to this.' I stormed out and headed upstairs.

My first thoughts were that Max clearly still had it in for Tony. I thought back to the night I first met him at his mum's house. The ring, he couldn't have known about the ring. Caroline said that Tony hadn't asked her to ask me to bring something. Caroline didn't even know I had it with me until five minutes before Tony did. I tried to recall his exact words. He said I was my dad's little Carol Vorderman - that's no coincidence. Then I thought about what Max said about Harry. There was no way Tony would have gone to Dumfries and spoke to Harry. Nobody could plan or preconceive a meeting like that. How was he even to know that he would give me a reading at some point? People can't make things happen like that. He would surely need to be psychic to predict something like that. He was psychic, he had to be.

As I tried to convince myself that he was, I found myself dialling Harry's number. He was drunk, as usual.

'Hey, sis,' he said cheerfully, then changed his tone as he presumably remembered our last encounter at Mum's house.

'Listen, Sis, I'm really sorry about asking for that money.'

'It's ok, forget it.' I had no time for his bullshit. 'I just want to ask you something.'

'What's up?'

'I need you to try and remember,' and I said this knowing that he probably couldn't remember half of the stuff he gets up to. 'Do you remember speaking to anyone about me and dad? About how he used to call me Carol Vorderman, or Mum, Meg?'

'No, why would I mention that?' he said.

'I don't know, what about Dad's ring? About him giving it to Evan,' I said.

'No, why are you asking this?'

'Because if you did, I need to know. There is a man who knows all this stuff and it's only us that knows, Harry. He could know where Evan is so think, please.' I waited while his brain searched through his hazy memories.

'Oh wait, there was this guy in the Crown. Nice bloke. We spoke for a while, maybe I mentioned it to him. I was wasted, he kept buying the rounds,' he informed me.

'What did he look like?' I asked.

'Tall, ginger, and come to think of it, he had a Fife accent. He said he was originally from Glenrothes but recently moved here.'

'That's him. For fuck sake, Harry, I suggest you better sort yourself out, in case you need to give a statement to the police.' I hung up and felt like such a fool.

Ray and Max were sitting at the table; the sound of me running down the stairs had caught their attention. 'You were right. Tony has been to see Harry,' I said.

***

D.I. McCabe and Emma didn't take long to arrive after I told them my filing cabinets had been stolen from the lock up and that I had new information for them. When it came to telling them, I stumbled on every word. Max was great and ended up explaining everything. *You stupid woman,* could be clearly read from both of their expressions. This I could bear, at least they didn't arrest me. I resisted the temptation to ask why not. They were more interested to hear that Tony spoke to Harry in Dumfries.

There didn't seem to be the same tension between Max and McCabe that had been there previously. Maybe they had reached a new level of respect for one another due to their shared interest in Tony - the subtle male bonding nonsense was enough for me to head upstairs. Only a second or two passed before Emma appeared. 'Can I come in?' she asked and instead of telling her I needed five minutes peace, I told her she could.

Curled up on the bed, I watched her as she padded about in front of the window. I waited on what she had to say. She didn't appear angry, but the silence reminded me of when I was young and my dad wouldn't say a word, as if he was quietened by disappointment.

'You should have told us, Rebecca,' she said finally.

'You should have known. Why keep my laptop until now if there is clearly no-one examining it?' I replied. 'I know it's no excuse, but if they were doing their job right, we would have known two weeks ago that it was linked to Evan's abduction.'

'I can't comment on that, but believe me the thought has crossed my mind too,' she said as she sat on the bed beside me. There was a tension between us that I had never felt before, some kind of mutual frustration, I presume.

'It just seems to be one thing after another. Why weren't we told about Tony's history of fraud?'

'Tony doesn't have a record, Rebecca. We had no reason to mention it.'

'But Max said he had a history, I presumed that's what he meant,' I told her.

'No. Tony's been up in court on a couple of occasions, but was never found guilty. I presume that's what he must have been referring to.'

'So, it's just more assumptions,' I said, shaking my head. 'I don't even know what to believe anymore.'

'D.I. McCabe has requested a warrant to check Tony's property, we'll be sending someone to speak to your brother and we have officers and forensics at the lock-up now. If Tony is involved then I'm sure we'll know soon enough.'

'Well excuse me for not holding my breath,' I replied. 'You already detained him and then let him go, remember? I should never have listened to you in the first place, about Caroline and Tony. I'm actually glad I met Caroline, but if Tony is involved, don't think I won't question why you pushed it.' I said this unsure of what I was accusing her of, but it was one of many things that had crossed my mind.

'That's not fair, Rebecca, you're just upset,' she said.

'Do you know what's not fair? Our son is missing and we have to rely on a bunch of people that are beyond incompetent, to find him.'

'We're doing our best, Rebecca.'

'Well it's not good enough is it?' I said. 'Please just go.'

I knew it wasn't Emma's fault but I was past caring enough to apologise. Apparently it was her job to prepare us for the worst, *statistics say this, statistics say that.* I wondered what the statistics would have to say about the number of lives that are lost due to police negligence. Maybe I was being out of order, but felt I had every right to be.

47
CAROLINE

I could barely make Tony out, sitting amongst the green carpet of Asda bags on my doorstep. 'What the hell are you up to?' I asked, the gratitude for the gesture spread over my face from ear to ear. 'Has Christmas come early?'

'If you're referring to me as Santa Claus, I'll take it back,' he said.

'What are you like? Come on you must be frozen.' I unlocked the front door and we both loaded our arms with as much as we could manage. 'Tony, this is far too much. You've already given me a loan. There was no need for all this.'

'Well I'm glad the money went in ok, but we were meant to go shopping on the way back from Anstruther, remember, but got distracted by your DIY ideas, and I knew you still wouldn't have been yet. Am I right?' he said.

'Yes, I just hadn't gotten around to it yet. I've just been to see Rebecca,' I told him.

'How is she?' he asked.

'Not good. They've hired Max Watson,' I announced and looked at him to see his reaction. He shook his head in what looked like disbelief. 'There is stuff going on but I promised I wouldn't say anything. We just went to her lock up and it's been broken into.'

'What's Max saying?' he asked as he started to put tins away in the cupboard.

'It could be something to do with money and Rebecca's past. Sorry I shouldn't really be saying anything, I promised. I know I always tell you things but I don't like breaking promises. You get that, right?'

'Of course,' he said. 'Say no more.' I could tell by his tone that he was either angry or upset about Max being back on the scene.

'I just wish there was something we could do. You were right about Billy being a twin, by the way. They're looking for him now.'

He was deep in thought, I could tell. I didn't see it coming but he turned and took me in his arms. He was holding me like he would hold a piece of jewellery he was trying to read. It was like he was in one of his meditations, calm and meaningful. I didn't resist him, but wondered what was going on in his head.

'I need to go, there's something I really need to do,' he said. He kissed my forehead before rushing out the door.

'But you've just got here,' I shouted after him.

I knew it must have been unsettling for him, knowing Max was now involved, but that reaction took me by surprise.

***

An hour later, I watched the police car drive off and dialled Tony's number. It went straight to voicemail.

'We're looking for Tony Delimonte. Is he here?' was what the smaller of the two officers had asked.

'No, why?' was my reply, and despite my persistence, they refused to comment.

'Come on, Tony,' I said as it reached voicemail once again. I had no idea what the hell was going on and I was not about to let it lie.

I grabbed my coat and car keys in the hope that he was at his mum's. Failing that, I was prepared to head up to his flat in Perth. Why couldn't they just leave him alone? It was

235

Max Watson, it had to be, I was sure of it. Some people are just born arseholes. I wondered how Rebecca and Ray had even come into contact with him. Did they look for him or did he approach them in his quest to ruin Tony? Emma could have orchestrated it of course with her gentle manipulation that she thinks goes unnoticed. However it happened, I was sure that he would now be pleased with himself.

As soon as I turned into Rowan Court I could see that Tony's car wasn't at his mum's. I checked the petrol gauge to ensure I had enough to get me to Perth and back, before turning around. I had only ever been to Tony's flat twice. It's only half an hour's drive but it was normally enough to put me off. It always feels longer for some reason, maybe because there's not much to look at on the way, a dull combination of country roads and dual carriage ways. It made sense for him to visit me while he was at his mum's. I left him a voicemail to let him know I was on my way.

When I arrived there was a police car and van parked outside, with three officers loitering outside the front door. 'What's going on?' I asked. 'Is Tony here?'

'Who's asking?'

'Me, I'm asking?' I replied.

'And who are you?'

'Caroline Frank, a friend,' I told him.

'No he's not here. We're waiting on a warrant. You don't have a spare key do you? Save the damage.' He was obviously the cocky one, the other two stood beside him trying to keep a straight face.

'You can't knock his door in, what has he supposed to have done?' I asked.

'We can't reveal that information but I would suggest you get back in your car. There's not much to see.' I didn't know if it was the way I was feeling but his tone made me want to punch him right in the face. I did as I was told, got back to the car and tried Tony's number again.

Unsure of what to do next, I sat tight in the hope he'd turn up soon and put an end to this misunderstanding, whatever it was. By the time it took me to have a cigarette and give dirty looks to the neighbours, I noticed the officers surrounding Tony's shed, taking turns to look through the window.

'This is harassment,' I shouted as I made my way up the path.

'Please Miss, leave us to do our job,' one of them said as if I was nothing more than a nuisance. The other was standing guard of the shed, while the cocky one spoke into his radio.

'Yes, we can certainly see something similar in the shed,' I heard him say.

'What's in the shed?' I asked.

'Nothing, please will you leave us to it.'

I ignored his plea for peace, walked around the one on guard knowing he couldn't stop me, and looked in the window. Although the window was partly covered by an old rag curtain, it was easy to make out the back shelves were lined with tins of paint, there was a lawnmower and just inside the door sat three tall grey filing cabinets.

'This is a set up,' I told them. I ran back to the car and called Rebecca. She didn't answer the first time but she did the second. 'Rebecca, what's going on?' I asked.

'The police are after Tony,' she confirmed.

'I know, but why?'

'Do you want to come over and I'll try to explain,' she said. 'Tony's not who you think he is, Caroline.'

237

'Bullshit, Rebecca. He's been set up. Tony's no criminal, and even if he was, he wouldn't be stupid enough to leave your filing cabinets in his shed for the world to see, would he?'

'They're in his shed?' she said then repeated this to whoever was in the room with her. I hung up in disappointment and got back in the car.

I had no idea what to do now so I left Tony another voicemail, begging him to get in touch. This had to be beyond anything he had had to face in the past and for all I knew, he had no idea what he could be walking straight into. This wasn't even harassment, it was incrimination.

48
REBECCA

1st April 2018

There had been a lull in the chatter for long enough to tempt me back downstairs, that was the first of me realising that Emma and McCabe had left. Ray was still seething but I knew that whatever he was going to throw at me, I deserved. I sat down without saying a word.

'What I don't understand, is if Tony is in on this with Billy McIvor, why did he have him arrested? Too much of this doesn't make any sense,' he said to Max.

'From what I know about Tony, it doesn't surprise me. They obviously went into it together with the intention of sharing the money and Tony got greedy,' Max replied.

'So why wouldn't Billy stick Tony in, now that's he's in the shit?'

'He won't say any more than he needs to. Nobody likes a grass, especially in prison, and when Tony goes down for this, he'll pay the price. You'll have no worries there.'

'How can he access an account with just an account number,' I interrupted, realising that having Max there to help us make sense of things was exactly what we needed right then. It made a change from Emma's, *Let's not jump to conclusions* and *I'm not quite sure*, and McCabe's, *It wouldn't be fair to say right now.*

'You'd be amazed at what goes on in the real world, Rebecca. They'll know a crook in the banking world or online hackers that'll do anything if the price is right.' Max replied.

'You of all people should know that Becky, what exactly was your price?' There it was, I expected it and had no comeback. 'Anyway, what makes them think this Gregory guy hasn't blown it all? How much was it?'

'Over a million,' Max and I said together.

'Fuckin' hell,' was Ray's response.

'They maybe know something we don't,' Max said, making me wonder if Gregory was dead.

'Yeah, they've probably killed the prick,' Ray said, thinking the same thing. The very thought was disturbing, blubbering Gregory pleading for his life.

'I could still track that account if there is any way of getting a hold of that account number. Are you sure there isn't anywhere else you accessed your off-shore account from or have your password saved?'

'No, the police still have my laptop and any paperwork or statements would have been in the filing cabinets,' I told him.

'Here, log in to your e-mails on this, I'll see if I can find anything.' Ray handed me his new tablet.

I googled hotmail login and typed in my email address and password before handing it back. I had faith that if there was anything helpful to be found, Ray would be the best person for the job.

'What's the name of the off-shore bank?' he asked.

'Internaxx with two x's.'

Max and I watched Ray intently as he tapped away on his tablet. 'Get me a pen & paper.' I ran to the phone where I always keep a post-it pad and pen.

When I gave it to him, he started jotting down notes. Trying to watch over his shoulder, I noticed he was on the Internaxx login page. 'Here, that's your account number you'll need to phone this number and say you've forgotten your PIN. They'll ask you a load of security questions so let's hope you know the answers.'

I did what I was told. I stood in the hallway with the door closed between us and went through the motions of verifying all the information that was required. They agreed to send me an email with directions on how to reset my PIN.

Ray received it straight away, followed the instructions and wrote down the new PIN he had created. Within seconds, he was logged onto the account.

'Have you got it?' Max asked.

'Yes, 24th March 2016.'

'Good work, Ray,' Max appraised. Ray wrote the account number down as Max double checked it. 'Now listen, I need to get to work.' He waved the post-it note. 'Three scenarios: one, they're all as dumb as they look and Gregory Fisher and his money are long gone. Two, Tony's managed to get to the money already and then I'll be right on him. Three, he hasn't quite got there yet, and if or when he does, he'll be traced immediately.'

'What about Evan?' I asked.

'We just need to say our prayers, Rebecca. You never know.'

49
CAROLINE

2nd April 2018

It was the following morning before Tony finally called me back. I didn't know whether to scream at him or cry. I did a little of both and despite my outburst he didn't attempt to settle my nerves. He insisted that I meet him at Falkland Hill and in my desperation to see him, I made it there in fifteen minutes flat.

I wondered if he had found Evan's body. He did say that there was something he needed to do and I couldn't shake the feeling that he had been given more information from the spirit world. The day when we found Jase came back to me as clear as a picture. The image, the shock, the smell, but my mind kept altering the details. It was Evan's skull and not Jase's. He was found on the hill instead of a field. It wasn't my boy, it was Rebecca's. I had no choice but to pull myself together and be strong. If he needed my help then I was going to be there, I owed him that much.

Tony's car was one of three that was parked. The other two were empty and I presumed they belonged to dog walkers or hill climbers. Pulling up next to him, he must have known that I was there, but didn't turn to acknowledge me. His hands were fixed on the steering wheel and his gaze on the view below.

When I opened his passenger side door, he was startled a little, but he still didn't look at me. 'Tony, what's going on?' I asked, placing my hand on his arm. He glanced at me for a split second and turned away.

'I'm sorry,' he said, slow and a bit vague. I wondered if he had been drinking but there was no smell or sign of alcohol.

'Sorry for what?'

'For everything,' he said.

'Tony, you're scaring me.'

'I've written you a letter,' he informed me.

'Why?' I could feel myself getting riled up at his lack of response. 'You better tell me what's going on, Tony. I swear to God I will shake it out of you. This is not funny. Have you any idea what I've been going through and all you can say is that you've written me a fucking letter!'

'I'm sorry,' he repeated.

'Yes, so you said, but sorry for what?'

'All of it,' he replied.

'What do you mean? All of what?'

'Ronnie, Jase, Evan, us,' he said.

'What are you saying?'

'I pushed Ronnie,' he replied.

'No you didn't. You didn't even know Ronnie. He jumped, he committed suicide. Why would you say that? Tell me he committed suicide.'

'I can't.'

'Look at me,' I screamed and he didn't flinch. Slowly, he turned to look me in the eye. I recognised that glazed look in an instant. 'What have you taken?'

'I can't go to prison,' he said. 'I have to explain. Please let me explain.'

'Explain what, Tony? You're telling me you killed Ronnie. Why are you saying this?' I opened the glove box and took everything out. I knew he had taken something so I searched the car looking for something that would answer my question. Tony didn't take drugs so whatever he had

243

taken he clearly couldn't handle. I got out the car and made my way around to the driver's door. I opened it and told him to get out. 'You need fresh air,' I said. When he didn't budge I pulled at his arm until he finally got out. Holding onto the car he told me again that he needed to explain.

'Well, get on with it,' I snapped.

'He's been…black…mailing me all this time, I'm being set…up. I can't… go to prison, Caroline.'

'Tony, breathe,' I said, noticing him gasping for air. 'Who has set you up? I saw Rebecca's filing cabinets in your shed. They won't get away with it.'

'Max,' he replied. 'I think he's going to kill Evan.'

'Max Watson?'

'He's after that money. It's just a game to him.'

'What has this got to do with you?' I asked, unsure of whether to believe him or not, hoping that he was so off his face that he didn't know what he was saying. It wouldn't have been the first time I'd seen someone that wasted, talking shit.

'I'm sorry. Max made me help him, I'm not psychic,' he sobbed and gasped and I couldn't believe what I was hearing. 'It was Max that made me come to the pub that night we met. He thought you had access to that money.' Hurt, pain and anger rose through me until they reached my fists and I punched him and slapped him and screamed. 'How could you do this? Why would you do this to me? You've known this whole time and you made me believe... I trusted you Tony. I trusted you.' I fought and fought until I fell to the ground.

'I'm sorry,' he said, cowering. 'I didn't know you back then. I had no choice,' he said, his words beginning to slur. 'The letter explains everything, I need you to tell Emma the truth so Max doesn't get away with.'

'Why didn't *you* tell Emma instead of bringing me up here?' I yelled.

'I can't go to prison. Please. The letter,' he continued to gasp.

'A letter? A suicide note? What have you taken?' I shouted and continued to check under the driver's seat, and there they were, two empty bottles of Oxycodone 'Have you taken them all?'

Tony closed his eyes and leaned his head back against the car door. 'Let me die,' he said. 'Please.'

'Don't you dare put that on me,' I cried. 'I thought I owed you my life. How could you? I thought you were my friend.'

'I was, I am. I'm so sorry. The letter please.'

It was too much to bear. As I got to my feet, I reached into his car to retrieve the letter from his dashboard, gave him one last glance before jumping back into my own car. As I sped off down the single track road, I phoned for an ambulance.

I didn't get far along the main road before I had to pull over; my tears were blurring my vision and it dawned on me that nobody else knew that Max had Evan, I dialled 999 once again.

50
CAROLINE

With my head resting on my arms as they hugged the steering wheel, I waited until I heard the knock on the window before I looked up. My eyes had caught a glimpse of the blue lights reflecting in my side mirror so I was expecting it. Partly relieved, I surrendered my need for control. Unsure of what I should be doing or where I should be going, when the female officer asked me to come to the station, I didn't question why or put up a fight. I stuffed the letter into my pocket and gladly let her guide me to the back seat of the police car.

'Mrs Frank, two phone calls were made from your mobile phone; the first one at 13.15 requesting an ambulance to attend East Lomond Hill. The last one came fifteen minutes ago saying that Max Watson is involved in Evan Shelby's disappearance. Can you confirm that it was you who made these phone calls?' she asked as her male partner watched me through the rear view mirror. 'Yes, it was me who called,' I replied.

'We're going to take you to Blackbridge station, where you will be asked some questions, is that ok?' he said.

'That's fine.'

***

When we arrived at Blackbridge police station, I was led to interview room one, and offered a cup of coffee. D.I. McCabe would be there soon, I was told. They couldn't tell me if the ambulance got to Tony in time or not.

Sitting on one of the black swivel chairs in an almost entirely grey room, there was nothing to do but think. My thoughts were non-coherent; they were flicking between Tony, sitting there next to the car, to nights we'd had together drinking wine and watching DVDs; how he was so concerned after I tried to commit suicide; that day we found Jase. I had so many questions, there was too much information that needed to be pieced together, but I didn't know where to begin.

I stood up and started to pace the room. I thought back to how I first met Tony, in that bar. That was almost two years ago. How could he have fooled me for all this time? What signs did I miss? Was anything real? I truly believed he was my best friend. It was obvious now that he hated Max, but back then, when Max made his life hell, that had to have been a show. How could I be such an idiot? I didn't even know how to feel; I didn't want Tony to die, of course I didn't. I wanted to believe him about our friendship being real, but how could I? I needed him right then to tell me everything was going to be fine, but that safety net that I'd had for so long was gone. If I were to call him, his mobile would probably vibrate in some hospital drawer, or in a sealed forensic analysis bag somewhere; all alone, like I was now.

After another half an hour or so, Emma and D.I. McCabe came in and took a seat. Emma was pale and there was no doubt that if she were in any other profession, she would have been sent home by now. I wanted to be angry with her for not knowing but I couldn't, she must have felt as stupid as I did. Knowing her, she probably didn't even believe that her precious Max was involved.

'We understand that this must be a very difficult time for you Mrs Frank, but we need you to tell us everything you know. Are you ok to begin this interview now? Is there anything you need before we begin?' D.I. McCabe asked.

'No, I'm fine,' I replied.

'Ok. This interview is being recorded. I am Detective Inspector Michael McCabe and also present is Detective Sergeant Emma Harper. For the purpose of the tape, could you please state your full name?'

'Caroline Marie Frank,' I said.

'Do you mind if we call you Caroline, Mrs Frank?' he asked.

'No, that's fine.'

'Ok, thank you. And Caroline, can you confirm your date of birth for me?' he continued.

'21.04.1973.'

'Thanks. Today's date is 2nd April 2019 and the time by my watch is 16.22. This interview is being conducted in interview room 1 at Blackbridge Police Station.

'Caroline, we would like to discuss the phone calls you made to the contact centre earlier today. Could you please tell us about the events leading up to the first call you made at 13.35?' McCabe asked, obviously leading the interview as Emma sat next to him looking a million miles away.

'Tony phoned me-'

'For the purpose of the tape could you give Tony's full name please,' he said.

'Anthony Delimonte.'

'Thank you, please continue,' he instructed.

'Tony phoned me this morning and asked me to meet him in the car park at Falkland Hill at one o'clock. I knew that he was in trouble. I had a feeling he was hiding because someone was trying to set him up. I just didn't expect this,' I said, unable to stop tears from forming.

'What made you think that someone was trying to set him up?' McCabe asked.

'The filing cabinets in his shed. It was so stupid. Only Scotland's dumbest criminal could be that stupid, surely?' I said.

'Ok. So what happened when you arrived at Falkland Hill?' he asked.

'I knew he had taken something. He was vague and just not himself. He kept saying that he was sorry for everything and that he had to explain.'

'He said he had to explain. What did he have to explain?' Emma finally chipped in.

'He told me he killed Ronnie, my husband, that he pushed him. I didn't believe him. I thought he was just off his face. It wasn't until he told me that Max was going to kill Evan and that it was all for that money that I started to believe what he was saying.'

'And what did you do?' she asked.

'I hit him. I kept hitting him. I couldn't believe what he was saying. I didn't want it to be true. I was angry at him,' I said.

'And are you angry at him now?' McCabe asked.

'I don't know. I don't know how to feel,' I replied.

'Is this when you phoned for an ambulance?'

'No. He wanted me to let him die. I wasn't thinking straight. I got in the car and drove away. When I realised what I was doing, I stopped and phoned the ambulance,' I said.

'What about the second phone call? Where were you when you made that?' asked McCabe.

'I was upset, so I pulled over. That's when I realised that nobody knew about Max yet and I couldn't let him get away with it, so I phoned. Then, I just sat there, for ages, not

249

knowing what to do and that's when the police car pulled up and brought me here. He said this letter explains everything,' I said, pulling it from my coat pocket and handing it to McCabe.

'Have you read it?' Emma asked.

'No, I haven't. I'm not sure I want to,' I admitted. Maybe it was because I couldn't physically or mentally take anymore; maybe it was because I had come to the conclusion that there was no way in hell that that letter could possibly contain all the answers that I needed; whatever prevented me from opening that letter, didn't really matter now.

'For the purpose of the tape Caroline Frank has just produced an envelope from her jacket pocket.'

I watched as he opened the envelope and removed the pages of folded A4 lined paper. I braced myself as I thought that he was going to read it aloud.

'Interview suspended at 16.39,' he said grabbing his suit jacket. 'Let's go.'

Emma looked as stunned as I was. 'An officer will be with you in a minute,' she said, before running off at the back of him.

51
EVAN

The footsteps above me sounded different. The familiar soft trainer-like taps were now heavy thuds of boots or shoes. Looking past the pipes and wires above me, I followed the sound until it faded. The key rattled around the lock before the heavy feet made their way down the wooden staircase. My heart was thumping in my ears.

'It's just me. You do remember me don't you, Evan?' he said. He sat down in the swivel chair and put his briefcase on the empty computer table.

'Yes,' I replied.

'You remember me from the underpass, don't you?' he asked. He started to remove one of his gloves before changing his mind.

'Yes.'

'Well I'm sorry about that. I really am. I need you to know that none of this your fault,' he said and I nodded back, aware that although he was calm and now drinking from a whisky bottle as if nothing was wrong, that any minute now he might hit me with it or make me drink it. He removed a small brown glass bottle from his coat pocket. The same coat he had on that day, only this time it was grey and not black. It was the same brown bottle though, with the same white label. I thought of how he put a cloth over my mouth in the underpass, and Tony telling me it's what he used to kill that other boy. *Don't cry,* I told myself. *Don't cry.*

'It's partly your mum's fault to be honest with you,' he gave a little laugh. 'Sorry, that's not fair. I won't slag off your mum.' I squeezed my teeth together so my face didn't

251

move. The thought of him being near my mum made me want to throw up.

'Relax, relax I'm not going to hurt you,' he took another swig from the bottle.

'So why are you here?' I asked, trying hard to loosen up my body, but it stayed stiff.

'You know Evan, let me tell you this,' he swivelled the chair so he was facing me directly. He put one finger in the air as if telling me to wait a second. He turned back to the table and lit a cigarette. As he blew the smoke in my direction, I took a deep breath and tried to inhale it in the hope it would make me feel better. He was too busy looking at the extension cable running from the stairs to the electric heater and lamp. 'Nice little set up you have here,' he said before looking over to the bucket in the corner and screwing up his nose.

'Can I have one?' I asked, nodding towards the cigarette packet on the desk. He looked at me and laughed like I was a stupid child before considering the idea.

'Oh, why not? Here,' he said as he flicked one over. I caught it and held out my hand for his lighter. He walked over to where I was sitting on the bed and held the flame out in front of me. 'You've done that before,' he laughed again as I let out the first puff from the side of my mouth.

The truth is, I didn't smoke but I had tried it before. My friends told me that the more often I smoked the more enjoyable it would be. Although it made me dizzy and sick to begin with, I did reach a point when it felt ok. Then we started trying vapes because of all the different flavours, so it had been a while.

'I was smoking at your age. I don't know how kids can afford them these days. I'm assuming your dinner money doesn't cover it,' he said and I shrugged.

I felt light headed like it was my first one all over again, so shuffled back on the mattress to rest my head against the wall. I closed my eyes. *Everything will be ok kiddo,* Tony said before he left. He lied. This was not going to be ok.

'Where's Tony?' I asked, opening my eyes to see Max handing me an ashtray. He opened the door to the stairs to let some of the smoke out that had gathered all around us.

'Why do you ask?' he replied.

'It's normally Tony that comes,' I said, not letting on that he had been here the whole night and had not long left.

'You won't be seeing Tony again, I can promise you that,' he said. A lump began to form in my throat, making it difficult to swallow. I'm not sure if he meant that Tony was dead or that I just wouldn't be seeing anybody ever again. I stubbed my fag out in the ashtray and glance over towards him. 'Tony is about to get in a lot of trouble,' he looked at his watch. 'This time tomorrow, he'll be wearing a grey tracksuit.'

I tried a smile, the way you do when someone makes a joke and you don't get it, but you don't want to look stupid. I thought he meant prison and I hoped he did because that would mean he was still alive.

'Let me guess, you think Tony's your pal. Books, blankets,' he said looking around the cellar. 'He's maybe even said you'll be going home soon. Correct?'

'No,' I replied.

'Look at me and say that,' he said. I looked at him but nothing came out.

'Listen kid, you can't fool me. There's no point in trying. I can tell. Just like I can tell you're thinking there's a chance you could get me on side; you don't smoke that often and the second drag on that cigarette made you dizzy; you're scared but you're trying to act brave. I'm a detective son, I know these things. Tony's no hero.'

'Are you going to kill me?' I asked.

'I'm afraid so. But you've nothing to worry about. It won't hurt,' he tried to reassure me, the way my mum used to do when I was younger and had to see the dentist.

I closed my eyes and tried to think about what this meant. I had never considered what it would be like to be removed from the world as if I never existed. When Grandad died it was strange that he just wasn't around anymore. Everyone was sad and cried a lot, especially Mum. But, I used to think about how he was the only one that it didn't affect. He was *none the wiser*, as Mum would say. I think that's why I wasn't afraid of dying. I knew that stuff didn't hurt. I was crying because of the things I was going to miss out on; I wanted to tell my mum that there are 2845 bricks down there; divided by four, that is 711.25. She would probably smile and cry. I wanted to see my Dad's face when I told him I asked for a book on computer science and finally understand what an algorithm is, and what codes are used for and that it has made me wonder, who's the better mathematician, Mum or Dad?

'I promise I won't say anything if you let me go,' I said, trying to stop my voice from shaking but tears were coming now and the more I blinked to stop them, the more they came. 'Please. I don't want to die. I want to go home.'

'I really wish I could, Evan, but it's not that simple-'

'But, I'll say whatever you want. That it was all Tony; that he tried to kill me. I won't mention you,' I pleaded.

'You can't talk your way out of this, son. I don't carry things out on a whim,' he said. 'Tony needs to be sent down for this, and I'm afraid that means there needs to be a body.'

'Like you used Jase's body to send down Patterson, and planned to do to Billy?' I shouted at him, before wiping my eyes with my sleeve. 'You're sick.'

'Oh, ho, ho. So you and Tony really are pals then,' he laughed but I could tell I had annoyed him. 'No I'm not sick, I'm smart. Smarter than anyone you know. And yes, exactly that. Fit up an orphan and there's no backlash; nobody to believe them when they *swear it wasn't them*,' he said as if he was talking about a child. 'Tony's mum's losing her marbles, maybe I'll just get rid of her too,' he shrugged. 'Not like your mum, she's a fighter. Did your pal Tony tell you she visited Mark in prison, demanded to know what he had done to you?' He laughed again and I wanted to punch him in the face.

'Yeah and she wasn't the only one, was she? Billy visited him too, didn't he? You messed up there, didn't you? Mr fucking smarty pants,' I said. I was surprised that he didn't get up and knock me out, instead he gave that same stupid little laugh.

'You know, Evan, I can see why Tony took a shine to you. You're right, I did mess up. Maybe I'm getting too old for it now. If Billy didn't have that alibi, he'd be banged up beside his pal Patterson. You would be dead, of course.' He took another long drink of his whisky before offering me the bottle. I shook my head and managed to stop myself from telling him to shove it up his arse.

'Here, that's your last,' he said, handing me another cigarette. 'I'd really love to sit and chat all day but I'm afraid I have to be somewhere soon.'

I started to cry again as I sat back on the bed.

'Once you've finished that, close your eyes and I'll get this over with,' he told me.

255

As I took small puffs to make it last, I considered how I could stop him. I could try to knock the bottle from his hand; I could put up a fight; 'I know where the money is,' I yelled, desperate.

'Nice try, son. I'm sorry,' he said as he pinned my legs and arms in one swift movement. The cigarette was removed from my hand and my mouth was held tightly against the cloth. With all my strength, I fought against him. The sweet liquid was now in my mouth and stinging my lips. My skin felt cold and tingly. I had no fight left.

52
REBECCA

With a police car parked outside our house and another two officers guarding the back door, the tension between Ray and I was the highest it had been. He was refraining from pointing the finger at me for what I had done, but the blame was still there, lingering around the house with him. That's the reason I asked Mum to come as soon as possible – I needed that unconditional love. When I told her what we thought was going on, her face displayed disappointment for a split second, but she carried on being supportive without further questioning. She was here to stay as long as I needed her to.

Mum felt safe knowing that the officers were surrounding us in case Billy McIvor's twin or anyone else became desperate enough to show up. Emma had called to ask if Max was here first and when I told her he wasn't, we hadn't heard from him, that's when said she would have officers securing the house as a precautionary measure.

Sitting at the kitchen table, I stared blankly at the silhouettes through the glass in the door – waiting once again.

'Come on sweetheart, you need to eat,' mum said, after suggesting every possible way to cook eggs. Despite me telling her I wasn't hungry, she placed a boiled egg in a cup with toasted soldiers fanned around the plate resembling the sun. *You just need a little sunshine in your life,* is the unspoken words that normally came hand in hand. I knew she meant well but all I could see as I removed each finger of toast was how my sunshine was disappearing.

That was when the house phone rang, I leaped from the seat and made a dash to answer it, but Ray got there first. I could tell that it was Emma's voice but couldn't make out what she was saying. I tried to read Ray's face as if it held the transcript. Something unfamiliar in his expression made me hit loudspeaker.

'We're on our way now. Sit tight and I'll phone again as soon as there's any news,' is all I caught before she hung up.

'Have they found Tony?'

'Yes, and now they know where Evan is,' he replied. 'Well they're pretty sure they do anyway.'

'Well where do they think he is?' I had a sudden rush of adrenaline.

'She didn't say.'

'We need to find out, we need to be there.' I began to slip my shoes on.

'No. We don't even know if he'll be dead or alive, do we? They don't even know for sure that he's there.'

'And what if he's alive, I want to be there, Ray,' I pleaded.

He held me by the arms in attempt to calm me. 'We need to wait until we know it's safe. Half an hour at the most and we'll have heard back from her.'

'He's right, honey. Come and sit down.' Mum's voice came from the doorway to the kitchen.

Ray gave me a firm reassuring hug. 'Now's the time to say your prayers,' he said. Ray is in no way religious so I didn't take it literally, but Mum did.

She sat down at the kitchen table, hands clasped and eyes shut. Once again we were waiting but at least we had some hope this time. We had no idea what the outcome would be so I joined her at the table and silently pleaded with God, over and over, to please let him be alive.

Ray was right - half an hour later we received the call and instantly put it on loudspeaker. Ray and I squeezed our hands together, bracing ourselves as we waited to hear the latest news.

'We've got him,' Emma said as Ray squeezed tighter and closed his eyes. 'I'm afraid he's unconscious, but the paramedics are with him now. I'm going to follow the ambulance to Ninewells Hospital. A car is on its way to pick you up and take you there. Please don't drive. It should be with you in the next few minutes. I'll meet you there.'

'Ok,' Ray replied and ended the call. He reached over, grasped the back of my head and pulled me in to his chest. 'They found him, Becks.'

'He's unconscious,' I said. 'Why is he unconscious?' I sobbed into his neck.

'I don't know, but he's alive. That's the main thing,' he replied before passing me by the shoulders to mum.

'I'll lock up here and take my car,' Mum said. She smiled as her trembling hands took a hold of mine.

'They've found him, Mum,' I cried.

'I know, honey, it's wonderful. Now go, go get your boy,' she said, patting my shoulder.

The police car was outside by the time it took us to grab our coats, phones and keys. Ray and I sat together in the back seat, clutching hands.

'Please let him be ok,' I pleaded once again.

53
REBECCA

The rest of the journey to the hospital was a haze of questions and tears and before we knew it we were outside the main entrance, where Emma was waiting by the door with another officer.

'Where is he? What's happened to him?' I asked as I climbed out the car.

'Mrs Shelby, is Evan alive?' I was asked as a camera was shoved into my face. Ray grabbed it and smashed it to the pavement before police officers intervened and we were led inside the hospital.

'Evan is being treated for acute chloroform ingestion. He has been taken to the intensive care unit,' Emma informed us as we raced through the corridors, following her lead.

'Is he going to be ok?' I asked.

'I'll try to get a hold of the doctor as soon as possible. He'll be able to answer your questions,' she replied. 'He's in the best place, Rebecca. He's being well looked after.'

'Where was he found?' Ray asked.

'He was found in a house in Newburgh,' she replied. 'There's a lot going on at the moment but I'll hopefully have answers for you soon.'

'We should phone Max,' Ray suggested. 'He'll want to know what's happening.'

'That's not a good idea. Along to the left,' she said, directing us along the corridor where two police officers were standing guard outside one of the side rooms on right at the far end.

'Wait, what do you mean it's not a good idea?' I heard Ray ask, as I caught sight of them, I knew exactly where to find Evan, and started to run. The distance between us diminishing with each step, closer and closer I was to him and I realised that this was real. I was going to see him with my own eyes in a number of seconds. The moment I had been praying for was here. The officers saw me coming and after some form of communication with Emma I presume, they stepped aside. Ray had caught up and as I opened the door to his room and barged in, I became face to chest with a white and blue checked shirt and stethoscope. I looked up to see the doctors face switching from shock to a sympathetic smile.

'You must be Mrs Shelby,' he said in a South African accent.

'Sorry,' I said before slipping past him.

'You must be Mr Shelby,' I heard him say then. 'I'm Doctor Marais.'

As I reached Evan's bedside, I collapsed to my knees and took his hand. 'We're here baby. Mum and Dad's here. You're safe,' I told him.

I studied him closely, taking in every inch. There were blisters and red blotches around his mouth that looked painful and his hair was slicked back with grease. His beautiful blue eyes were closed, but the heart monitor was beeping and his chest was gently rising and falling, he was very much alive and that was the main thing.

'He is responding very well and quickly to the treatment we have given him. His vitals are stabilising and we've taken bloods to check his serum enzyme levels,' the Doctor informed us.

'Is he going to be ok?' I asked.

'He's going to be fine.' He smiled. 'I suspect he'll have his eyes open very soon. He may vomit and have a headache, but that's to be expected.'

'Oh, thank God. Thank you,' I said.

'Thanks, Doctor,' Ray said as he reached over to shake his hand.

I looked to Ray for a solidarity connection, but he was distracted. His jaw was tight and temples pulsing.

'What's wrong?' I asked. He looked towards Emma and I followed his gaze.

'Max has been arrested on the suspicion of child abduction,' she said, quietly and composed.

'Max?' I looked at Ray who now has his head resting on him and Evan's joint hands. 'That's crazy. That's ridiculous.'

'They wouldn't arrest him without good reason Becks,' he mumbled.

Emma left the room with her vibrating phone in her hand. I followed her into the corridor. 'How could you not have known?' I demanded.

'I think we need to establish the facts first Rebecca before we start making accusations,' she said. 'I need to take this, it'll be an update from D.I. McCabe.'

Despite the tear in her eye, I dismissed her with a drawn out sigh as I returned to Evan. Through the blinds to the corridor, I could see her with her back to us, her hand raised to her forehead. She didn't believe it. Either that or she did and felt as betrayed as us.

'Do you really think he could have done this?' I asked Ray as I reclaimed Evan's hand.

'To be honest, I don't want to think about it now, Becky. Let's just concentrate on Evan. Whoever done this to him is going to pay one way or another,' he replied.

Emma came back in to let us know that she had to go to the station to finish interviewing Caroline.

'Please tell me Caroline isn't involved too,' I said.
'No. She was fooled too.'

54
CAROLINE

I waited at the station for another two hours because I was desperate to find what was written in that letter, that made them run off like that. It didn't take too long to find out.

I recognised the officer – Paula - who had obviously been asked to babysit me. She was lovely and I was grateful to her for sharing that moment when we found out through a radio call, that Evan had been found alive. I have a feeling she wouldn't have experienced her first ever 'happy tears' if I wasn't such an emotional wreck, falling to my knees and wailing with relief.

Emma finally returned without McCabe and I couldn't read her face when she first walked in. There was a smile when she told us that Evan was going to be fine but it soon diminished when she removed the white envelope from her inside pocket.

Paula left and Emma informed me that there was no need to carry on the interview.

'I think you should read this,' she suggested. 'It's not going to be easy, Caroline, I have to warn you.'

I took a deep breath and considered this for a minute as she removed the letter from the envelope. Part of me wanted to forget all about it and pretend that it didn't exist. But, I knew that wouldn't be possible - I would read it sooner or later. So, I decided to get it over with. I sat down and Emma placed the sheets of paper in my hand. In Tony's quickly scrawled handwriting, it read:

Caroline,

Evan is in the basement of St. Mary's Cottage, Lonse Drive, Newburgh. The police will have time to get there before Max.

Now I need to tell you the truth. This has been a long time coming and I'm sorry it's in the form of a letter. You deserve the truth, you always have done. I will make no excuse for my involvement or behaviour. I'm not looking for pity or forgiveness. What I have done is unforgivable.

I got myself into trouble a few years back; fraudulent credit cards, bank loans etc and that's when I first got involved with Max Watson. He had enough evidence against me that could send me to prison, but he offered me a way out. He's always been bent Caroline, I just didn't realise back then how fucked up he actually is. I didn't know what I was getting myself into, all I knew was that I couldn't go to prison. You know as well as I do that I wouldn't cope in there. All I had to do was help him out with a job and he would forget all about the fraud shit.

Max had been protecting Ronnie and Gregory, so that they wouldn't get questioned about the dealing - for a price obviously. He must have gotten greedy. All I had to do was push Ronnie off that cliff (his words not mine). He said he'd take care of the rest, the staging, the forensics. I didn't know about the money at the time, I just thought he was some power crazed vigilante. Max told me about Ronnie and what he had all been charged with in the past, and what he had done to you with the cigarettes, his own wife and it made it easier for me to do it. After hearing what he was like from you, I can't really say I'm sorry for killing Ronnie because I'm not sure if I really am. Don't get me wrong, taking another man's life is soul-destroying, especially when he has a child, but saving you from him, made it worth it. I am remorseful for everything else I've done though.

265

I thought we were quits after Ronnie, but looking back, it was just the beginning. He said that he would decide when enough was enough.

A year went by without hearing a word from Max and I was hoping he had changed his mind. He found out I was making a living from conning people with psychic readings- another thing I'm not proud of. He liked the idea and said he would make me a star. I was just grateful that I didn't have to kill anyone else. He found out personal information about my clients and it made the readings a lot more convincing. That's when I met you.

He sent me to the bar that night we met - he knew you'd be there. Jase was already dead and I knew I was going to have to lead you to his body. I should have killed myself then. That's my biggest regret.

That's when it started getting weird. He joked once about being the puppet master and how I was one of his many puppets. That's when he told me about the money too. He told me everything and I knew then that I had no way out. He threatened to hurt my Mum.

Gregory Fisher is dead. Max tried to blackmail him after the funeral but Gregory had the money transferred to an overseas account and made a run for it. Max caught him on the way to the airport. Max threatened to kill him but he refused to give it up. He stabbed him to death and had someone else get rid of his body.

I honestly don't know why he thought you had the money or access to it. Maybe he was just getting desperate. He prides himself on his ability to cover things up. Even when things don't go to plan he finds other ways. That's what happened with Jase. He took him that night because he knew he'd be assigned to the case. He could investigate you and try to find out about the money without suspicion. He said he didn't mean for Jase to die. He used some equivalent to chloroform and misjudged the strength or something. He didn't suffer Caroline, I hope you can take some comfort from knowing that. I know that's been a huge thing for you and please believe me when I say, it broke my heart every time you spoke about this and I couldn't put your mind at ease.

Max told me that I had to lead you to Jase's remains so that Patterson could be charged with his murder. He had to cover his tracks and stitch somebody up for it. I shouldn't have done it. I hate myself for giving you that image and the pain it has caused you since. Believe me Caroline, I hate myself for everything I have put you through but everything else was real, I promise. I stopped the psychic stuff so I wouldn't have to pretend anymore. Our friendship was real. I love you Caroline, I really do, you have to believe that.

You told me when you were drunk that you knew nothing about the money and when I swore to Max that you weren't involved I thought that would be the end of it, but he wouldn't give up.

Somehow he managed to find out that the money had been transferred into Rebecca's account but because it was an overseas account, the trail was lost, so he went after her, after Evan. I've never understood this because it's not like he was going to be assigned to the case. Emma still trusts him though so I'm sure that's one of the things he was relying on. I kept hoping that because it was her job, she would see right through him, but she didn't.

He wanted me to put ideas in your head about meeting Rebecca because he knew that if the two of you got together, eventually she would want my help. I didn't need to though because by the time you finally got in touch with me after Evan was kidnapped, you had already made that first move.

I need to hurry. I need to get this to you. I managed to convince Rebecca I was genuine because about a month before this, Max had me going through to Dumfries to quiz her brother, Harry. Again, he knew exactly what pub to find him in. He had asked me to do this before with people so I didn't think anything of it at the time. The whole thing was planned down to the last detail. He had Billy McIvor lined up to take the blame from the start He already had the boots with his DNA on and other stuff too but that's when it all went wrong. It was Max that put it on Facebook about the ruin- he thought it was funny to begin with, until Billy's alibi fucked everything up.

He panicked. The only thing he could come up with was pointing the blame at Billy's twin - I was to put the idea in your head while he put it in Emma's. But, I had already messed up by then by mentioning St.Mary's. Evan was being held in the basement of St. Mary's Cottage and I was supposed to say Billy's street because he had planted more evidence. He's had it in for me since then, saying that I was deliberately trying to mess things up for him.

Evan had already told us, well me, about the lockup and where to find Rebecca's files. I took those files and left them in the back of a van for Max to search through them, he said he'd get rid of them. As soon as you told me that the Shelbys had hired him and that she knew they were missing, I had to find out what he was up to. When I spoke to him, he told me that the only way I would escape prison now, was to make a run for it. I knew exactly what he had planned – while the police were busy looking for me, he would kill Evan. If Evan was killed after I was found then the *pathologist (or whatever you call them) would be able to tell and he didn't want to take that risk.*

I should have written this letter before now, and sacrificed myself for him, Caroline, but today's that day. He's a good kid, the smartest kid I've ever met and he deserves to go home. I've known where he's been all along. When I had to carry him in, his body was lifeless and I thought Max had killed him too. Luckily he came round and I tried my best to look after him, honestly I did.

I wish things could have been different, I really do. I just need you to know how sorry I am for all the pain I've caused and that I love you more than you'll ever know.

Take care of yourself,
Tony. X

I closed my eyes, wishing it all away. Emma came around to where I was sitting in an attempt to console me, but there was no point.

55
CAROLINE

My thoughts didn't wander far from Tony that day. Rebecca's prayers had been answered and I was so pleased for her, for all of them. There were celebrations going on in the streets but I didn't have it in me to join them. Piecing together all this new information was what I needed to do, in order to save what sanity I had left.

With the wi-fi reconnected from the money from Ronnie's jewellery, I searched Facebook and newspaper reports because I was sure that somewhere I could find out if Tony was still alive. There were many about Evan being found, and on Max's arrest, but nothing about Tony.

How did I feel about him killing Ronnie? I couldn't decide. Deep down, I guess I always knew he didn't jump. I was there that night. On the night Ronnie died, at about 6pm he told me that I needed to go to the Crags with him later on about 9pm. He was to meet someone there and I knew it was none of my business to ask who. I remember he was a bit shifty, something was bothering him and my guess is that he didn't know if it was going to be some kind of set up. He never asked me to go with him on business and to this day I still don't know why that night was different.

Jase was lying on his bed watching a film when it was time for us to leave. I kissed him on the forehead and told him that we wouldn't be long.

Ronnie insisted that we walked so that we looked like we were just out for a stroll. He often met acquaintances at the Crags and despite it being at least a mile and a half away, he refused to take the car, probably in fear of being pulled over by the police; it was easier to hide on foot.

'Speak if you're spoken to, but otherwise keep your fucking mouth shut,' he said as we sauntered up the brae. By this point in life I despised him, there was not an ounce of the Ronnie that I fell in love with, left.

Facing the open sea, the wind blew bitter against our bodies. I wrapped my big grey cardigan around me and wished that whatever was about to happen would be over soon. We came to the old wooden bench that marks the peak and I took a seat. Ronnie pranced around rubbing his bare arms, with his eyes on the path we had just climbed.

As the minutes passed, he kept looking frantically at his watch. 'Fuck sake, just go home will you.' This wasn't to save me from the cold, it was because he didn't want Jase to be left home alone for too long.

I've thought about the last time I saw Ronnie, many, many times, and he showed no signs whatsoever of being suicidal. He judged himself on success, and by success I mean money; in his eyes he was definitely succeeding in life. And there's Jase, he wouldn't have left his son by choice.

In my mind, he fell by accident. Why the police ruled it suicide, I had no idea and didn't care to question it. Max could explain that one, I'm sure. He was the one that made that decision after reviewing all his own planted evidence.

Tony had a conscience though. I don't believe for one minute that he didn't suffer after taking another man's life, even if it did belong to a wife-beating, drug-dealing scumbag.

Jase was a different story; all the lies. I could see it now, Tony's reaction to us uncovering his bones, the depression that followed, his concern towards me; it was guilt. When

Max interviewed and accused him of killing Jase, what was that? Was it performance or genuine? Had Tony pissed him off then too?

Tony had betrayed my trust repeatedly and that was unforgivable. Our friendship was over and that was what I struggled most with. I had that grief whether he was dead or alive.

Just when I wondered how I was going to get through the day, Margaret's white Micra pulled into my driveway. I still hadn't adapted to the new view I had from my living room window now that the conifers were gone, so the sight of the little car driving along the road first was a strange one.

I opened the front door to welcome her. 'How's Evan?' I asked, wondering why Rebecca's mum would be visiting me now.

'He's going to fine,' she said and our hug turned to a celebratory one. 'Are you OK?'

'No, I'm not. I'm really not,' I replied. I didn't have it in me to put a face on it.

'Come on, we'll deal with this together,' she said.

'I don't know if Tony made it or not,' I cried.

'I don't know either, honey. Why haven't you called Emma? She would be able to tell you.'

'I should, I really should,' I replied. It wasn't like the thought hadn't already crossed my mind.

'Do you want me to do it?' she asked.

'It's OK, I'll do. Come and sit down.' I felt brave having Margaret beside me as I no longer had to face it alone.

Emma didn't answer her mobile but within seconds she called me back. 'He's in the Vic,' she said, meaning the Queen Victoria hospital in Kirkcaldy. 'He's in a coma,

Caroline. From what I can make out, it doesn't look good. He's in the ICU.'

'I need to see him,' I told Margaret after I hung up.

'We can try but they might not let you in, sweetheart.'

'We need to try,' I said.

'OK, let me drive,' she replied.

The journey to the hospital took about twenty minutes and Margaret was trying to figure out how I was feeling but I couldn't help her because I didn't know either. I had no idea how I would react if I did get to see him. Who knew the damage he had done to himself? All I knew is that I had to see him and I'd take things from there.

'How are you feeling?' I asked Margaret. 'You must hate him for what he's done.'

'I don't know exactly what he has done, Caroline. By the sound of it, if it wasn't for Tony, Evan might have been dead. So no, at this moment I don't hate him.'

'How do you feel about him lying like that? He lied straight to your face, to everybody.'

'Sometimes people do things for reasons we'll never understand. Things that are out with our control can affect us mentally or change us. Maybe he didn't have a choice, who knows? But I believe that even the worst of people have some good in them. I find it hard to believe that people can be pure evil. So, to answer your question, I'll make up my mind when and if I ever find out the truth.'

This made me think about that bastard Patterson, I could have sworn he was pure evil until it hit me for the first time that he had been set up. Patterson was innocent. I had hated him for so long and it wasn't even him that killed Jase. It was Max that was the evil one.

'What about Max? He killed Jase and Gregory Fisher, he had my husband killed, tried to kill your grandson,

273

blackmailed goodness knows how many people and that's only the stuff we know about,' I said.

'Oh my goodness. I had no idea. He killed Jase? What makes you say that?' she asked.

I hadn't even thought about the fact that nobody else knew what I did. I filled her in about my last conversation with Tony and his suicide letter as quickly as I could before we reached the hospital.

As soon as the car stopped, I jumped out and found myself running ahead of Margaret. I ran past the police cars and ambulances that were parked outside Accident and Emergency and headed for the main reception. One of the receptionists was on the phone and the other one looked at me and smiled. 'Can I help you?' she asked.

'I'm looking for Tony Delimonte. Anthony Delimonte. I was told he was in the intensive care unit. Overdose, probably escorted by the police,' I blurted out.

'Just a second,' she nodded. 'Are you family?' she asked as she picked up another phone and dialled an internal number.

'Sister,' I said quickly.

'Hi May, there's a lady here to see Mr Delimonte...his sister...thanks,' she said before hanging up.

'Take a seat please, someone is on their way down to see you,' she informed me and by that point Margaret approached.

'We've to take a seat,' I told her, so that's what we did. As we sat my legs restlessly tapped away until Margaret put her hand on my knee to calm them. We didn't speak, we just waited.

A male and female officer turned the corner and headed in our direction. The female whispered something to the male. 'Mrs Frank?' he asked.

'Yes, can I see him?' I asked.

'Let's just hang on a minute, his Auntie and his Mum are on their way down to speak to you.'

'OK,' I replied. I wasn't prepared for that answer. I had no idea how I was going to face her.

'Is there a room we can use?' the male officer asked the receptionist. She pointed to a room at the side that I could see had children's toys in it.

Mrs Delimonte and a similar looking woman that I had never met before but presumed was Tony's Auntie Dina, turned the corner that the officers had just come around. Mrs Delimonte was crying and it was enough to set me off. She didn't deserve any of this. The male officer placed his hand on her shoulder and told her we could use the room but she kept walking towards me and put out her arms. As I held and tried to comfort her I could feel her tiny fragile frame pressing into mine, not a bad bone inside her.

'Oh Caroline, honey,' she said.

'Come on,' I said guiding her to the room. Margaret and Dina followed but held back unsure of whether to come in or not. Mrs Delimonte and I simultaneously invited them in. The female officer closed the door behind us and waited outside with her partner.

'How is he?' I asked.

'He's not good,' she managed before sobbing uncontrollably.

'He's in a coma, they think he could have brain damage,' Dina told us.

'What do you mean they think?' I asked.

'They can't tell us anything for sure,' she replied. 'They need to carry out further tests. They're not even sure he'll pull through.'

'Don't say that Dina,' pleaded Mrs Delimonte.

275

'It's OK Maureen, I'm just telling them what was said. I'm sure he'll be fine,' Dina said as if speaking to a child.

'Why would he do this Caroline? I don't understand,' she sobbed. They hadn't told her. I didn't know what to say so I looked at Margaret.

'We should maybe come back later,' she said.

'No, I want to see him. Can I see him, Mrs Delimonte?' I asked.

***

Watching his defenceless body lying there in that bed, unable to run or hide from what he had done made me realise how vulnerable Tony was. Police were guarding the room, so in the event of him awakening, he would be arrested. He was a grown man, responsible for his own actions, was what I kept having to remind myself. Max had apparently made him do those things, but he didn't, he blackmailed him, the consequences of not going through with them, was prison. And, *if you can't do the time, don't do the crime*, goes the famous saying. But, he threatened to hurt his Mum too, so could I blame him for that?

I didn't know what I was hoping to achieve by going to see him, or what good would come of it, but for some reason, I felt relieved. I remember hearing once that you should always assume that a person in a coma can hear what you are saying, something about the hearing being the last thing to go. An officer in the corridor outside, insisted on watching me through the little window, I'm not sure if it was in case Tony woke up or if I tried to turn off the machines that were keeping him alive, probably both. But, the officer thinking I was off my rocker was the least of my worries.

With a chair pulled up to the edge of his bed, I rested my elbows on the bed at his side. I thought carefully about the message I wanted him to receive. Should I make him feel guilty for everything he had done to me or simply make it clear that our friendship was over? If he didn't pull through did I want the last thing for him to hear, to be a rundown of all the bad things he had done in his life and the hurt he had caused? Maybe I should have spoken to him about all the good moments we shared, how we became so close and how he helped me through some of my darkest days. But, I couldn't, because all of those memories were tainted now. It was impossible to tell what was real and what was not.

'I don't know who you are,' I said with a large lump forming in my throat. 'You're not the person I thought you were. I think that's probably the reason that I don't even know what to say to you. I know you might not be able to hear me so it probably doesn't matter anyway. But if you can, I'm sure you don't need me to go over all the things you've done. You did the right thing sacrificing yourself for Evan and I'm sure Rebecca will be grateful for that but the only other positive thing to come from all this, is that now I know the truth about how Jase died. I don't have to tell you how much the lead up to his death haunted me, because you already know. He didn't suffer in any way and probably not even aware of what was happening to him, and I can't explain how much relief this gives me. It's like the missing piece to the puzzle, the closure that I never thought I'd get. You've caused me a new kind of pain, Tony. But hopefully one day, I'll get my head around that too.

'I'm not going to beg you to wake up, because I know that's not what you want. But, if you do wake up, you need to be man enough to face the consequences. Don't be a coward all your life, Tony.'

277

I stood up, knowing that under any other circumstances I would hold his hand or kiss his forehead, but I couldn't. My barrier had gone up. 'What's meant to be, will be,' were my final words to him.

56
REBECCA

'It's ok, Mum and Dad are here,' I said as I held the cardboard sick bowl to Evan's chin. Ray and I exchanged a smile after we both recognised the moment of realisation in his face that he was now safe. After a five hour agonising wait and worry that the doctor had gotten it wrong, he was finally awake. Ray pressed the orange buzzer for the nurse while I stroked his hair with my free hand - he sobbed helplessly as he continued to throw up.

'My lips are stinging,' he cried when there was nothing left to come and needed his face wiped.

'Wait a second.' I went to the sink to wet some cotton wool. 'It'll probably sting for a few days, honey. You have blisters from the chemicals.' Gently as I possibly could, I dabbed around his mouth and looked into his deep blue eyes that I had sorely missed.

'I thought I was going to die,' he said as he reached out for the long awaited group hug.

'Well, you didn't, you're here and you're safe,' Ray said as he pulled us in tight. United in tears, sobs and smiles, we held on until the nurse's cough interrupted us.

She shared our joy as she clearly recognised us. 'How are you feeling, Evan?' She eased her way in to check his vitals.

'My head hurts.'

'I'll get you some painkillers for that, sweetheart. The doctor will be in soon and we've saved you a little side-room in one of the wards, to give you some privacy. You're a bit of a celebrity about here, you know.'

Evan gave us his cringing look that we knew so well. 'No way.' Ray nodded in confirmation, 'I'm afraid so.'

Within an hour, we were in the side-room and Evan was beginning to take on a new lease of life- whether or not it was the medication he was given, I'm not sure. He started asking questions about Max and Tony.

We reassured him that Max was locked up and that we knew that Tony had been taken to hospital but that was all we knew.

'He's not going to get into trouble, is he? He's not a bad guy, Mum, Max made him do things.'

'Nobody can make you do things, son,' Ray replied.

'I know you hate him Dad, he told me. But you're wrong.'

At that, D.I. McCabe knocked on the door and let himself in. He was pleased to see Evan and came straight over to shake his hand. 'Nice to finally meet you, Evan. I'm Detective Inspector McCabe, but you can call me Mike.' It was a nice touch I thought. We obviously weren't special enough to call him by his first name, but clearly Evan was, and that was ok with me.

'You two must be feeling a bit overwhelmed, I would imagine,' he said.

We both smiled. 'Yeah, just a tad,' Ray replied playfully, making Evan laugh while trying to keep his poor blistered lips pursed.

I was surprisingly glad when he walked in because I could tell from the way Evan was talking, that he had a lot to say and I knew McCabe would want to hear it too. But I needed to speak to him first.

'Do you fancy coming to the coffee machine? I'm sure we could all do with one,' I said to McCabe.

'Certainly.'

As we walked down the corridor, he spoke first. 'Emma's been suspended with immediate effect,' he announced.

'Why?'

'The letter that I told you about - the one from Tony to Caroline. It suggested that Emma may have breached confidentiality procedures. An investigation will be carried out obviously, but it will mean you'll have no further contact with her, I'm sorry.'

I stopped in my tracks. 'Do you think she knew?' I had to ask, although I knew the answer. Or at least I hoped I did.

'No. I don't believe she did. But, I do believe she trusted him. That's no excuse though for sharing confidential information or acting unprofessionally.'

We carried on walking as I considered the fact that I would not see her again. She had been our rock – there from day one. We had our ups and downs but I had no doubt I was going to miss her.

'Has Evan said much about what happened?' McCabe asked.

'Not really but I have a feeling he was going to start just before you arrived. I asked him if they hurt him in any way, because I had to know, but he said that apart from Max knocking him out with those chemicals, that they hadn't.'

'That's good. You might find that he'll be eager to tell you everything, and it'll be good for him to get it out into the open. Because of his age, we can't hold an interview until he's been allocated a social worker. We then need to have a pre-interview briefing and a practice interview, so there's no rush. But, if he shares any information when we get back, I'll take down some notes, if that's ok? It'll give us a clearer picture of what we're dealing with.'

'That's fine.'

When we returned with three coffees, Evan was clearly in the middle of a story.

'Wait a minute, son. Could you say that again so that Mum and...Mike know what happened.' Ray got up and started pacing, like he always does when he's angry, but he sat back down when I gave him the look to stop it.

'I was just saying that I had been running back to school because I was going to be late. As I was sliding down the banking, Max held up his badge or identification, whatever it's called, so I stopped. He said I had to go to the station with him and that the school knew about it and that mum was already there. I know I shouldn't have gone with him now, but he was a policeman wasn't he, I could hardly say no.'

'It's ok, son, you're not the only one he fooled,' Ray said. 'We all fell for his shit.'

'Do you want me to tell you the rest?' Evan asked, looking at the three of us in turn.

'It's entirely up to you. You don't have to though. D.I. McCabe was just saying out in the corridor that an interview will be set up after you have been allocated a social worker.' I looked towards McCabe for confirmation.

'That's right. It'll be a couple of days at least.' His notebook sat open on his knee in the hope Evan would carry on. I'm pretty sure we all wanted him to but there was no way anyone was going to force it.

'I'd like to tell you everything. Mum, you always say it's good to talk.'

'It is, honey,' I smiled.

'Ok. So, when we were walking towards the underpass, he said there was nothing to worry about and that I wasn't in any trouble. When we were in the tunnel, he stopped and told me to wait a minute. He asked me if I knew any of the

282

boys' names that were sprayed on the walls. I remember reading them and the next thing he was holding something over my mouth. I tried to get him off me but he was too strong. I remember tasting that chloroform stuff. The next thing I knew, I was in the cellar.

'How did you know it was chloroform?' McCabe asked.

'I didn't at the time, it was Tony that told me what it was,' Evan replied. 'Tony was in the cellar when I woke up and he was telling me I was going to be ok. I kept being sick.'

'Was Max there?' Ray asked.

'No I never saw him again until this morning when he came back to kill me.' He paused as he reminded himself where he was in his story. 'So, when I stopped being sick, Tony went away and left me. I didn't know if I was being left to die there or if they were maybe a bunch of paedos.

For the first couple of days, I slept a lot. I just didn't feel well. It was cold and dark so Tony brought down pillows and blankets. He had to run the extension cable from upstairs so he could plug in the lamp and the little heater. He couldn't come too often so he made sure I had plenty to eat and drink. He gave me books and magazines to read so that I had something to do.'

'Did Tony tell you why you were being kept in the cellar?' McCabe asked as he continued to scribble down notes.

'He didn't to start with but then he told me everything last night when he stayed over. That was just last night wasn't it?'

'It was, son.' Ray answered first.

'I thought so. The police were looking for Tony because Max had set him up. He told me how Max had killed Jase Frank and his dad's friend - I can't remember his name. He said they were drug dealers together and that Max was after the money they had made. That's why he made Tony push Jase's dad off that cliff. Then he kept blackmailing him, that's why he was looking after me. He didn't want to do it anymore, that's why he was trying to help me. He was crying and everything. He didn't know Max was going to try and kill me, did he?' Evan asked, looking hurt at the thought.

'We don't know,' I answered. 'We don't really know anything yet.'

'He's not going to get into trouble, is he?' Evan looked at McCabe. 'He saved me. If it wasn't for Tony I would be dead right now. He didn't want to do any of it. Max made him do it,' he pleaded.

'I'm sorry Evan, but it would be unfair to answer that right now.' McCabe let out a sigh as he carefully considered his next words. Shaking his head, he decided not to share them. It made me wonder if Tony had died. We knew he was in a coma but given Evan's unexpected admiration for him, I suspected McCabe felt it was better not to mention it.

'What happened this morning with Max?' Ray quickly changed the subject.

'He just came in and sat down. He was smoking and drinking whiskey. He said that it wasn't my fault and tried to blame Mum. He said that he was going to have to kill me so that Tony could get charged with murdering me. I said to him, 'What like you did to that Patterson guy and was going to do to that Billy guy,' because Tony had told me all about that too. He said he does it to orphans because they don't have family to fight for them and that they all deserve it anyway. He kept laughing. I had my eyes shut when he put that stuff over my mouth again. I can't believe I'm still alive.' He gave a little laugh as he realised how lucky he really was and we all shared that same thought. We had our boy back, yet we were so close to losing him forever.

I watched as Evan lay his head back on the pillow and considered how lucky I was. I could easily have been in the same position as Caroline – without my son forever. I was going to watch him grow and knew I would never take another second with him for granted.

'I'm going to let you get some rest,' McCabe said. 'I think you all need it. It's been a pleasure, young man.' He held his hand out once more to shake Evan's, followed by Ray's. When he turned towards me, I put my arms out to embrace him. I no longer disliked him but couldn't really say why that was. Perhaps all the hate I had left in me was now directed towards Max. If he could suffer all the pain he had caused, then justice would be served. But unfortunately that's never the case, is it?

57
EVAN
4 Months Later

So much has been going on that it feels good to have a day at the beach away from everything else. Everybody knows who I am and it's so embarrassing. At least when we're in Elie people don't come up to me all the time and ask me weird questions or ask for selfies. I'm not going to complain about the attention I get from the girls in Blackbridge though, because that's kind of cool.

I've been coming here a lot with Gran because she's been helping Caroline get moved into her little cottage, but Mum just lost her job so she wanted a chilled day to 'think things through', so that's why we're here today. She was found guilty of misconduct and has been barred from something called the ICAS, which basically means she can't be an accountant anymore but she doesn't seem that bothered - especially now that Caroline has just pulled out a bottle of Prosecco and plastic wine glasses from her picnic basket.

'Come on, let's see who wins at skimming stones,' Dad says, nodding down to the water below in the bay. He gives me that look that means, *Let's leave mum and Caroline alone to talk.* I am kind of glad because listening to women chatting is like torture. Maybe it might be interesting to hear what they were talking about after everything that happened, but from experience, especially Gran, it's usually all feelings and clothes and who they bumped into recently and always the weather; like who really cares?

I know all the other stuff anyway. They'll talk about Max and how a guy called Timmy Boylen came forward and told the newspapers a story of when Max used to work in the children's home where Billy McIvor, Caroline's husband and the rest of them grew up. They had to call him Uncle but he abused them so they all battered him. Apparently that's the real reason Max wanted them all to suffer.

They'll also talk about how Max might get off with murdering Jase Frank and Gregory Fisher because there's not enough evidence and how Caroline wrote a letter to Mark Patterson (my Gran's idea of therapy) and how she's going to try and help him get out of prison. I think it's stupid that they don't just let him out but apparently it's not that simple.

Then they'll talk about Tony. I tried not to cry when Mum told me he died but I couldn't help it, I really liked him. Caroline said that it's what he wanted so I kind of understand why it was for the best. I wanted to go and see him when he was in the hospital but Dad didn't think it was a good idea. But, Tony was good to me, though, and he was the only one that knew my secret…I was just convinced that if he heard my voice he would wake up and we could talk about it. I've been keeping it to myself for so long because Tony told me I had to wait until things had settled down. That's why I think I'm going to tell Dad when we get down to the water.

'I'll play you for a tenner,' I say, knowing I always win.

'Go on then,' Dad replies.

It's roasting hot so we both have our shorts, t-shirts and shades on. I look quite good. Mum's bought me lots of new clothes, and Dad, well he looks like a middle aged man trying to look cool – luckily nobody knows us!

As we walk along by the front of the water we both immediately start looking for flat stones. I always knew my

Dad was the only person I could tell what I did but I am worried about my mum finding out. She blames herself for what happened to me but I know the truth - it was my own fault.

My dad counts to four as his stone bounces along the top of the water. 'I'm out of practise.' He laughs.

'Dad, there's something I need to tell you,' I say as I release my stone. I get five jumps.

'What is it, buddy?'

'I've been too scared to say anything because I know I'm going to get in a heap of trouble.'

He stops and turns to look at me, worried all of a sudden. 'Don't be scared to tell me anything, if there's something wrong then we'll fix it. It can't be that bad.'

I pick up another stone, aware that mum will be watching us from the top of the hill. 'Remember that time you taught me to use remote assistance on the laptop?'

'Yes,' he replies as he raises his eyebrows and pretends to scratch his forehead.

'Well...I had been doing it on mum's laptop. I just wanted to see what it is she does, with her accounts and stuff. I knew she wouldn't have a clue, you know what she's like. I was sitting in my room, watching what she was doing. Anyway, I needed a bank account set up so that I could register for bit-coins. You know that digital currency thing that all the famous people use-'

'I know what bit-coins are, Evan.'

'Well, I managed to get an online bank account set up in my name, with mum's authorisation.' I look at him to see his reaction.

'Shit, Evan, that's fraud. That's illegal. You can't be doing stuff like that.' He continues to throw stones without any effort now. 'Tell me you closed it.'

'No. You see, the thing is; I was watching mum that night she was about to transfer that money into another account, the drug money. I didn't know it was drug money. I just saw the amount and couldn't believe it. I quickly phoned mum's mobile and when she answered I told her I was starving. Do you remember I used to do that?'

'Yes, and she would bring you something to eat.' I can sense his anger now, or maybe it's dread or worry or something. 'Then what happened?'

'I typed in my account details and transferred the money. I left mum's screen saying that the transaction had been processed and the next thing I knew she was through the kitchen doing the dishes.'

'Evan, son…I don't believe I'm hearing this.' He sat down with his elbows resting on his knees, so I do the same. 'Throw stones as far as you can,' he instructs; we're both aware that mum will still be watching.

'I was going to tell you. I kept expecting you or mum to bring it up but nothing ever got said. You both just kept being normal all the time. It reached a point when I knew I had gotten away with it. I had exchanged all the money into bit-coins and I was worried that if you checked my computer you would see all the e-mails they kept sending. As soon as you told me I was getting your old laptop, I reset my one to factory settings and set up a new e-mail address. Remember you gave it to Gran or Uncle Harry or whoever?'

'So you're saying that you have a bit-coin account with a million pound in it and nobody else knows?' he asks.

'Tony knew about it. I told him when he told me that's why Max had kidnapped me. I thought if I could give it back he would let me go. Tony insisted that I shouldn't tell anyone. His plan meant that I could come home and Max wouldn't get the money. I had no idea he was going to try and kill himself. I offered Tony the money but now I understand why he wanted me to keep it. There's no trace, Dad.'

'I'm afraid there will be, son. It's more a case of, is anybody going to care enough to look?'

'Are you going to tell mum?' I ask.

'I have no idea, buddy. I have no idea. Well, I'll need to but let's keep it between us for now. Shit.'

H rubs his head again.

'Ok,' I agree.

'Beat that,' he says after using all his strength to throw his stone. I try but only make half the distance. He takes my head in his hand and pulls me towards him. 'Come on, we'll take a walk to the lighthouse and walk back the other way.'

We look up to see mum and Caroline still chatting away. He puts his arm around my shoulder. 'I'm glad you told me, and we'll sort something out,' he assures me.

I have no idea what will happen now but I decide not to mention the things we can possibly do with all that money. It's not like I haven't thought about it.

'One of those houses next to Caroline would be nice though, wouldn't it?' I wink at him.

About the Author

K.T. Marshall lives in Fife, Scotland with her partner and two children. Being a huge fan of psychological thrillers, writing a novel was always on her bucket list. After studying creative writing with The Open University, and countless nights writing when her children were in bed, it became a reality. She now hopes to write full-time and is working on her second novel – *I Should Have Known.*

You can follow her on Twitter:
https://twitter.com/KTMarshwriter

Or Facebook:
https://www.facebook.com/k.t.marshwriter/

Acknowledgments

Thank you to everyone that has supported me on my journey from first draft to published novel. I have been lucky to have so many supporters from day one – there are far too many to mention!

A special thanks to my parents who have been full of encouragement my whole life and made me believe I could do anything I set my mind to.

A huge thank you to my beta-readers, proof-readers (especially Kate) and fantastic editor Anne Hamilton, who kept me going when things got tough – this wouldn't have been possible without you.